The Blue Man Dreams the End of Time

Michael McIrvin

Fearful Symmetry Publications

Fearful Symmetry Publications Edition, 2020

Produced by Fearful
Symmetry Publications
(USA)

First published by BeWrite
Books (UK and Canada)

Printed in the United States of America
Second Printing
00 01 02 03   7   6   5   4   3   2   1

ISBN: 978-1-7341970-3-7

Cover © Tony Szmuk 2009

Acknowledgements

An article John Leonard wrote for *The Nation* many years ago inspired the short story that became this novel. The writer wishes to acknowledge the late Mr. Leonard's inadvertent but seminal contribution to this project.

For my family.

The Blue Man Dreams the End of Time

Prologue

We deny a beginning because that would imply an end, and the idea of the end, of ourselves, of time, scares the hell out of us. So, we begin in the middle. It is the American way.

Those with longer tenure on this planet can say, *In the beginning …* or *Before the time that is our time …* We say, *Oh by the way …* as if everything that happens in this expanding universe, primordial starstuff blowing outward from incipience toward oblivion and the entire lot in between, were incidental. An accident, that's the word.

And because I have come to realize that I am quintessentially American, all foible and excuse, delusional on a good day, I begin this tale with now, which is certainly the product of, the beginning of, nothing. A coincidental alignment rolling out of the confabulum of space and time to bring me to this moment.

So, by the way, I woke up blue today …

Part I

To wake someone from sleep
is to saddle some other with the interminable
prison of the universe
of his time, with neither sunset nor dawn.
It is to show him he is someone or something
subject to a name that lays claim to him
and an accumulation of yesterdays.
It is to trouble his eternity,
to load him down with centuries and stars,
to restore to time another Lazarus
burdened with memory.

Jorge Luis Borges

Who can deny the savagery of God?

Sophocles

Chapter One

I woke up blue today. Not sad as in the cliché, but actually, absolutely, from head to toe, blue. Ultramarine, Chanelle says. Cerulean, says Justine.

All I know for certain is that I passed out drunk in an alley halfway between the Lucky Satyr Lounge and my apartment, and when I woke up shivering in the cold dim light before dawn, to the smell of stale piss and rat droppings, I was naked. My clothes were neatly folded in a pile by my head, my cheap, size 13 shoes resting on top with their tongues lolling like thirsty dachshunds. My hands, my genitals, even the soles of my feet were a deep blue, and the cold and broken asphalt had made little blue indentations in my shoulders, ass and legs, like craters on the moon, shadows within shadows.

Before I realized my change in hue in the small light of the alley, I checked my back pocket to see if I had been robbed, a perplexing glimmer of other possible violations to my naked self beginning to surface in my imagination. The seventeen dollars I had when I left the bar were still there, along with my comb and the map to Chanelle's new apartment she drew for me on a bar napkin the night before. The directions are poetry: *down the alley between 3ʳᵈ and 4ᵗʰ, a silly Caucasian titty-pink stucco story-and-half in the middle of the block, up a flight on the outside to the only door, also pink but Pepto-colored.*

Now, as she stands in my tiny, greasy kitchen with a cup of tea steaming between her long black hands to

13

warm them, she worries that the "perpetrators," as she calls whoever painted me blue, will use the map to find her, steal her stereo, violate her, maybe paint her too. Justine is sure Chanelle watches too much TV.

"Witness your use of the word perpetrators. Hell, why don't you just call them *perps*, or *alleged perps*. TV is making you paranoid, girl."

"There ain't no alleged about it," says Chanelle. "Poor Sonny is blue, isn't he? Not *allegedly* blue. That crap is for the weak-kneed, for liberals who think the whole human-damned-race is innocent instead of fallen."

Chanelle puts one hand on her hip and leans slightly forward, as she always does when she is about to wag her index finger in her sister's direction and make a not necessarily cogent point that she thinks is so obvious it's a major tenet of native wisdom.

"You're guilty, or you're not; and a man is blue, or he isn't." She smiles smugly and Justine rolls her eyes, as she always does when it's obvious her sister has settled into a final certainty no matter the violence to reason.

I sleep with both women, but one at a time. The only thing they agree on to my knowledge is that all of us in one bed would be a perversion. I met them just over a year ago at the Lucky Satyr where Justine serves drinks. She took me home one night when I couldn't take my eyes off her beautiful ass in the ruffles of an over-tight uniform that accentuated everything, all those Pavlovian signs in search of a response, and I went home with her twin sister by mistake the next night. They thought it a damned funny joke to play on a drunk white man, and had probably played it on many – or so I think in my most cynical mode – but when I mentioned the possibility of, "you know, uh, us all together," they said the word in unison, drawing out the middle syllable

14

and their voices rising in volume and tone like school girls: *perverrrRRRsion.* Then they giggled until they actually hurt my feelings, which I thought impossible after all I've been through, and I haven't said a word about the three of us together since.

So we have a schedule, "our arrangement" we call it when our three-way relationship is mentioned at all: Monday and Wednesday Justine stays at my little apartment over a dry cleaner, Tuesday and Thursday Chanelle stays, and Friday through Sunday I sleep at one of their places or the other, alternating weeks, like a kid in a complex custody arrangement.

Just because you sleep with somebody doesn't mean they have the right to laugh at you when you're blue.

"Know what happened to Little Boy Blue when he grew up?" Chanelle asks Justine, her eyes sparkling at me like Fourth-of-July rockets from where she leans against the ancient gas stove, a pot of day-old soup still on the only burner that works. "He became a drunken Seven-Eleven clerk, changed his name to Sonny so people would stop asking him to blow that damned horn, and he got bluer and bluer."

"I heard Boy Blue's mama warned him he'd turn darker and darker if he didn't stop playing with his pee-pee, but he wouldn't listen," says Justine, and she laughs at her own joke, bending over and slapping her thigh in an exaggerated pantomime of laughter. Her voice echoes in my nearly empty apartment.

"I heard she told him if he slept with black women it'd rub off. If we were triplets, he'd be indigo." The sisters fall into each other's arms with laughter, tears flowing heartlessly down their cheeks.

I am wondering how to become unblue. I have already taken a half dozen showers, hoping an onslaught of hot water and hard scrubbing will at least

15

fade me to something like gray, a sign I will be my pale self eventually. But soap hasn't lightened me a shade, and the scrub powder for sinks and toilets I used just now left me severely chafed, which seems to add to these women's enjoyment. I return to the molding bathroom to stare into the mirror at the abomination of my face – which is bluer than Krishna's it occurs to me– to consider my options in some semblance of peace. I am due at work by noon, which requires either a cure or calling in sick again. It's likely that the just-beyond-acne kid who is the manager, Bob something-or-other, will fire me this time. Lately, I can't stand the thought of waiting on morons who don't know which self-service pump they got gas from or delinquents who have $20 worth of store merchandise stuffed in their pants – like I care – or some minimal semblance of a human being screaming-pissed because the milk he bought yesterday is rancid already, as if his sanity depended on this retribution against a minor functionary in the corporate infrastructure who couldn't do anything about his dilemma should he want to, so I call in sick and go to the bar instead.

An angry contusion is trying to force its way through the blue darkness of my left cheek where I used the chlorinated powder most vigorously, panicking when I realized that this may not be something applied to my skin as a prank, that this blueness might be systemic. A wave of unmitigated horror, tinged with an awed appreciation for the multiply-leveled irony in my blueness, is pushing its way to the surface, too. It's been a long time since I looked over my shoulder every few minutes, since I fled from job to job at least monthly, and town to town nearly as often, for fear they'd somehow trace my fake social security number back to me, for fear that the thin shield of my various aliases would crumble like tinfoil.

16

But who else would do this, use a systemic agent both reprehensible and, as Justine and Chanelle's reactions only hinted at, funny in a macabre way, in that darkly ironic way that seems to characterize the age? Who else? If they only knew, the sisters would probably appreciate the scope of the joke, the time and energy it must have taken to produce a systemic agent just for me so *I* can fully appreciate the seemingly cosmic scale of this prank. So I can completely grasp the fate rolling at me like a train sans brakes just before it runs me down. So much for beginning in the middle, for coincidence, accident.

The hand of fate is not cosmic, however, but very human in this case, if my fears are correct. I close my eyes against the blue specter of my face, and for a brief moment, I am caught in that uncomfortable land between laughing and crying. In fact, I feel like I could do either, and I have not shed a tear or let loose even a minor snicker for what seems like years.

Fate. I consciously stopped using the word a long time ago because it can't exist except as a sum of random forces, at least to my saner self. The cosmic dice roll and one of an infinite number of permutations is, momentarily or for the duration of one's life, depending on scope and context, fact. A life only looks like a whole thing, something that could have been scripted, after the bleakest of facts, when you're worm shit. A man is simply born what he is, when he is, to whom; which is to say, all of us are merely a bundle of peptides twisted just so, born into class X, untouchable or Brahmin, slave or master, into nation Y in the first or third world – the existential albatross or the existential brass ring just like that. Random as a lightning bolt. All subsequent permutations the result of human interaction, the force of the impact as we run headlong into other lives and career off in some new direction as circumscribed by those first factors, as circumscribed by the simple facts of one's birth. No, Einstein would not have dreamed relativity if he were born into a Guatemalan slum. Instead of an equation that falls just short of the unified field, he would have seen a half-baked god dressed in feathers and a breechcloth in an impoverished Guatemalan version of Nirvana – and he probably would have gone mad. And I would never have dreamed myself a hero if I were born anywhere but in America, land of the ostensibly free and the brave only when absolutely necessary or utterly deluded.

I dab some Vaseline on the abraded skin of my cheek, wincing ever so slightly, and try to decide what to do, but no ideas come to me. Instead I am assaulted by the inane memories of how I arrived here, if my suppositions about this blueness are correct, the long road to becoming this blue man in the mirror.

When I was young, I had a strident sense of destiny. I knew without doubt that the universe had something in store for me, a heroic role to play in the grander scheme that I could barely touch with my mind, like groping in the dark for an object you can run your fingertips over but can't identify as vegetable or mineral. In my delusion, I intuited that I was somehow special, but I couldn't quite bring to the full light of consciousness exactly why or how. I thought I was a work in progress and the eventual sum of all my experience and thoughts and stupid dreams would be a man well suited for an extraordinary purpose.

Then came my fall and subsequent banishment. And even then, like Oedipus after he knew he'd killed a king but had no idea he'd killed his own old man, I was stupid enough to think that I simply hadn't discovered what I was to do in this world, even rationalized that my *mistake*, the reason for my dismissal, had been somehow foreordained, woven into the very fabric of the universe and was thus meaningful on the largest possible scale. Two men had not merely died, or hell a hundred or more men and women and children had not merely died, at these blue hands, but the world had inched closer to its own destiny, a blossoming into fulfillment that required my sacrifice and penance.

What crap. My so-called fate has always been engineered by men. Men with power or men who are merely petty bastards like Bob what's-his-name, just men – and this blueness may be the final proof.

Justine is jiggling the doorknob as I put the Vaseline back in the medicine cabinet with the cracked hinge that sounds like a cat when its tail is pulled. She tells me that she and Chanelle are sorry if they hurt my feelings. "Go away," I say. "I think I may be ill. I'll be out in a minute." She walks away and there is a burst of female laughter from the kitchen. It's wonderful to be loved.

Chanelle is probably closer to right than Justine – ultramarine. The blue is darker than my eyes, which are closer to azure, sky blue, but I'm not as dark as the nearly purple Chevy I drove in high school. The color on my body is just as immaculately even, however, as if sprayed on with an airbrush. The wrinkles at my eyes are as blue in the valleys as at the peaks. I have a day's growth of beard, which makes the color appear to be deeper at my cheeks, where I'm going soft around the jowls, where the stubble remains dark, but it's an illusion of contrast. At my temples the gray looks snow-white because of the deep blue background.

I look at my cock when I take it out to pee. It is the exact same shade as the hand that holds it, as my face in the mirror a moment ago. I can't stand to look long and close my eyes, miss the eternally stained toilet to the left for a second, and open my eyes again to adjust my aim. Who else could have devised this agent just for me, just for the joke that is another man's terror? Who else could make a metaphor reality just for a laugh? I shake my blue dick with my blue hand and fold it back into my pants.

Before I was Sonny the drunken Seven-Eleven clerk, before dozens of other names I culled from obituary columns and then enacted as I had been trained, before they threw me out for what they called my *mistake*, my code name was Blue. As in sad but also faithful – true blue like an old dog named Blue – as in heavy-hearted music played by John Lee Hooker, as in out of the blue, blue Monday, blue skies, bluebells, faded blue jeans and a Chevy so blue it was almost purple with blue interior and discarded blue panties to reveal the magic pink passage beneath a blue dress.

That was my problem at the Agency. I was a romantic in a world of cold-blooded killers incapable of poetry, unless you consider the condensed lingo of the trade, the bloodstained words that represent an entire body of macabre knowledge, poetry. Never mind that I became one of them; somehow I stayed a romantic even *after* the bitter end, but the clues were in the name I picked the day I lost my virginity, as they called it, the day I "played my first solo" and took out a Colombian diplomat suspected of being a commie drug runner. Suspected by whom and based on what evidence no one ever said, and I didn't expect them to tell me anything but the target and the date of his exit to the Underworld – that ancient Greek destination for all the dead whether they were saints or sinners. The Mayans believe the same thing, that all the dead are gathered in the dark below ground, but how I know this is a long story. I stare at my face again in the mirror, and I swear, this tale gets funnier by the minute in a bleak kind of way, like a joke told by a demon, and not the Greek version but the medieval Christian one with a hot fork and vicious sense of humor – you know the punch line is going to hurt but can't help but laugh.

Only later did I figure out that the Company never cared about the latter charge against the Columbian, not then and not now. Being killed for running coca must be one of those bleak jokes at the Agency these days, since the boys in the Company have made money selling that product themselves to finance a covert war, if the news reports from a few years after my departure are to be believed. Maybe it's accepted as a business thing, taking out the competition, and maybe it was even then, even as the man's windpipe buckled in my hand and he gaped like a posturing orangutan at the zoo and his eyes bulged and he went nearly as blue as I am now. Or maybe the current war on drugs taking place on foreign shores just gives the foot soldiers in the Agency something to do since the former charge became the biggest joke of all, the communists now mostly gone or doing their best imitation of capitalists. Maybe the war on drugs is just blood and maneuvers to keep agents occupied and the machine of covert operations greased, that omnivorous handmade clock finely tuned and blood-hungry. Just in case. Maybe that was the reason I was told to kill the diplomat, just for practice.

It was the other charge, the diplomat's politics, that made it OK in my own mind to kill the man: my *raison d'être*, his *raison d'mort*. It wasn't about economics then, not explicitly, which is maybe the greatest act of legerdemain ever performed – to associate closed markets with evil in the popular imagination, to convince the hero that he serves good no matter how evil his tactics – a joke told by a demon. The Christian kind with a forked tail and a pointy beard.

That day in the back of a limousine with tinted windows, in a perverse rite-of-passage for which my fellow agents slapped me on the back and bought me drinks when I returned to the States, I became Agent *Blue*, and the name became part of an elaborate illusion wherein I could believe I had become a hero and the Agency could forget I am a man. After all, the hero is always incognito, pretending to be just a man until he dons his other identity and his true name, something elemental and beyond the understanding of common human beings, those who are not heroes, who might condemn the hero's methods as too brutal, too inhumane, if they only knew. And my handlers could punch in the instructions for the next mission, encode them in my synapses as into a machine.

My code name also became part of an elaborate misunderstanding between the Agency and me. It was not the name itself, but the differences between what we heard in it. It was only during my excommunication that I realized that my colleagues didn't hear my name the same way I did. For them, blue was part of a football cadence, *blue-31-hut-HUT,* or the color of a fast and brutal car with no panties or other trappings of a life, or the word was short for the infamous blue streak that all fast talkers are capable of, or the color of a gun barrel. Or blue was past tense for blow: *she blew me and I blew her away.* Or blue was the color of suffocating men, men with smashed windpipes, Colombian diplomats who run drugs and stupidly call themselves communists in a hemisphere patrolled by cowboys in dark glasses who will make sure the profit goes to one of us, a *Norte Americano*, or to nobody.

The day I figured this out, the Company heard my name the way I heard it, and consequently that was my last day as an operative, an agent, a spook, a cowboy riding the geopolitical range in the clandestine service of America. My last day as a hero. It was the end of our misunderstanding, but not the end of the illusion, which is of course just a diminished version of that larger illusion the powers-that-be perpetrate upon us all like a perverse Platonic paradigm. We are the good guys and all who would oppose us are the bad guys, the old white hat and black hat thing from childhood. But the illusion in my case is stronger than most people's reality, which is to say, than other people's version of the illusion, which is the crux of the joke. I actually thought I wore a white fucking hat and the people I killed wore black hats.

Now the joke has apparently become palpable. Today, I woke up actually, absolutely, from head to toe, blue. I could almost laugh.

Chapter Two

Justine and Chanelle are stifling giggles in the background as I call Bob at the convenience store to tell him I have the flu. He says he knows I am hungover again, just like the previous six times I've called in sick in the last month. "By the way," he tells me, "you're fired." Then he says, like a remembered punch line, "There were two men in the store looking for you today, an hour apart: one in dark glasses like cops wear and expensive-looking driving gloves, and the other a darkly complected man in an expensive suit, maybe your lawyer. I assume a guy like you has one of those."

Bob what's-his-name says, "The men are probably your past catching up to you," then laughs like a madman as if this were some kind of culmination in his pathetic little life I can't begin to guess the meaning of, probably having to do with my fate being darker than his own. My good deed for the day maybe – to make this idiot feel better than somebody else for a few minutes. Normally, I would tell him to shove his stupid job up his ass, but I have other worries today and merely hang up the phone and stare at the back of my blue hand.

I wish Chanelle and Justine would go home. I called Justine for help, because she is very bright and I thought maybe she could help me figure out how to become unblue. Chanelle tagged along for the spectacle. They have finally run out of blue jokes, and my jobless situation is at least nominally sobering for them. At least they are now quiet, no more jokes. They are even uncharacteristically compassionate for a minute or two. Justine offers to ask her boss if he still needs a bouncer, as if a guy getting as gray as I am could bounce the young toughs who drink at the Lucky Satyr – former CIA bad boy with all the requisite skills or not. Age is age.

Chanelle had offered to cook something, but she apparently forgot when the perennial argument between these two over politics and TV as metaphors for human endeavor broke out. I have heard it all before and, although I am usually amused, listening but never participating because the argument is as much an elaborate family ritual as it is a real discussion, I just want quiet right now. I need a plan, and I am years out of practice planning much of anything, let alone escape from the best assassins the world has ever known while apparently permanently marked for slaughter. I can hear some Company hack now, asking John Q. Citizen in Anytown USA, "Seen any blue guys lately?"

Both sisters have a linguistic tic, which, besides sleeping with me, is about all they have in common. I mistook one for the other a year ago while very drunk, but Chanelle's lips are larger and her nose flatter, like her daddy's she mentioned once in passing, and Justine has offset nipples – the right is higher than the left. One watches cop shows religiously, and the other reads about political action, although she doesn't participate in any such action herself. One likes the top, one the bottom. One is quiet but insatiable, one loud and truly attentive to my needs. One throws a fit if she gets pickles on a burger as if it were vermin poop, and one eats anything considered food by any culture on earth.

But they both say *GirrRRRLLL* to preface at least one half of all utterance when in this argumentative mode, one hand on a hip like the first step in the little teapot dance they make kids do, the other waving downward as the speaker shakes her head from side to side with her eyes closed. An anthropologist I knew with the Agency, a man who helped manipulate and destroy whole cultures in Southeast Asia and Central America, would probably get much out of this exchange, but it's merely an annoying affectation after all the times I've been subjected to it.

"GirrRRRLLL, what you mean cop shows are to comfort white folk? They comfort you, Sonny?" Chanelle says now, her hand swishing through the air as if swatting invisible flies. The question is rhetorical. I am never expected to say a word and probably wouldn't be heard if I did.

"You know they're all scared to death," says Justine. "They like to pretend they don't know how they got to the top of the pile or how they stay there, by keeping their thumb on the rest of us, but deep down guilt works on 'em until fear busts out into the open where they have to deal with it somehow, someway. Don't you see it in 'em? All black folk could see it in 'em if they dared look because we the biggest reason they feel it.

"All that fear-that-is-really-guilt projects out into the world and shines back at 'em off of our black faces. So TV helps 'em out so the whole white world don't come to a stop. That show you watch every week has pages and pages of nothing but black faces in mug-shot books every episode. It's simple, really. The cops are all white knights, even the black cops, taking care of those evil black faces so guilt-become-fear won't reflect back at white folk. They can sleep at night because TV tells 'em it's all under control." She pauses to catch her breath and I half expect her to request an antiphonal "amen."

"GirrRRRLLL," says Chanelle. "Where you get this uppity soci-Oh-logical bullshit? TV is just the way things

26

are in this world. Evil is evil and its everywhere. You called me paranoid earlier, but this blue-thing that happened to Sonny just shows that too many people has evil in their hearts. Cops hassle too many brothers for being brothers, but we needs 'em to keep the darkness from taking over the world."

"GirrrRRRLLL," says Justine, "you're so full of shit. The cops are part of the darkness, a big part, keeping control for the one percent of the population who own everything ..."

They go on like this for hours when they're in the same room together, which is another reason I haven't mentioned us all together in the same bed since that one time. After sex, my primary and perhaps only function in their lives, there would be no sleep.

I close the door to my tiny bedroom and lie down on the bed in what sunlight can sneak over the building across the street at this time of year. If I looked out the grime-streaked windows, I'd see the first snow of the season falling prematurely on the cars in the street below, provisionally painting over this bleak street in the Ohio Valley, this tattered remnant of a place. It's a wonder I didn't die of hypothermia last night, naked in the alley and with so much booze to thin my blood.

I'm exhausted from too much drink and too little sleep, but I need to think. If it's the Agency, and I can't imagine who else it could be, why now? I was kicked out nearly two decades ago, and I got complacent about hiding my tracks after about ten years because no one showed up at the door with a loaded automatic, and because deep down I knew they could have found me even if I hid inside the Arctic Circle. I haven't bothered to cover my tracks at all for at least the last five, except to use this same alias, Sonny the drunk, because this one suits me just fine. So why now? Did some agent take offense after all these years, or did he want to kill me at the time of my transgression but couldn't get authorization and only now went rogue? Maybe my head is some moron's retirement present to himself, some friend of Rudy's from the old days who decided to even old scores. The front door to the apartment opens and closes, and I hear someone moving about in the kitchen. I put my hands behind my head and try to remember the old connections, who might be sufficiently deranged to carry a grudge this long.

I'd love to believe that my code name and my being actually blue is just coincidence, but as Rudy, my partner in South America, used to say in his Texas drawl, "Coincidence is only the unexplained relationship between cause and effect. We got to get as close to the beginning as possible to get to the truth." A succinct enough definition of the way the world works for a spook, an epistemology of paranoia in practice perhaps, but accurate all the same. At least you can build one hell of an illusion this way, by connecting the dots to make a picture that conforms to what you need the picture to be. A Columbian diplomat is the enemy because Castro visited his country and the two played golf.

Rudy was truly paranoid toward the end. He saw intrigue in a loaf of bread, in kids playing in the street, and he would level his gun at them from a hotel window and make gun noises like a kid playing at violence. It makes sense to attempt to correlate a physical effect to a possible sociological or historical cause, simple logistics, but for us the beginning was always *our* first experience with the constituents of a situation. We might ask a previous operative in our arena what he knew of X or Y, or maybe even have a professor of history or anthropology on the payroll put in his or her two cents, but in our arrogance, that was as far as our

28

investigation went. For all practical purposes, time began for us with US involvement in any situation. The truth, I discovered most painfully, is another animal altogether.

I met a Mayan in the museumed ruins of a dead civilization in late 1978, and again coincidentally – miraculously, suspiciously – in the ruins of another dead civilization on the outskirts of Guatemala City six months later. He told me the *Popul Vuh,* literally The Book of the Community, begins with the creation of the beginning. As far back as it gets. I shivered when he said it, although a full-blown sense of foreboding was probably beyond me then because a beginning implies an end, but I was whole heartedly a killer by this time anyway, incapable of anything like rumination let alone conscience, and completely enthralled to the carefully constructed rationalizations of late Western Civilization. Chanelle is now humming loudly from the kitchen, a popular rhythm and blues number about lost love and revenge that would be playing on the stereo if we were at her place. I envy her the ability to take the song's lyrics at face value. I tried to explain tragedy and the revenge motif to her once as the song played just loud enough to talk over in the background, and I even invoked the few plays by Seneca I could remember, but she only smiled at me with a puzzled look in her eyes and declared me overly serious, as if knowledge, a recognition of cause and effect, of meaning, were merely a bad mood one refused to get out of and a stupid smile the answer to everything. Can I get an amen? I thought her the anti-Rudy at the time, and not without affection.

I stare into the dark spot on the ceiling where the upstairs tenant's unwatched bath water soaked through a few months ago as if it were a map to the encoded truth of my blueness. The center is now mold black, like the interior of some far off continent yet to be explored, but the edges are brown lines of varying density that actually look like topography. I know the morass of unanswered questions, the chaos of history, comes unhinged from our neat arrangement of the facts in the service of dominion, that those questions are the unmappable territory in the dark region. I know a man's life is a drop of spit on the outgoing tide. Chanelle drops a bowl and curses, but almost immediately she is humming again.

Several years before I ran into the Mayan, the governments of Guatemala and Mexico asked the CIA to help them control their indigenous populations. The powers-that-be were afraid of people who think in such grand terms, who can wait a hundred years, or a thousand – five thousand – to regain what has been taken from them. The powers-that-be could feel them waiting and claimed the tribes were a hotbed of communist dissent to get US attention. I thought at first the secret policemen in Mesoamerica had read Engels, but they just understood us well.

My partner and I were sent in answer to their request. We taught representatives from both governments how to destroy their tribals via conscription into their armies, overt or covert, or into the drug or timber trades, by exploiting latent tribal animosities or by creating the necessary tension in the absence of ancient hatreds. The method our students seized upon as holy writ was to scare the hell out of the populace with the dead bodies of loved ones, the more mutilated the better. Heads chopped off were good, heads placed into the abdomens of the dead like a perverse pregnancy were better, and genitals hanging from gaping mouths were best. The image of the victim devouring his own manhood is deeply symbolical no matter the culture, the source of an atavistic fear to buckle the psychological defenses of the strongest warrior. It happened all the time. One day a village would be on the verge of insurrection, the next the men were easily herded into trucks to be hauled to a place too far to walk home from and put to work on a plantation or cutting trees.

I would shudder with this memory, but a man who is responsible for such tableaux of gore and human parts is incapable of remorse, even after all these years. The risk is madness, which I can feel staring at me out of a dark cave behind my eyes sometimes, the darkness to which I have relegated it – if the mere possibility of remorse occurs to me. What penance could I possibly perform to expunge this memory? What return sacrifice could I make in the name of the Western gods of control and commerce but of my paltry self? No, best to think in the old terms, at least when it comes to the many dead: they are markers in a game their betters play on a scale they can't possibly comprehend. It's a strange irony. The hearts and minds of the body politic must be won at all costs, but at the same time, the masses really don't matter a whit.

In the museum in Mexico City, the Mayan stood in front of a large stone pillar covered with images of headless sacrifices, or rather heads and bodies separated from one another. I had come to see this particular set of hieroglyphs on the advice of one Colonel Cordova. He told me the stone's message was a centuries-old validation of our methods, but mostly he wanted to take cultural credit. "The people of Mesoamerica were taking heads to maintain order when your country was overrun with savages," he told me later, beaming like he'd just told me he fucked my girlfriend before I met her.

"My great-great-grandmother told me about the

creation," the Mayan said out of the blue and in perfect English, as if he had been waiting here to tell someone, to tell me. "How she knew I can't say, because that portion of the *Popul Vuh*, the origin, was stolen and burned by the agents of conquest, missionaries." He was about my age and dressed in a dark blue suit, and he wore expensive sunglasses. I thought at first he must be a well-to-do local in the museum for a dose of his heritage. The people milling around us were tourists and a few children in greasy clothes begging for coins. One couple to the Mayan's left, Americans judging by their garish dress, looked up when he spoke but went back to conferring over the museum brochure they held between them when it was clear his comments were meant for me.

"I have, we have, no such concept of time," I told him. "We have cause and effect on the finite plain of history. All we know for sure is what we ourselves see and hear, and we doubt even this sometimes." I was not feeling well. The famous water was attacking my lower intestines, and I was also pissed at Cordova when I realized what he wanted me to see in the hieroglyphs. I was distracted, the worst mental state an agent can be in because you can't see what's coming at you, but my notion of my destiny had shrunk to this at the time anyway, to an easy equation: all the blood and terror were the coinage of heroic acts and I was destined to perform them.

"What do you see in this picture?" the Mayan asked me. As he turned toward me, for an instant, I saw a bulge in his linen suit jacket, under his left pectoral, to match the bulge under mine. I was immediately alert. I knew he must be Mexican Secret Police, but I didn't recognize him as one I'd trained. Was Colonel Cordova playing with me, sending one of his elite killers to teach me a history lesson, or was this guy here to remove me from the picture for some reason all Cordova's own? I then sensed the man next to me was dangerous, but I couldn't tell whether this was a response to the killer in him, the same foreboding I felt around all members of the trade, or an intuition of imminent mayhem.

"It's a warning, I would guess. The strong reminding the weak of their relative size," I said. I pointed to the lopper-of-heads, a huge beast with a sword in one hand and an ax in the other. He was ten times the size of the dead. "I guess you don't fuck with the ruler of the realm."

"And who is that big one?" he asked.

"A mighty king, I suppose." I waited for the man to tell me who he was or to go for the gun. I stretched my fingers like a movie gunfighter. I'd practiced the postmodern equivalent of the quick draw ceaselessly: my hand flying to the cold metal of the 9 mm, flipping the leather thong from the hammer and swiping the safety with my thumb, pulling the night-dark weapon out into the light of day, as if it were a nocturnal predator aroused from its sleep, and aiming in a single fluid motion. I was very fast, and there was always a bullet in the chamber of the 9 mm. I half hoped to prove my prowess right there in the museum. I wanted this guy to be a double agent, a provocateur, so I could drop him where he stood to the awe and amazement of the couple gibbering over the brochure in their K-mart spiffies even as the effluvial dross of the Mayan spewed over them.

"Yes. A king," said the man. He smiled a humorless smile, and he paused to look at me for several seconds as if for effect. There was hatred in his eyes, which burned through the dark lenses of his glasses, and something else I couldn't name, a knowing, a sense of witness, something beyond my tiny *Norteño* sense of time maybe. I stretched my fingers again and ran through my moves in my mind.

"The king is Death," he said. "Which my people have known since the beginning and yours have yet to discover. The reason you can't win here is that the king of everything is Death. One can be sacrificed to the universal order or one may be executed, his blood run over the ground for nothing, to no purpose but as food for the ever-hungry mouth of Death. It's our choice, an individual's choice. *We* always choose the former, and you gringos, and those of my people who have become like you, always choose the latter. To be sacrificed makes all the difference."

Chapter Three

I must have dozed. I swim up from dreams of the world covered in deep blue snow as a man coming up for air from the depths of the ocean – soaking wet and gasping. The smells of coffee and tuna casserole, Chanelle's specialty, are in the air. Justine must have gone to work. Her shift starts at five and it's now half past. She would have had to go home first to get into her tight little uniform of crinoline and cheap lace.

"You feel better, Boy Blue?" asks Chanelle as I emerge from my room, and she pecks me on my abraded cheek as I lean against the kitchen counter. "Don't worry. If this doesn't start to wear off in a couple of days, we can take you to a doctor or something. I know it's Justine's night, but I wanted you to eat right when you woke up." She pokes gently at the abrasion on my cheek with a look of exaggerated concern on her face. The end of her finger makes me cringe, but her touch feels good too.

Chanelle is the least tender of the two. Her sister is not prone to acts of overt affection either, but at least she smiles in my direction once in a while and treats me as something more than a shared sex partner. Chanelle tends to go about her business, delivering flowers for a shop not far from her new apartment, keeping her place up, and haranguing her sister. Unless naked and intent on lively interaction, we tend to move around the same space as friendly strangers.

I thank her and kiss her on the cheek, which makes her laugh almost shyly. She pats my chest on her way

35

to the door, tenderness a novelty between us. "Be good, Boy Blue," she says as she closes the door behind her.

Before I eat, I look out the window at the street a floor below. Justine once described this neighborhood as she remembered it from childhood as a living thing, but the place melted into this wasteland long before I came. She told me the neighborhood was once filled with families and family businesses, and her eyes grew moist as she talked. Babies were born here, and their brothers and sisters played stickball and tag as their parents watched from stoops, talking of weather and baseball. And the old hung on until the final exit, knowing that the space they left would be filled with another soon enough, here, on this very street. Now the storefronts are mostly empty, gaping into the streets like corpses, the upper floors either empty or where a handful of people like me live, people who don't want to be found.

A few blocks to the west are crumbling row houses with mostly hookers and junkies for tenants, a few families struggling to stay clear of the dark drama all around them, and most of them failing. The street outside my window is more like no-man's land, the wretches like me and the few old folks who still cling to the place as home all but invisible, a few small businesses to serve us. A couple of blocks to the east, a brave new world encroaches – self-service gas stations and strip malls and liquor stores with bars on the windows and convenience stores with quaking clerks waiting by turns to be robbed by the desperate citizens to the west or to sell them the daily necessities of life.

I can see my blue reflection in the window, and through it, I see a man I don't recognize standing in the doorway of the empty storefront directly across from my apartment building. He is wearing sunglasses in spite of the darkness in the street at this hour of an October afternoon. His hands are wrapped around a steaming paper cup and he is wearing tight gloves. He is looking up at the window. I step back, a reflex, but he can't see me without the light turned on behind me, and I turned the lights off when Chanelle left, before going to the window, an old habit from the Agency days and my incognito life afterwards.

For a moment I am afraid for Chanelle, afraid this bastard might indeed follow her as she feared when she found out that I had the map to her new apartment on me when rendered blue. I am afraid he might use her to get to me, the oldest terror tactic in the book, but then I remember that she uses the back door to the dry cleaners like I do. She always pats old Liebowitz on his ass and tells him on the way out that he's beautiful, Liebowitz who is eighty-three and still engaged in the ritual of hissing steam and razor-sharp creases to keep himself alive.

Chanelle and I are both creatures of the alleys, using them to scurry quickly from one place to another like our own private walkways, stepping over drunks and circumventing the nodding junkies when we run into them. Justine thinks the habit strange and dangerous. In fact, she can't imagine how a woman as paranoid as Chanelle – who thinks evil truly does lurk in the hearts of men just like the old radio program used to say, merely waiting for the right circumstances to hatch – faces the risk that traveling through town this way entails. But the truth is Chanelle thinks herself invincible, a power for good bolstered by her faith in God, a power to be reckoned with. She carries a can of mace at the ready and an attitude, and in truth I've seen grown men of a certain desperate demeanor step back into the shadows as she passes.

The man across the street doesn't even pretend he isn't here for me, to send me to the Underworld where my ancestors mope about in the dark. He has to know he looks out of place in his nice overcoat and his upscale haircut. He must know that incognito is out of the question anyway because there are so few people left on the block and any new face is duly noted and reported to any other neighborhood face until we all know a stranger is among us. He just stares up at the window. A taunt. A promise that he wants me to know will inevitably come true. He wants me to know that he is the author and agent of my fate. It is the most heartless of games.

The fading light makes it hard to see, but I swear he is smiling. I swear there is nothing in his expression but unwavering intent and a malicious lust. He dumps the contents of his cup onto the sidewalk, drops the cup, and walks away to the east as if out for a stroll. He looks up at the window until he has to crane his neck around. Then he turns the corner and disappears.

I watch the corner for several minutes as the dark grows by degrees, then stare into the dark where he vanished. When I return to the kitchen, the tuna casserole is stone-cold, but the coffee is strong and hot. I eat like the condemned man I am, deliberately, tasting every bite. I imagine each swallow is a tiny victory against time and circumstance, against fate.

Chapter Four

These were the days of green fatigues and riding around in an army-issue jeep checking on our former students. Many of those students had also been through the School of the Americas and graduated peasant-loathing "counter-insurgents."

Our job was to hone their skills as destroyers of cultures and controllers of the populace, and we had flown in three months earlier to bring them up to date on the latest methods, a kind of post-graduate brush-up for soldiers in the service of American interests. In fact, this was the early 80s, and one of their own had recently taken the Guatemalan presidency by force, General Efrain Rios Montt, a graduate of the School of the Americas. Reagan praised him as a "born again" reformer and sent the old boy arms, but it was Rios Montt who instituted Civil Defense Patrols, our students, to control the population. During the seventeen months of Rios Montt's "Christian" campaign, 400 villages were destroyed, an estimated 20,000 Indians were killed, and more than 100,000 fled to Mexico.

Vietnam had been a prime proving ground for ever more innovative ways to make a human being suffer, and my partner Rudy had written the actual book, the training manual used at Fort Benning, Georgia, and in Panama before the school moved to US soil. The training manual was based on his experience in that far off jungle country fighting people in quaint clothes. He had been in Vietnam from the beginning, which is much

39

earlier than any but those involved could possibly guess. His expertise was in how to keep a body alive under the brutal assault of prolonged torture, how to shoot the heart full of just the right mixture of drugs to keep the "client," as we called them, going; but he was also a master of psychological brutality.

"Fucking with their mind is as important as making them scream," he said. "You bring a pair of bloodstained panties into the room and tell a guy his old lady or his daughter is next door, and I guarantee he'll sing like a parakeet, tell you his mother is an insurgent, and offer to drive you over and introduce you." He proved the point again and again in those three months.

This particular day we are creeping up a rutted jungle road toward an Indian village the local cowboys think is filled with communists. For proof they ask rhetorically, "Would anybody but communists pool the crops grown in little slash-and-burn plots and divide the proceeds evenly after what isn't needed to survive is sold at market in the provincial capital? Would anybody but communists vote on absolutely everything, raise each other's kids like their own, and share tools and even clothing? Why," they would answer themselves without a hint of sarcasm or irony, "it's un-American."

The jungle sun is scorching in the open places, old slash-and-burn gardens just beginning to be reclaimed by the wilderness around them, but the jungle air is stifling in the places where the trees form a wall of green right up to the edge of the rutted two-track road. The bugs buzz in my ears like the drone of a plane or a demonic voice, and I am wondering how anybody lives here at all. I am wondering if these poor bastards wouldn't be happier in the city anyway, where the government is trying to force them to migrate. As we have taught those in power, the masses are easier to control if they give up their folkways in favor of living in the squalor of squatters' ghettos and maybe working in a factory for wages.

We have been on this road for half a day, Rudy blathering nonstop about whatever comes into his pea-sized Texan brain. The oppressive heat leads inevitably to the heat in Texas, where it is of course worse, then to a story about a colony of Vietnam vets living in a dry wash on the outskirts of San Antonio, which leads to another tale about a hooker in Abilene, then to a hooker in Southeast Asia Rudy tortured and executed on a tip from an informant, which leads to an admission that he tortured other hookers in Texas after the war because he had done something wrong in that former case, because his drug mixture couldn't pull the woman back from the brink and he just had to figure out why, the nuances between her breathing and not breathing. On and on he goes like a tape of nightmares. Rudy the perverse perfectionist, the artist who sees nothing wrong with this admission to a comrade-in-arms, another expert. The man is the least likely of agents in one way, a motor-mouth, but by all accounts he is good at his craft, a born killer who loves God and his country. Then I smell burning leaves, sharply aromatic and ever so illusory, the smell of memories: the backyard in Nebraska, the autumn rite the old man practiced as if a holy calling and he a high priest, the chosen one, diviner of decay. The piles of leaves had to be just so big, all equal in size so there was no unwarranted danger – and he said it this way: no unwarranted danger – but big enough to yield a column of smoke to deliver this same sensual punch. I remember he told me once when I was the high priest in training, a twelve-year-old with a rake, that the piles were to be as big as an average-size man, no more and no less. He lay down next to one of mine once for a visual aid, then

41

stood and chewed me out because the pile was twice his girth.

Then the smell grows acrid, sharper, sickening for a few bumpy minutes, then it turns sweet as the most tender meat on a brazier, aged prime rib or a well marinated London broil – singed hair followed by roasting human flesh. I want to vomit at the recognition, at the charred bodies lying everywhere in the village that is a single torch as the jeep jumps abruptly from the trees and into a circle of thatched huts all aflame, but I don't. I don't even let my face show the horror that threatens to overwhelm my heart when I see the tiny corpses of children burning, some in pieces where they'd been hacked apart before they were set alight. It is part of our code, our own kind of cultural relativism: we never bat an eye at the horrors perpetrated by an ally, especially one we have trained to keep order ruthlessly.

I don't even flinch when Rudy says, "Sheeeeit. Just when I think these spics the dumbest sons-a-bitches on earth, they go and do me proud, outdo the teacher." And he smiles like a father at his only child's graduation, like a jazz man smiles at his apprentice as he riffs on the music the older man taught him – the master now mastered. Rudy beams at the soldiers standing around smoking cigarettes, at the soldiers still torching what little is not already on fire, at the soldiers idly hacking the charred remains into smaller and smaller pieces like bored gore hounds. He smiles, a man much pleased with himself and the world just as it is, his big hick's thumbs hitched in his blood-red suspenders, which look ludicrous against the camouflage green of his fatigues, as we sit in the jeep in the middle of a circle of flame like supervising demons in the seventh circle of Hell, as if waiting for the punch line.

Then, as if the aesthetic of terror demands that smoking corpses have accompaniment, Rudy begins to hum an aria. I am looking the other way, trying to ascertain the number of dead by the parts scattered over the ground – ninety, a hundred? – and for a moment I think those first eerie sounds come from the gaping mouth of a char-black corpse in front of me, a scream so beautiful to behold I could weep. For this split second, I could be gladly burned alive if to be aflame meant to make such a noise, if agony birthed such beauty.

Then I realize it is Rudy's fat Baptist lips that drip song, which could easily be dripping blood. The corpse I had been staring into breathes only the smoke of his own organs as they smolder. For the first time ever, I hate the race. Not just Guatemalan soldiers but the race entire: the victims, Rudy, me. We are such weak bags of bones and shit that time will inevitably undo. And we can't wait to see others undone while they are still under-ripe – hacked or burned or broken to pieces. Damn the desire to break another, and damn human weakness too, our brittle nature that sends us to our knees before the executioner, that sends us reeling into the earth under machetes and bullets. First our metaphorical hearts break and then our actual bodies. And Death stands grinning to our left and to our right, urging us on to draw blood, to fear, to our own pathetic undoing. Screaming. Pissing ourselves. Bleeding.

And then I remember the Mayan and his unholy picture in stone, the lopper-of-heads. What did he mean that his people choose to be sacrificed while mine opt for execution? Aren't these corpses descended from his line? Did none of them beg, weep, die thinking *why me*? Death is death. What is there to choose? These are words on the wind, a different thrust of lips and tongue for the same end, a semantic quibble.

Two soldiers have thrown a man's smoking corpse on top of a dead woman whose clothing has been torn away. She was obviously young and beautiful when alive. You can see it even now in her drooping features, her sunken eyes. She is a tribal goddess who must have all but floated over the ground as she went, buoyed by the power flashing in every eye that beheld her.

One of the soldiers pours gasoline on the couple and sets them alight, then a dozen soldiers laugh at the tableau: lovers writhing in flame as corpse muscle shrinks in the heat. Here is the punch line of the only joke told by demons: love is death, desire is death, everything is death. I stretch the fingers of my right hand like a movie cowboy as Rudy whistles on. I want to shoot them all, but I don't. This is our own peculiar brand of cultural relativism, and I sit as stoic as stone in the jeep. My right hand aching, my heart on fire, a relentless scream in my head matching Rudy's aria note for note.

Chapter Five

A stain. That is what Justine calls her hometown in its present state of decay, this rust against a shit-brown sky. The old-timers who hang out at the liquor store where I buy an occasional pint, an old-neighborhood place barely holding its own against the new cut-rate stores with bars on the windows a few blocks away, say that it wasn't always this way. The textile and steel mills grew out of the earth like natural things, a mechanized extension of the garden that is America, the flourishing products of dream-seeds spread by their forefathers, the luscious fruit of bygone days filled with money and beer and beautiful girls who smiled at you in the local pub, even if your hands would never again come clean of the daily grease and your clothes were the color of your work, even if the old lady was pissed at home feeding the kids fish sticks and macaroni, the kids who dream of nothing but escape.

When they wax rhapsodic this way, for a few minutes these old codgers forget that Robber Barons grew fat on the carcasses of their fathers and grandfathers. They forget the bad faith contracts they themselves worked under. They even forget the years of cheap imported steel and cheap imported textiles, cheap imported everything, which became the years of unemployment because global capitalism was hatching on the horizon to feed on whatever was warm blooded and moved and was within its reach.

Justine turns in her sleep, an angel in repose. She is one of the few people, besides any child on earth of course, who is actually beautiful when asleep. Her face is less stern than when she is awake, but she is merely composed and not sleep-stupid with her mouth open and air rushing in and out of her nose. She came in around eleven, off early because the bar was slow, and we made love like we never have before. Sex with this twin was always good, but her enthusiasm last night was extraordinary. Probably the blueness. Everybody appreciates an exotic.

I got up at first light to stare down into the street. I had set an empty beer bottle on the doorknob to warn me of danger in the night, but I am certain the assassin will come in daylight, and in truth, I slept soundly. The point of his game, the blueness and showing up across the street, is to let me know the bullet is coming, to let me see the engine of my destruction from a mile away as it runs at me headlong. The object is to grow the target's despair until it turns to paranoia seeping out of his pores, and then to step close enough to see the accumulated fear in said target's eyes so the assassin can get the peculiar buzz of power over another, the concupiscent surge as death flies from his hand and life flees the target's body. My body.

My plan, as far as it goes, is to deny him that rush, to look at him with these big baby blues and not blink. I might even thank the fucker for ending my walk through this stain of a town, of a life. I look down at Justine again and feel a momentary pang of remorse for not knowing her better, but it fades in a single heartbeat.

It snowed hard through the night, an early heavy snowfall even for this town of northern latitude. Justine had to stamp the snow from her shoes when she came in last night, and she headed straight for a hot shower, complaining that the wind cut through her tiny uniform even though she wore an overcoat. Now the earth is covered in perfect white.

46

At around seven, a black Chrysler pulls to the curb across the street, a great cloud of exhaust rising in the cold. The windows are steamed over, but I can make out the man from yesterday, his gloved hand around a steaming paper cup, his dark glasses in place. He sits there for fifteen minutes, looks up at the apartment one last time, then pulls away slowly.

After sex with Justine in the wee hours of the morning, I lay awake thinking about all the corpses I have bequeathed this planet, and then about my own, and I was actually trembling as I listened to Justine's gentle breathing. When I fell asleep, at first I dreamt of the big sword-wielding figure in the stone tableau from years ago, the one the Mayan told me was King Death. Eventually, however, the thought that this assassin will punch my ticket to the Underworld struck me as a good thing, and I fell into the deepest sleep in years.

If this were a sanctioned assassination for a political end, no matter how reason may have to be stretched to achieve that end, most agents would have moved in already because the price for missing is always deemed too high. But I also knew guys like I assume this one to be, agents who would have stalked the president of some upstart country ten steps behind so he knew his death was lurking seconds away, so the buzz would be there for the shooter. Such killers could not live without this jolt.

Traveling the world to do the bloody deeds of the State tends to turn any man, the crazies right along with the rest, into an automaton, though. All emotion attenuated until it warps into something only barely akin to what our fellow citizens know as human. Inevitably, the suffering of others becomes a marker for something larger, something inchoate and strange, but the center of everything too. Purpose reduced to its gore-stained elements.

47

For Rudy, murder in the name of the State was a religious and sexual compunction, good-with-an-erection dealing a hammer-fist blow to the face of evil. The Other, the doppelganger, the agent provocateur was the force of darkness made manifest, and murder was a function of doctrine, biblical or constitutional. "And who could tell the difference," Rudy asked me once without a hint of irony. After he killed, Rudy always had to find a prostitute, and he frequently made an appointment before doing a job so he could drive straight there. As far as I could tell, he never consciously connected this habit to the killing.

For Buffalo Bill Custer, our section chief in Mesoamerica, murder was a way to clean up the gene pool. He gauged the worth of a human being by his clothes, what he drove, how ugly or stupid he was, which I thought at first was a rationalization, a way to answer the questions few agents ever asked: Why does the peasant die and not the lawyer? Why the lawyer and not the banker? Why the banker and not the Prime Minister? It could all seem pretty random if you let yourself think about the growing list of the dead in countries run by buffoons in military regalia who salute other buffoons as they march by the grandstand.

In the end, Rudy was losing it for just this reason. We were becoming the *random* fist of God, like a tornado or an earthquake, and evil didn't have a damned thing to do with it, no matter how you twisted the narrative to fit the circumstances. For a while he quoted scripture, dark things from the Old Testament and Revelations, to justify all the gore, but he started to lose sleep in the last months and confused the Bible with Shakespeare and TV commercials: *Suffer the little children to be or not to be and never forget you can't eat just one.*

But for Buffalo Bill, moral questions were strictly

48

sartorial, all a question of decorum – of manners and bearing and wealth. A man or woman was worthy to draw breath on the same void as Bill himself or they weren't. Simple as that. They were worthy enough to eat and laugh and fuck on this dimming planet, or they weren't. He once shot a fishmonger for wiping his preternaturally slimy nose on the back of his fish-slimy hand. The story was legend. Bill wrote up the report as just another dead leftist, the accusation enough for any Company man if made by another Company man.

But some agents were actually recruited for their inability to make moral distinctions all together. How else can I explain bastards like I suspect my assassin to be, born psychopaths who toy with their clients for no purpose beyond their own warped lust. The battery of psychological tests to which the CIA subjects potential agents is designed to select for traits like the ability to follow orders or to rationalize bloody acts in the name of God or country or good taste even, but also to select out the outright crazy, for the most part, because they are unreliable. I've heard Middle-Eastern terrorist groups don't want crazy men for suicide bombers for the same reason, a telling coincidence perhaps. The man with the bomb strapped to his back has to believe in some higher calling or who knows where he might set it off, maybe too soon after it is armed.

But Rudy gave the CIA entrance tests for a year while healing from a gunshot wound, and he told me that some operatives are hired precisely because they are beyond all moral compunction, because they do not need to subscribe to a contorted metanarrative in order to sleep at night. Rudy knew a couple of these guys personally and brought them in on a few missions early in our association, former Long Range Patrol recruits he met in Vietnam. Guys so feared by their own, he said, that no one ever told them to do anything when in-country. They were merely stationed along the DMZ and went into enemy territory of their own accord to collect ears or heads, spending weeks at a time killing in the dark and sleeping in the jungle by day as if on a bloody nocturnal vacation. I used to imagine the mythology that must have grown up around their deeds in the north, stories of ghosts that kill you in your sleep and eat your ears. Rudy said the Agency keeps a close watch on cowboys like these and puts them down like dogs gone bad if they kill too many friendlies, but a few such casualties are considered part of the cost of doing business. "The key," he said, "is to keep them busy. Idle hands ..."

The black Chrysler drives by slowly again, the driver looking up, and then the car stops in the middle of the street. He gets out of the car. His breath steams on the air and he pulls at each glove in turn, stretching his fingers spider-like, all the while looking up at the apartment as he performs this pantomime of preparation. Then he climbs back into the car and drives away, still grinning as a death masque grins on into eternity. Maybe the Agency is just keeping this one busy by giving him a graying former agent to turn blue and taunt unto death. How long until his desire is sufficient to require release? How long do I breathe?

Justine sleeps on, her beauty deepening in the rising light, a black angel in snowy reflection. I stare at her for a while, remember how she placed her hands over my blue face after sex last night, more tender than all of the other nights we have spent together combined. I remember the tune she hummed, a hymn that I almost recognized before she fell into the arms of sleep in the same position she is in now, her hands pressed together as in prayer and poised in front of her face, her knees drawn up in a semi-fetal crouch as if she were a child.

Then I stare up into the undifferentiated sky, white folded into white, then into the white earth doing its momentary imitation of perfection. For the first time in years, I want to believe in something big and ominous, something with a profound name I don't dare repeat, but I recognize this wish as absurd even as I think it. Belief is just more romantic bullshit to be deconstructed by the big hammer of reality, like patriotism or heroism or love. By the time I awoke from my dreams of King Death, I was wondering why I wanted to breathe any longer anyway, and now here I am thinking about prayer. Again, I could almost laugh.

I tell myself to shut up and take it like a man, whatever the hell that means, but I can't keep the stupid questions from arising in me like any other condemned bozo. "Why does a man breathe?" I tell myself to shut up again, the voice louder in my head this time. I tell myself that this is *particularly* grandiloquent bullshit, worse than the other bullshit I have lived on over the years, but then I think almost immediately, as if in self-defense, "It's a simple enough question, a primary question, and anyone has the right to ask it, especially a blue man who knows he is about to die." The problem is, the older the race becomes, the worse our options, and the answers I hear tumbling in my blue man's brain are not comforting. Now, there is not even the slightest chance for absolution and redemption. That old story is long dead. I have done what I have done, simple as that; and some dark hole to fall into is all there is.

Hell, we aren't even the agents of history anymore, however illusory that may have been from day one. The ebullient individual now utterly a drone, a tiny click in the unemployment figures, a purchaser of Chevies and Mitsubishis, and not only without gumption, as my grandfather called it, an animating verve that at least

51

borders on will, but we are now just vaudeville dummies without even a cosmic or cultural or historical hand up our collective ass. Once, we recognized ourselves as starstuff shot through with sublime essence threatening to blossom as an extension of the universe, which was also a blossoming, outward and forever. But now, we are so much clothing temporarily given form and stumbling about the rotting earth. I draw a stick man in the steam on the glass of the window, and then immediately wipe it away.

I envision a great machine swallowing everything beyond this room, the few people on the street below, and the dead steel mills in the distance, and the line of Seven-Elevens some blocks away that demarcate this no-man's land from the rest of the world, and even the Guatemalan corpses smoldering in my memory along with the other many dead. I envision the machine now coming for me but overlooking Justine, letting her sleep on, and then I tell myself to shut up again. The thought that I may have put this woman in harm's way makes me shudder, and I consider walking down to the street and up to the driver's side window the next time the assassin parks his car.

Then, as I look across the street, I find myself imagining I am Van Gogh and the snowy earth is a canvas demanding paint. Even as I go mad, even as the machine swallows it all down, I would paint this perfection that covers the defunct steel and textile mills along the blackened river, paint this ground that is a war zone of burned-out cars and smashed windows, walls tumbling down. I would turn the whole vision shades of violent blue, a visual treatise on this crumbling civilization that would melt with the snow, but not until I was no longer here to see the war zone underneath, the stain, emerge again.

Then, when I turn around to look at Justine as she

stirs, I wish instead that I were Rilke. I'd write an ode to this beautiful woman in my bed, bearer of good tidings, dispeller of this industrial-strength depression as she wakes and stretches and smiles and calls me to her, even as the assassin parks across the street once more, even as he smiles without mercy up at the apartment, smiles across the perfect white expanse of the street, even as I kiss Justine's imperfect breasts and the machine swallows us all.

Chapter Six

Once upon a time, I'd have tracked this bastard down, his mirror image but blue as I lurked in the shadows outside his hotel or the whorehouse where he's staying. I would have stalked him back, tit-for-tat, let him see me waiting in shadows, let him know I was going to send him to the Underworld. I would have confronted him from behind a Glock, asked him to say one true thing with my free hand at his throat and my knee in his nuts, my spit flying into his open face as he sweated his last, as he knew with certainty this would be his final breath.

Justine is making coffee, and for some reason, the smell of it is a reminder of being in my parents' house, something I have not thought about for years. I don't allow myself to think of them, of that place. I never smoked cigarettes, and I genuinely hate the damn things. Exposure to the smoke fills my sinuses with snot and makes my head ache. But my old man smoked with his coffee in the morning, and the smell of his Camel mixed with brewing coffee was somehow comforting. The petty tyrannies, the bigger ones too, all forgiven by this simple ritual. I lay here and let my mind wander to their faces over that same table, but it is not long before I am back to the present, to my blueness.

I can't decide if I am resigned before the inevitability of a bullet to the back of my skull at the point where it sits atop my spine, or if this is fear and I just don't recognize it because I haven't really known fear on this scale and I'm frozen like a deer in the headlights. Maybe my self-loathing is calling the assassin to me like a beacon atop the lighthouse nearest home calls a sailor from a thousand miles in the dark. Maybe I just want to get the hell off this planet, exit this tale told by an idiot that is the story of my life and of the whole Western world. Maybe I'm just ashamed of being blue.

And ye shall know the truth. And the truth shall make you free. It's from the Bible, John VIII, 32; and it's carved into a marble wall in the lobby of CIA headquarters in Langley, Virginia. Some archaeologist of the future will stand before those hieroglyphs in utter dismay. What kind of people were these who made it all up as they went along, a self-serving history, a self-serving truth? That is, if truth can be revivified in any but a solipsistic sense so that archaeologists of the future even know what the fuck the word means. Maybe the concept will be so defiled as to be but a quaint remnant of a former time when people were naïve enough to believe anything written in a book, stamped on a wall, carved into their flesh as they shuffled into trains like cattle or went to their knees with the sad realization that someone had written a different truth, one that excludes them utterly, someone brutal enough to make it so the whole world over.

Bribery, forgery, blackmail, fraud, assassination, extermination, infiltration, re-education. This is the vocabulary of the Company and it represents a complete body of knowledge, a civilization's composite vision of the truth as it is thrust upon the rest of the world, making conscripts of those backward savages silly enough to believe *they* had the universe figured out, as the members of the civilization are themselves conscripted into this single monolithic thing, this culture that is all cultures and no culture at the same time. Coca-Cola and Prozac. Johnny Walker Red and Marlboros. Dot-com everything and the nightly news read by a drone in tweed. Pop Tarts and sports facts, the new opiates of the masses, over coffee in an ersatz Navajo mug from Wal-Mart. Nike on the radio, the goddess of victory co-opted and complacent and turning tricks, whose entry in the dictionary is just before nil, which means nothing, zero, which is derived from the Greek *nihil*. And damn if it doesn't all come to this: Nihilism. The doctrine that says all values are baseless and nothing can be truly knowable, so we make it up as we go along, whatever suits us; the rejection of all distinctions of moral value and a concomitant willingness to refute all previous theories of morality as well, as backward, as strange, as arcane and thus dead. The doctrine of some 19th century Russians, romantics whose dreams were sucked out of them, whose optimism turned sour as month-old milk, who believed terrorism and assassination the valid tools of social engineering. *And ye shall know the truth.* And the truth is we have become agents of nihilism, one and all.

Chanelle and Justine come into the bedroom together. Justine was making coffee when her sister used her key to get in, and Chanelle asks about the beer bottle that had been sitting on the doorknob, which fell and broke into a thousand pieces on the linoleum when she turned the knob. I know I have to tell them, not about the bottle but what it represents, the danger. But why would they believe me? I have never let on that I was ever anything but what they know, a hard-drinking convenience store clerk.

Justine is now sweeping up the broken glass as I sip coffee. Chanelle has her arms crossed and is staring at me like I'm an errant child. "Why you set that bottle where it can fall and break like that, Sonny?" she asks me again. I had passed off the question the first time and brushed past them to get to the coffee pot. Justine pauses in her sweeping to look at me too. I had put the bottle there after she fell asleep. She crosses the floor to lay her hand upon my blue arm.

"What's the matter, Sonny?" she says, and the look on her face is of genuine concern.

"There is a danger I need to tell you about," I say, but then I falter, unsure of how to tell them about my assassin without admitting everything, my complicity in the end of the world. It comes to me like one of those proverbial bolts from the blue, what it is I'm facing, and why.

The place I start the story surprises me. "In the *Popul Vuh,* an ancient Mayan text that I read in a Spanish version many years ago in the basement of a museum library in Mexico City, that I read more than twenty years ago because a man asked me questions I could not answer ... In the *Popul Vuh* is the story of Blood-Girl, a goddess of sorts who finds the Twin Gods hanging from a tree in Dusty Court after they were murdered by the Chiefs of Hell. As the skulls of the Twin Gods speak to her, telling her their tale of woe, they drip spittle into her womb and she becomes pregnant."

"That's so gross, Sonny," says Chanelle. "What kinda story you telling us here?" The sisters share a twin look of confusion.

I continue, not knowing where this story leads, but knowing it is the answer I need, a way to explain not just the danger but my blueness. "Her father is outraged by her pregnancy and sends owls," I say, "preternatural winged creatures with great glassy eyes to seek out Blood-Girl in the dark where she is hiding from her father's wrath. When the owls swoop down on her, she sees her own reflection in their eyes and is sad beyond all reckoning, which is important, which says something about the human condition: that it is grave, that it is deceptively difficult, that the fact that we exist

57

and know it is important. The owls' orders were to tear out her heart."

Chanelle and Justine are very attentive now, obviously confused but also curious. Justine for the tale's coming meaning, I imagine, sensing this is a morality tale, and her sister, bless her, because she hears Stephen King in the details. In any event, they are listening.

"It seems that her father, Blood-Chief, is in league with Hell. It isn't clear to me whether he's pissed because his daughter lost her precious virginity, which he needs intact to make alliances with some other household via her marriage, or if he's doing the bidding of the Chiefs of Hell because they fear the Twin Gods' progeny; but the owls take pity upon the girl and fly back to her father with a piece of wood covered in blood-red sap. The whole host of Hell dances around the ersatz heart as it roasts, savoring the smell they believe is her flesh burning.

"While all of Hell is busy partying, the owls fly the girl through the hole in the sky that the smoke from the fire makes and take her to earth, where she will be the source of all that is human, all suffering and all prayer." Both sisters start to speak now, to voice their confusion, but I interrupt them.

"In the beginning," I say, "all was in suspense, calm and silent and without motion, waiting; and the sky was as blue and empty as my hand." I hold my palms out, blue palms toward the ceiling, the prop for this tale that exceeds all others.

"In her womb Blood-Girl carries the Truth, and Truth's twin, Death. Blood-Girl is Destiny, you see, the first mother but also the world's story as it must be told, as it must unfold, as it must end, and when her children meet, together they are the end of time. And the agents of Hell are afraid, so they make up lies. They retell the story casting themselves in a better light, stretching and warping the twin Truth and using the other twin, Death, to their own unsavory ends. The agents of Hell kill whoever disagrees, you see, or they torture their loved ones until they give in to their stunted version of the revised story and play the part the agents want them to play: killer or slave, agent in the service of Death, or blue man soon to be executed.

"Do you understand?" I ask almost rhetorically. I know this tale as I've told it is beyond even Justine. Both sisters look confused, but there are tears in Justine's eyes.

"What you mean that you're about to be executed?" she asks.

I tell them the truth as best I can, but I cannot bear to say it all, outright, that I was an agent in the service of Death, that the blood on my hands would drown the Ohio Valley and wash all this rust to the sea.

Chapter Seven

I went to the ruins in Guatemala City to kill time, and to get away from Rudy. Rudy had taken to drinking first thing in the morning, and his quotation of scripture mixed with Shakespeare and TV had become increasingly strange and increasingly violent: *Blessed are the meek in spirit who clamor for us to release the dogs of war, whom the dogs of war eat like ballpark franks roasted fat and juicy for the big game. Forever and ever. Amen.*

The Mayan from Mexico City, the man about my age and height but dark and with high cheek bones, the man with the bulge in his coat over his heart that mirrored the bulge in my coat, sidles up to me as if we had an appointment to meet in front of the hieroglyphs on this stone stele I had stared into for ten minutes. He has his hands behind his back in a gesture of neutrality, but the shock of seeing him again after so many months makes me more than wary. I am again prepared to shoot him on the spot, this time just for being here, surprising me with his presence.

In the picture, a woman sits under a tree that is before a great door, and she appears to be sleeping. The door has been shattered. To the woman's left, three men kneel before three others with long blades at the ends of long shafts. The kneeling men's throats have been slashed and flowers bloom where their blood spills over the ground: daffodils, daisies, other flowers with delicate lips, delicate pincer-like stamen on tender stems swaying in a stone breeze.

The Mayan looks at the picture incised into the stone. He speaks without turning his head. "Do you know who the woman in the picture is?" he asks.

"More questions meant to tell me my people will fail and yours survive?" I ask. "Shouldn't you get to whatever point you are about to make and save us both the time and effort of this little game?"

"She is Quiché, the people and their place and their religion all rolled into a single symbol. Those are the gates of Hell she sits next to, and they are shattered because the people survived the tortures there."

The man turns to me then and I instinctively stretch my fingers, ready to reach for the gun in my coat quick as lightning, to deliver nine millimeters of hardened copper and lead to his cerebral cortex before he can blink.

His eyes are dark and stern in a way I can't imagine my own in spite of the deepening cynicism that the job is bringing on like a terminal disease, but there is something else in his face – a smoldering rage that has at least partly transubstantiated to a level of focused purpose that I have never read in another man's face. His hands remain behind his back, and his voice softens to a harsh whisper, half-conspiratorial and half admonishment.

"The tree is the tree of life," he says. "Those sacrificed and those doing the sacrificing are shamans, holy men who kill and die for Quiché because there is no greater human desire. But also because it is their destiny, their lives as played out in the dream of Quiché where she sits sleeping outside the smashed gates of Hell, where she sits under the tree of life."

"What is it you want?" I ask him then. "I don't see how any of this has anything to do with the politics of this place that so occupies us both." I am fishing, trying to get the Mayan, whose long nose and high

61

cheekbones bespeak his heritage, to reveal his allegiances, his reason for singling me out twice in six months without a word in between, as if he knew I'd be in the museum and in these ruins so he could give me riddles that went nowhere.

"I am a shaman," he says without a hint of irony or movie cowboy grandiosity or ego. "And neither of us is interested in politics."

"Sacrifice to Quiché or sacrificer?" I ask, my hand still flexing.

"For now, the latter," he says. "Someday, the former." He turns back to the picture on the stone. "You will be both one day too, although you don't know it yet." He turns his back on me and walks away into the crowd of milling tourists. Just like that: he appeared and laid a bullshit riddle at my feet and disappeared again into the chaos of the world.

I haven't seen the man since, until today. Today, he is across the street, standing before the same storefront that the assassin stood before yesterday. His hair is white at the temples like mine, but otherwise he is unchanged. He is in a deep blue linen suit, like a banker or a lawyer, presumably the second man Bob what's-his-name told me came to the store looking for me the day I was fired.

Like the assassin, he looks up at the apartment. He raises his head a little, as if to acknowledge me in the window, but I know he can't see me. The light, as always, is in my favor. He looks even more out of place in this neighborhood than the other one. His suit is too well tailored, his features too Indian in a region of black faces, and here and there, a Latino or a Caucasian. I can't imagine why he is here, unless he's with the other killer. But why would it take two? Did the psychopath tire of the game? But no, that would bring about his fulfillment of my fate, my death. Is it perhaps a game

62

within the game, a contest to see who can find me first, torture my psyche best, then beat the other to the deed? But the man I saw only twice in my life would not play such a game – my intuition says so anyway. There was too much history and mythology in his stories, too much intense purpose in his eyes.

"But a man changes," I say aloud, especially after enough blood accumulates at his feet and he wonders if he might drown and so becomes a killer completely, whole heartedly. "I did," I say.

Chapter Eight

I dreamt of the Underworld last night, the endless ranks of the fallen, the gone-eyed dead in an ambivalent light. The Underworld of the ancient Greeks, where the victims of tragedy go after the fact; and we are all victims of tragedy. A place of great stone stelae standing idly about and covered with gruesome figures, heroes and sacrificial lambs, and here and there *The truth shall set you free* cut into the rock like a bad joke on these souls imprisoned in the Underworld for all of time.

My grandparents were there, each numbered among the dead by natural causes before I turned twenty. My parents were there too, although they were still alive the last I knew. I have stayed away all these years, at first to protect them because the Agency might have been looking for me, or maybe only because I feared being found and one's ancestral home is a logical place to look. Then I stayed away because they seemed to belong to another life, family a concept I never really understood anyway, all that pain confined to such a small space, and after my banishment I accepted family in any yet to be discovered positive sense as a luxury I would never be allowed. The year I've been with Justine and Chanelle is the longest I've stayed with anyone.

The old man was in the shabby overalls he wore to work in the yard, to change the oil in the car, to paint the fence. My mother wore a floral print housedress and held the scissors she used to cut our hair, mine and the old man's. They were younger than the last time I saw them, staring stone-faced from somewhere in my childhood. Postmodern American gothic. The Underworld smelled of new-turned earth, like a spring garden after the previous year's remains are turned under to rot, to make the circumscribed plot of earth green one more time.

I realized as I stared at my parents in my dream that these were images from a photograph, the means by which we trap a memory to keep it from escaping altogether. The dream of them was a copy of a copy of their flesh and blood selves, and I could not remember them any other way, could not conjure any image but this one captured in black and white by some relative or other.

Then I saw Chanelle and Justine among the dead and my heart broke. They looked at me with accusing eyes frozen in that last grimace of disappointment. After the Blood-Girl story, I had told them what I could of my past, leaving out the many dead with their throats slashed or crushed or bullets to their brains, all the terrible photos stored in my memory like a macabre album of my life, my real family, all those I sentunder.

By the way, I told them, when I was with the CIA, the Other was everywhere – the mole, the infiltrator, the incipient traitor waiting for the right moment to blossom into something terrible. The Other was everywhere and trying to break into the heart of the Agency, which was the heart of America as far as we were concerned, which was the heart of democracy. It remains our favorite myth in that most diminished sense of the word, a lie we need to account for our behavior on the global stage, which has always been atrocious.

Chanelle started to speak at that point, to defend her country to the death, but I wouldn't let her. I went on, hoping to get it all out before I lost my nerve.

65

Justine just looked sad.

We looked into other men's eyes, I said, as if looking into a mirror for our reflection, one mirror in a wilderness of mirrors that might reveal our opposite number. We looked for signs those eyes belonged to cowboys from the black side of someone else's house, the doppelganger of evil intent, our malevolent twin.

In Guatemala, my partner, Rudy, saw me in the eyes of a down-and-out balladeer named Miguel Santiago. I used to stand at the corner where Miguel sang and played his guitar, his beat-up hat upturned on the ground, passers-by throwing in coins. I stood there every day that I could get away because I had never heard music so pristine, so sad, so extraordinarily human. The clarity I knew standing in the dirt-poor streets of Guatemala City listening to this man sing was the only religious experience I could lay claim to.

You see, in those days I had forgotten what a human being is. I had become wholeheartedly what the Company hired me to be, completely a destroyer, which is to say, I had not been human for a few years. And the sound of Miguel's music alone was a terrible reminder, a bleak mnemonic that sent me cold inside. I could not stop listening.

And his words, his words were all about death. They carried death in themselves like dark envelopes you open and then stutter and quail at the contents. But death beyond anything I could imagine. Death as motive force. Death as creative, as oxymoronic as that sounds. All I knew was the scattering of flesh and blood over the ground as a perverse sacrifice to ideals that had disappeared years ago, that maybe never existed.

But Miguel sang about death as if it were a twin to God, God's dark sister in everything, that feeds everything even as it feeds *upon* everything. Death walks the world and death sleeps in our bones and death hovers over us in the market and death wears a sequined gown to the ball and death carries salvation in her pockets and death springs to our lips and shoots down our throats the moment we are born and death sings the blues like John Lee Hooker and death is a becoming and a presence and a goal we strive to make golden if we have a clue – and death is forever and ever, amen.

The sisters were looking at each other now, then back at me, then at each other, confused. Justine had tears streaming down her face. Chanelle looked like she wanted to leave the room.

One day, Miguel wasn't on his corner, I told them. His hat was still there, still full of coins, but he and his guitar were gone. I just caught a glimpse of Rudy driving away. I followed him in a cab. We drove for miles, to the outskirts of Guatemala City where garbage smolders in heaps as big as mountains. We'd been there many times because the death squads dumped bodies there and Rudy insisted we take a peek at the dead at least once a week to measure how well we'd trained the killers.

At this image, the sisters closed their eyes in unison and tipped their heads back. Tears now streamed down Chanelle's cheeks too. I went on, trying not to look at them.

I sent the cab driver on his way and walked among the rag pickers, mostly children and the lame who sift through the smoking refuse for anything they can sell. The smell of rotting vegetables, rotting flesh, mixed with the smell of burning rubber and plastic and cloth and all other detritus of the industrializing third world. The rag pickers parted as I walked through their ranks, barely noticing me in my suit and shining shoes. They were used to men dressed this way, and to men dressed in camouflage, walking among them in broad daylight. These were the days of terror in broad daylight. I could see Rudy and Miguel ahead of me through the smoke. The trunk lid of the car was up and Miguel was on his knees in the dirt. Rudy was above him, his gun drawn and pointing at Miguel's head.

"He's you, partner," Rudy said when he saw me. "He's your evil twin come to break into your defenses. I can see it in his eyes. Sheeeit, brother. This goddamn guy's gotta go. You know how it is."

"I've never even talked to him, Rudy," I said, thinking even at this point that the situation was controllable, that Rudy could be reasoned with like any other cold-blooded killer with the Agency who subscribes to so malleable a code as ours. Little did I know how unreasonable *I* sounded, how removed from reality, how mad. I helped Miguel to his feet.

"Look at him," Rudy said, and he pushed Miguel's cheek with the barrel of his gun, pushed his head around until I could see his eyes.

Blood ran from the corner of Miguel's mouth and from his left nostril. His left eye was swollen shut, the eyelid gashed. He looked pathetic in his rags: once white smock and pants like peasants wear, a once colorful poncho like the highland Indians make, which lay crumpled on the ground, his huaraches made of vines and an old tire for the sole all but worn out and barely on his feet. He looked confused but also resigned. These were the days when everyone in Guatemala City knew what a trip to the dump meant.

In Spanish, I told him that it would be OK, that my partner was confused about Miguel's identity and this would be over soon. The rag pickers moved like apparitions in the distance, in the smoke, and never looked up from their work. No one in Guatemala ever looks directly at a man with a gun, at the victim pleading or bleeding or past all hope.

"Look at him," Rudy said again. "He has the same sad, stupid eyes you do. And those songs, what kind of dumb commie fuck sings about death all day? He is you, man." All trace of his Texas accent was gone. I'd known Rudy for years and not once did he sound this way, like he was from the Ohio Valley.

"I only listen to his music," I said.

"There are no coincidences," said Rudy. "He has hold of you because he is you, your reverse self, which is the way we are drawn to them because we are looking for someone to call our brother, because we are looking for our prideful selves. He is in your life for a reason. Look at him, look at him, look at him," Rudy said like a mantra. Then he laid his big hand on Miguel Santiago's shoulder and forced him to his knees in the smoking dirt over my protest.

On the endlessly self-referential stage of counterintelligence, there can be no accidents, it's true. Rudy wasn't so much crazy as he was completely an Agency man, and I knew he was right in that perfect moment of absolute knowing. I looked at Miguel and he was my romantic self turned brown and poor and kneeling in the dust of a garbage heap, of Western Civilization, and I was Civilization's protector.

Terminal impasse. It was both a truism and a joke. Death was the only absolute truth we knew. Not the death that Miguel Santiago sang about, but the absolute negation of life, which is the end of doubt. Rudy suspected Miguel was a communist plant sent to infiltrate my life even from that grave distance of poverty and song. Rudy saw devious counterintelligence in his eyes to mirror my own black purpose, but he had no proof one way or the other. *That* is terminal impasse.

Rudy had told me the first time we met, "Err on the

side of caution. In death there is no equivocation. All supposition becomes a null set. A man is dead," he said, "or he isn't."

The truth is limited to the perceiver's ability to comprehend it, and Rudy had the most rudimentary imagination. He was a Company man to the center of his grain-sized soul, a distinguished member of the empire stalking his own dark Other through the jungles of Mesoamerica, looking for an enemy he could embrace because he was his brother, his inverted self scuttling around the world with an ersatz dialectical signature doing the bloody work of that other empire. Maybe that's how Rudy would know him, by this quirk, and when he heard the accent disappear from his speech, Rudy would pull his gun and kill the bastard.

And what would the Other look like now, I pondered aloud as the sisters stood before me with their eyes closed and tears running down their faces and dripping on the stained and crumbling linoleum? Now that the Cold War is no more. Maybe Rudy's double would be a Japanese information technology entrepreneur in red suspenders like Rudy wore everywhere, business now openly the auspices for espionage, sabotage, assassination. Maybe he has Rudy's Texas-sized grin with gold capped teeth peeking around the edges of his mouth. Maybe he's a Baptist with a taste for hookers big as sumo wrestlers.

But what would make him *not* Rudy, since the doppelganger must stand in elemental opposition to the Agency's version? His broad nose and epicanthic eye fold? His syllabic language without L sounds? His loyalty to Toshiba and Mitsubishi rather than GE and Chevrolet?

Or maybe the double has split in two over and over, the double doubled geometrically until the world is a funhouse of mirrors within mirrors and the race entire is the enemy. An agent merely walks into the street and picks one, the one to follow home, to poison or shoot or blow into tiny pieces of atomized flesh, to blow back into carbon, the pieces already turned back into earth before they hit the ground.

Terminal impasse. Even as I knew with certainty what Rudy was about to do, I could not move. I froze for a split second, knowing in my heart Rudy was right. He was only about to do what we had always done. Err on the side of caution. "There are no coincidences," Rudy said in the dump at the edge of Guatemala City, in the smell of rotting things, in the smoke, ghosts moving on the horizon, and he shot Miguel Santiago through his heart.

The sisters were sobbing now, but the story was not over.

I knew Rudy was right, at least that Miguel was somehow an inverted version of myself and, by the code, he could not exist another moment. I managed to yell at Rudy to stop the same second his gun went off. Then, as if my hand were not my hand, I pulled my gun from the shoulder holster, faster than Bat Masterson, than Billy the kid, and shot Rudy dead. On his way to the ground, Rudy said without any trace of a Texas accent, "Wrong move, Bubba." Or maybe he said, "Why me?" Like any stiff he ever sent tumbling into the Underworld.

Chapter Nine

Buffalo Bill Custer, the section chief, was a collector. He had all kinds of artifacts looted from the locals in his office in Mexico City, more in his office in D.C., and Rudy said his house in Virginia looked like a museum. Buffalo Bill had his number one, Henry Bagby, actually pilfer the things: pots from museums, stone tablets with Aztec figures on them from archaeological sites, even old bones of former Aztec kings he said came from a private collection, which means that Henry broke into some rich guy's house.

Buffalo Bill spent much of his time cataloging his acquisitions, handling them for hours with surgical gloves on his hands. Not to protect the artifacts, but to shield himself from some imagined contagion from ages past, the reason he believed the Aztec Civilization disappeared. He knew all the stories about Cortez, and in fact Cortez was his hero. He came with a handful of men and conquered this mighty force of heathens and this massive land in the name of God and country, he told me once as he fondled an ancient Spanish blade that undoubtedly lopped many an Indian limb before its wielder was brought down. "What men. What times," he said. But he thought only a plague could have wiped out the civilization so totally. "After all, it wasn't in Spain's interest to kill them all, just the ones who were a pain in the ass. The rest would have made fine slaves. There were an estimated twenty-five million Indians here when Cortez landed, and within fifty years, that number was down to less than a million. Who in his

72

right mind would waste such a fine resource?" A rhetorical question to ponder unto the grave.

We called Bill's assistant, Bagby, Hank Butterbuns when he wasn't around, because of the close relationship he seemed to have with Buffalo Bill. I always heard the name and its implications figuratively, as an insult to Henry's servile obeisance to his boss, but Rudy took it literally, which made his Baptist heart skip a beat every time he thought about it – sodomites in his midst.

Rudy said that Buffalo Bill had been a collector in Vietnam too, plundering what little he could find of worth in that long-embattled land. He also collected ears, or rather his First Sergeant, a psychopath named Mankin, collected them for him. Rudy said that Custer mentioned the ears to him once in passing, mentioned Mankin by name almost as an aside, and never said a word about them again. But, Rudy told me, rumor had it that a Lieutenant in an outfit near the DMZ had a string of ears that stretched some twenty feet by the time American troops pulled back, that one third of the string came from a single village that this Lieutenant and one other soldier wiped out on their own and set alight while the rest of the platoon marched south to escape the coming horde. He said he never heard names, but he had little doubt that Buffalo Bill and Mankin were the authors of this farewell note to the insurgents, this tiny footnote to history, this rear guard action par excellence.

"Heroic deeds," said Rudy, "are more often than not left out of the official record." He was forever ambivalent about Buffalo Bill, the possibly-faggot hero, killer of VC. But Mankin, who he never saw, who probably lives on in the local mythology as a ghost marauder of central Vietnam, who collected ears for the

Lieutenant but not as gifts like Bagby's pots, or so Rudy surmised the pots to be – *the buggers*, he said – was indeed his hero. Rudy deemed the string of ears testimony to the Sergeant's wisdom, his understanding that "you gotta fuck with their minds. He probably gave them to Custer to catalog, as any collection should be cataloged," he said. "Date and time and age and circumstances. That kinda thing. The *real* history boiled to fact and represented by a part of the person in question – who died and where. That's what it's about in the end. No more and no less."

Rudy said that Mankin's reputation for lethality was legend in-country. The man could run through the jungle at night and he lived without sleep and he used a knife like an artist and his aim was never off the mark a millimeter and his eyes were coal black and did not reflect light and his hands both deft and strong and he never made a sound as he cut a throat or caved in a skull and he almost never talked but to curse his enemies and no order eluded his precise execution and no man was ever his match on earth or in Hell and he tracked his victims like they were prize game and he never lost them, never once, but killed them like a machine made of stealth and a fierce efficiency to make the devil proud and he never missed, not once, and the enemy trembled at his name and dreamed him in the night cutting their throats shooting them through the heart cutting off their ears. Mankin the apocalypse. Mankin the end of the world.

Mankin could have been one of us.

Chapter Ten

When Truth and Death meet, it is the end of time, and now time must be ended by this blue hand that I stare into as into an abyss. Justine is dead.

"Why this happen, Sonny?" Chanelle asks between sobs, slipping in and out of ghetto argot as she always does when wracked with emotion, although I had only witnessed the change when she was angry before this moment. Her face is bruised and puffy, her right eye almost swollen closed. She says, "This man kicked in my door while Justine and I was throwin' my clothes into garbage bags so's we could carry them to Marlene's like you said, so's we could be safe. He hit us. He tied us to chairs in the kitchen with duct tape and put tape over our mouths. He called us everything but a child-a-God. And he hit us some more, Sonny. I didn't think he was gonna stop until we was dead.

"Then he did it," she says, her eyes big with the horror of what she is about to say, what she is about to see in the shifting light of her mind's eye, the mental photo she will never be able to lose or forget, that will surely return in dreams to break her heart over and over again. "He hit Justine in the throat with the edge of his hand and she went bug-eyed with panic. Then she went blue, and my dear Justine was gone, just like that, Sonny. She was with me, and happy as a girl can be whose man is marked to die, and we was both commiseratin' over this terrible thing that happened to you, to us, and Justine was sayin' how she thought she loved you, Sonny, and I was sayin' it too, and then this man shows up and she wasn't there. She was blue and gone, just like that. Why did he kill Justine, Sonny, if he wants to kill you, if he knows where you are?" The look in her eyes is all sadness, but there must be blame soon. This I know with absolute certainty.

After I confessed, I had tried to explain to the sisters the reason an agent does what he does. I tried to explain malevolence itself used as a political tool, evil as something else. I had tried to explain my old way of seeing it all as of a piece, how the world moved around US interests as if our nation were the sun, tried to explain the terror and blood as just collateral minutiae to a Company man. But I gave up. Justine insisted that only the crazy kill without cause, the abused in childhood, the torturers of animals as prelude to mass murder. Chanelle said evil was always random and seemed to feel safe playing the odds that it would not hit her even if it took me out, that she had at least a fifty-fifty chance of being the bloody detritus of happenstance, and she insisted we call the police who would take care of the assassin. "Like they do on TV," Justine had said sarcastically, and they went into their endless argument about the nature of man.

That they might be targeted merely to torment me was beyond them, and I gave up trying to warn them. They only agreed half-heartedly to stay with Marlene, another waitress at the Lucky Satyr, until I figured out what to do. I told them I could never see them again and would have to leave town if they didn't take this meager step. But I knew I would do nothing, that I would just wait as fate approached, pulling at his expensive driving gloves, and left again with my blood on his shirt. My only hope was to keep them out of the way until it was over.

Chanelle says the assassin hit her some more then and whispered the worst things she ever heard into her ear, things she could not bear to repeat, things she will hear forever in her mind to accompany the mental photos that won't erase or burn or get lost when she moves. "Then," says Chanelle, sobbing great sobs that make me want to look away and cover my ears, "he made me watch as he cut off Justine's ear, and I couldn't do nothin' but scream inside myself like in a bad dream and you can't wake up." The mask of horror that threatened to become her face forever now turns to a countenance of grief so fierce I can't look at her, and I stare at my cheap size-13 shoes. I am to blame. My fault, my fault, my fault.

"God, what we gonna do without our Justine, Sonny?"

"I don't know," I say, and I have never meant any words more in my life.

Chanelle lays her head across my lap, and I stroke her black hair with my blue hand. She sobs for a while, then just rocks back and forth in my lap, half sitting on the couch, half lying down. I want to dim the colors of the photos in her brain, change the lighting to better effect, do something to ease what she felt and I can't feel for all the terror and grief for which I am responsible. Terror and grief just like this terror and this grief embodied before me, a thousand loved ones wailing in the night and beset by dreams like snapshots of Hell.

"I wish I could tell Mama that Justine still went to the church we was in from grade school, the one I still go to most Sundays, that the whole congregation will miss her and cry her into the ground." Justine and Chanelle's brother had taken their mother to Chicago to live near him several years before, to escape this city, this stain.

"Didn't you know she went to church every Sunday morning?"

"Justine didn't go to no church, Sonny. Not since we
77

was little girls. Justine had the world figured out without Jesus, who she called 'a symbol and means of white oppression' or some such nonsense. You know how she was with that soci-Oh-logical stuff, always explaining the world, and without help from no Jesus. I go to the same Baptist church on 4th we was baptized in, and I've asked her sometimes if she wants to go with me. She always says no. I appreciate you want to comfort me Sonny, but you can't make this up, not this." Chanelle wipes her nose.

"She was even in the choir. I followed her once," I say quietly.

Chanelle sits up to look at me, her grief now combining with an intense curiosity. Her hurt eye is terrible to look at, and I get ice wrapped in a washcloth to soothe it. Her good eye is swollen from crying, and in all, she looks like raw meat left too long in the sun, bruised and mottled beyond healing.

"She got up every Sunday she stayed with me, saying she had errands, and disappeared until noon or so. She was evasive when I asked about her weekly tasks, so I followed her once. She went into the Sacred Heart Baptist Church on 1st and Carnegie, and I snuck in at a side door to get a closer look at Justine in that strange setting, to see the novelty of her there among the parishioners all dressed up and smelling of a thousand flowers."

I didn't admit to Chanelle that I was jealous of Justine's Sunday mornings, that I thought she might have a married lover who could get away only on Sunday and felt as stupid as I was curious when she entered the church. I couldn't find her there among the few faces in the pews, mostly the faces of the old still in the neighborhood, a few people the approximate age of the twins. But there were no kids there in that sacred space, no one to step into the shoes of the old ones

78

someday. Someday, it occurred to me as I looked about, this church would house only pigeons and winos who needed a place to sleep.

"She came out with the choir," I told Chanelle. "And they sang as they walked to their places behind the altar. They were a dozen voices but sounded like three times that number, a raging sound of good will and heavenly purpose. They were singing a song about their god being angered by the hopelessness of humans, then started humming like a huge motor made of flesh, and Justine stepped to the front. She saw me standing in the wings then, or whatever that space to the side of the altar would be called, and she looked guilty for a second, maybe a little ashamed she was there after all her posturing, her secular ranting and disdain for the faith. Then she let loose a gut-wrenching tremolo like I had heard on my one mission to the Middle East, in Iran when the Shah was still there and killing his own right and left, a cosmically orgasmic yodel that echoed in the rafters and made me shudder.

"Those singers in the Middle East were women mourning the loss of loved ones – the slaughtered, the stolen, the tortured – and that sound is the most powerfully mournful sound on earth."

Chanelle sucks in her breath, a stutter of wind.

"There is an eerie ecstasy in that wail too, and that wail came from Justine's mouth. The choir clapped and swayed and hummed like kids playing they are jet fighters, but in tune, in multi-part harmony, and that wail just kept coming out of Justine's mouth, so strange and yet so completely human, like all emotion a person could ever feel, all joy and suffering and love and hate and everything in between, was represented in that sound at once, but boiled to essence, to a longing so big we cannot stand it, and the noise from her mouth rose to a painful pitch. She didn't breathe except

79

outward, as this wail, this sound-to-get-God's-attention, and I literally felt my heart jerk and stumble and my own breath grow desperate as I sucked in like I was trying to breathe for her, and then she stopped. Just like that, and the choir stopped humming at the same exact second, and the silence that followed tore at me even worse than the sound she had been making.

"The quiet after that storm of sound was pristine, as clean as the first day of creation maybe, not a cough, not a sniffle, not a sigh, as if there wasn't a human being in the place, not a human being on earth, as if Justine's wail had exploded us all like fine glass. Then Justine sang *Amazing Grace*, a song I remembered from my childhood. A song I never heard before Justine sang it in that clarity of being she had given everyone in the church at that minute, and the choir hummed along and swayed in the background, and I could see several people in the congregation weeping for what they are, an enormous joy shot through with a terrible longing."

Chanelle is crying again, into her hands, and I touch her swollen face and stroke her black hair again with my blue hand. "Stop, Sonny," she says between sobs, and I do, but I want to tell her that Justine smiled at me when the song ended like she knew her power, what she had just given to the entire race, that sound to sweep away everything and make the creation new again, clean and beautiful beyond thinking. My atheist body swayed with the choir as they hummed and swayed, and I bowed then, as I had seen a man bow to figures carved into stone once, to a picture so horrible I could not ever understand his bowing until that moment in Justine's church. He bowed to the truth, the clarion truth of the universe he had been given by an artist dead 500 years, maybe a thousand. Justine had given us all that same thing, the truth on an extraordinary scale, and I bowed and backed toward the side door

80

and left before I cried like a baby, before I buckled under the weight of this knowledge I had no right to have, before I burst into flame. Before Justine's gift destroyed me.

Chapter Eleven

When Truth and Death meet, it is the end of time, and now time must end.

Chanelle said Justine had convinced her as they packed that there could be someone among the police who would give me up to the assassin, that certainly CIA-types had local contacts. "Who else is a more logical contact for Big Brother than the cops?" Chanelle said she remembered these words even in her grief and did not mention me to the policemen who came to her apartment to investigate. They told her to go somewhere safe and are now looking for the killer based on her description, perhaps a deranged veteran of one war or another given his taking of Justine's ear as a trophy. She says the cops are concerned because this guy seems so efficient in his methods, but mostly they consider Justine's murder the act of a madman, a random act of violence in the sea of urban violence that is late civilization, an accidental alignment of life events resulting ironically in death, a cosmic coincidence. One cop tried to comfort her, Chanelle said, by telling her it just must have been her sister's time to exit and not her own.

Chanelle borrowed Marlene's car, an ancient Buick with peeling paint and cankers of rust that threaten to separate the chrome from the body, and I drove her to the train station. She will go to her mother for comfort and to comfort the old woman in return. She says she wants to tell her mother of Justine's death in person so her mom can see with her own eyes that she still has a daughter, this remaining half of a more-or-less matched set, the one with the broader nose like her father and balanced nipples.

I wore my overcoat with the collar up around my ears, a stocking cap pulled low and wrap-around sunglasses to diminish the blue that was visible. I knew I'd be stared at like any other geek by anyone who saw my blue face, and I didn't want everybody in the station watching as Chanelle and I said our goodbyes. I just wanted a few minutes with Chanelle to tell her I'm sorry one more time, to wish her luck and say good bye as if it were the final time, because it must be the final time.

My worries proved unfounded. The station was packed with commuters, as I assume it must be every weekday morning, but most were either absorbed by their newspaper or talking on a cell phone. Conversations buzzed around us, but none of the participants was talking to anyone they could see or touch. They sent their voices writhing over the airwaves to some apparition on the other end of this apparitional tether, and as if this act were desperate proof against solipsism (*see, I don't have to be present in the same room, to touch and smell and taste them, for the other to exist, which by extension must mean that I exist*), their focus on the conversation was absolute. No one looked up. No one noticed the blue man with the weeping black woman as we made our way to the ticket counter.

I wrote a very hot check for Chanelle's ticket to Chicago. The old black man who took my money nodded solemnly into my blue face as if looking into a future too bleak for words. Then we sat down in one of the long rows of hard seats to wait for the train. Chanelle was crying the entire time, quietly, her tears running from under dark glasses that hid her bruises and contusions only slightly. She wiped her tears from

83

her cheeks, more fell, she wiped them away, and more fell.

A kid of seventeen or so sat across from us, his hair flaming orange. His skin was pierced, his eyebrows and his lower lip and completely around the outside of his enormous ears that reflected the flat light of the train station. And he was tattooed with pictures of naked women, pictures of men engaged in violent acts, pictures of two dogs fucking on the back of his left hand, pictures of corporate and rock band logos at his neckline. There was hardly a clean spot on him to indicate his ethnicity. He wore earphones for the disc player he carried, but the heavy metal music was turned up so loud I could hear every note.

The boy was the walking paradox of American identity I'd seen in many young people across the country. He'd covered every square inch of himself so he disappeared, made himself a walking billboard of corporate sponsorship and violence and lust, but there was a perverse aesthetic in the whole package, an alternative persona he projects into the world to stand as a marker for himself; or maybe those images just oozed to the surface and really are him as walking pictograph, the real person, corporate logos and all. This portion of the paradox, the projected self, screams for attention. Look, it says, here is the truth as I am capable of understanding it. But no one but me was looking at *him* either.

The man next to him wore a suit and was working on one of those hand-held devices for storing addresses and checking e-mail. He looked into his hand as if reading his own palm, as a man lost in the wilderness stares into a compass, disbelieving true north could really lie in that direction. The woman next to him typed away on a laptop computer. Nobody noticed the blue man and the weeping woman.

Then the sonorous voice over the P.A. said the train to Chicago was boarding, and I kissed Chanelle on her cheek and told her I would make Justine's death right somehow, but that she wouldn't see me anymore so had to trust me on that count. I knew she'd think I meant I'd avenge her sister's death, kill the killer, torture the torturer, but that was not to happen. I would be sacrificed to the dark gods all assassins worship – terror and power and perfunctory death – because assassins are the instruments, and sometimes the authors, of fate. The killers are the ones who move the world, move history, and these are the gods whose combinatory dance is the great motor driving it all. I would die and get it over with, this bleak game I'd been in for so many years without knowing it until I woke up in the alley actually, really, absolutely blue. I would die so Chanelle wouldn't have to worry about being killed like her sister. I kissed Chanelle and told her that I loved her, and I meant it. She didn't say a word, just wiped the tears that would not stop. She walked away without looking back. The boy with the orange hair stepped in front of me then. "Cool," he said, "the ultimate tattoo."

I left Marlene's rotting Buick in the alley outside Chanelle's apartment where she could pick it up, but first I went to my apartment over the dry cleaner to leave a note on the door. I left the same note on Chanelle's door, taping it on top of the yellow crime scene tape, a note cryptic enough to confuse the police who would make erroneous connections to their case, but they would never catch this killer anyway. I doubted he'd return to the site of the murder, but I wanted to make sure that the assassin would get the message, and these were our points of overlap, as we used to say in the Company, the interstices of our separate jaunts through time. I also put the message on the storefront window across the street from my apartment that he was so fond of posturing in front of, the site where he left me threatening messages with his body, his presence, his dark glasses and leather driving gloves.

The message read: *The blue man has dreamt the end of time. All the eyes I have blackened with my fists or the soles of my shoes have come home to my dreams to stare me into oblivion. All the teeth I have knocked out have been made into an amulet against me. All the scrambled brains I have blown out have been served up to the dogs of Hell hot on my scent. The blood I've spilt has been mixed with everything I eat in perverse communion of killer with killed. Now it is time for the blue man to die. My skin must be made into blue shoes for the Other, the doppelganger, my bleak reflection in goblin light. My hair must be worn on the belt of the Other, my blood caught in a bowl to be served to the Other without his knowledge, so blood of killer and killed, sacrificer and sacrificed, will always be the same. Blue awaits you in the alley where my fate first became apparent. Yours in destiny, in blue flesh, in truth, The Blue Man.*

Chapter Twelve

I assume the assassin will see the note sometime today, but if he doesn't, the police may well drive up and down every alley in the neighborhood looking for the author of that strange missive. I can't afford being found by the cops. I couldn't possibly explain this blueness, and even the stupid patrolmen who spend their time in the neighborhood, eating or sleeping in their cars in abandoned lots, will remember seeing me with the twins. Our arrangement is something of a legend in the neighborhood. I am both the object of envy, by those who would like to have two women on alternating days, and of pity, by those who know better, who either know the twins or have tried a three-way relationship themselves. If Hell hath no fury like a woman scorned, what about two women? Our capacity for metaphor fails to do the pyrotechnics justice.

I also do not want the old guy who owns the building to have to clean up the mess. Liebowitz is a nearly blind old man who still dry-cleans clothes, breathing the fumes of the chemicals that will put him under the ground one day, because he can't imagine doing anything else. He doesn't need my blood on his linoleum. If I can do anything at all as regards my fate, it is to set the day and hour, an irony of biblical proportions that makes me smile for the first time since becoming blue.

I walk from Chanelle's toward the abandoned and falling down mill district. She lives only about six or seven blocks away, and I pass no one walking on this chill day. Even traffic is minimal. The buildings are all cast concrete or cinderblock and surrounded by the detritus of manufacturing – broken machinery and broken crates that held spare parts and broken barrels that held God-knows-what-chemicals or perhaps grease for the machinery. But the mills are also surrounded by the general detritus of late civilization: abandoned cars, cardboard boxes big enough to hold washers and refrigerators, discarded washers and refrigerators shot full of holes by gangbangers practicing their quick draw, condoms in the weeds, underwear worn out by the weather, lost spoons and broken crockery, bicycle frames and sprung doors, trash with the logos of every fast-food chain in America. There are chain link fences around all the mills, but they are falling and rent and haven't kept people out for many years. In front of an abandoned steel mill there are sculptures made of junk that look somehow both out of place and completely natural, if indeed that word can be used to describe this place at all. There are five- foot tall birds with legs made of angle iron and wings of sheet metal and sprockets welded in descending order by size for the crests. There is a rebar stick figure of a man with a tuba for a top hat. There is a spaceship made of corrugated roofing material. There is an empire state building and a space needle and Rube Goldberg contraptions made of pulleys and hand winches and railroad spikes, made of millions of flat washers of all sizes welded together to form steal ropes, made of cables and bumpers and drive shafts and the buckets off front-end loaders, made of wire and industrial doors, made of implements I cannot name, parts of machines I've never seen.

Rumor has it that the man who made these sculptures, a former steelworker laid off with all the rest, went mad after a while. That he tried to weld his hand to a knob that would open the door to another future and died of the infected wound. I suspect he realized that his art, like all art now, is the art of death, an attempt to conjure some small aesthetic triumph from the junk heap. And like all art now, his is both elegiac and nostalgic, longing in scrap-steel, an improvised whole made of the broken pieces of something else, some other dream. A tough realization to withstand, let alone to live. I imagine the ghost of this man weeping inside his welder's mask, turning garbage into art, and dreaming the end of time right along with me.

For years the mills have been the last home on earth for those completely outside the economy. The prostitutes and dealers who live and work in the tenements a few blocks away represent the shadow economy, the mirror image of the sanctioned exchange of money for goods and services that carries connotations of mythic proportions: America as commodity wet dream, her inhabitants stoned on possession. But if those in the shadow economy fall one more rung down, they are banished from the concept of money altogether except as a travesty of absence. They then move to these bleak spaces to become beggars and thieves, the homeless – that quaint euphemism for all-the-way-down and all-the-way-out – who eat at soup kitchens and wear Salvation Army-distributed clothes. They are drunks and drug addicts, the sick with AIDS or schizophrenia or some other utter disaster of mind or body who have nowhere else to go.

I heard once that a man with tuberculosis was in one of the abandoned textile mills, living in a former VP's office that had been stripped of everything but the walls and ceiling and floor. He just huddled in a Salvation Army blanket day and night spitting blood and waiting to die; but another man, his friend who had shared a bottle when the first man could still walk, got tuberculosis too. When the friend started spitting blood, someone who lived in these rundown industrial sites noticed and, soon after, the textile mill went up in flames, the TB guy in the VP's office too. His friend escaped to Florida to die in the warm air. Or so the story goes, but if the tale of the fire is true, it suggests that there is a social order here that I may have to deal with for my one night in the ruins.

Amazing how there seems no end to the caste system in America. Just when you think you've seen the bottom, can name it even, you discover that those you thought had fallen so low they left the scale, these men and women and children who must certainly comprehend the dark permutations of possibility – there but for the grace of God etc – actually have a hierarchy of some kind to enforce such accidents of fate. That word again, but in this sense the random weight that brings you all the way down, that pushes you into the earth, the existential albatross of TB for instance, whatever reason your fellows decide you must be banished or killed. You'd think they'd say things like, "Oh the poor man." Like, "God help him." But they torched him, which isn't certain proof of social organization, I suppose, but a pretty damned good sign.

Tomorrow night I'll go to the alley as the note says. Tomorrow night fate can have me. But tonight, the abandoned steel mill with the abandoned sculptures made by the mad steelworker-turned-sculptor in front will hide me.

I sit down on a pile of burlap and cardboard in a corner of a room that is an entire building. Steel was fired here, cooked in great pots from some original recipe, I suppose. An I-beam runs the length of the place that would have been used to carry the cooking

90

steel from one end to the other. The light is already dim from the low clouds that have hung on after the snow, that threaten to dump more. It is unseasonably cold, even for this latitude, where summer seems to have just arrived when the leaves begin to turn colors again and the old man in the dry cleaner says things about the changing season and his aching joints instead of hello. "Oy, the back hurts today. The cold rides my spine like a rail, the cold that sleeps in the body awakened to join hands with the cold outside for a few moments, the promise passed between them of a reunion one day for eternity. Winter will be here soon."

I can see my breath, but I'm warm in this big overcoat the old man gave to me, that someone left to be cleaned and never came to retrieve. It's only slightly too big, but I have room to pull my feet up under the hem and fold it under my ass while I sit, snug as in a sleeping bag almost. The burlap and cardboard are enough insulation to keep the ground from sucking all my body heat away.

When night falls in this warehouse, it falls utterly. The space of the building is dense black but filled with noise – pigeons flapping to a new roost, rodents walking on tip-toe, the moan of metal contracting, pieces of metal somewhere above swaying in the small wind through a great rent in the ceiling. There are also sounds I can't identify. I think I hear voices once, far off, maybe the down-and-out tenants' association come to evict me with flames, I think – a goddamn blue undesirable bringing trouble to the neighborhood – but then nothing but rat scurry. I am listening for the approach of the assassin, but I also know I wouldn't hear him coming. I also know he can bide his time, if he knows I'm here, and would wait for daylight so he can look into my eyes.

I dozed just before dawn, and when I awaken, the

Mayan is squatted before me not ten feet away in the gloom, hunkered down as they said in Nebraska when I was a kid. He is looking at me with curiosity in his eyes. No, it is hatred. But I blink and he's gone, an apparition, a projection, an unanswered question because I can't figure out how he's involved in my fate.

As the sun rises higher, the mill becomes a cathedral-like space, a great distance of pigeon wing-beats reverberating and slender particles of light through the hole in the ceiling and some windows high up at the far end. This place is filled with ghosts so thin, so long gone, they don't even make the clichéd cold spot in the air where they stood before the great blast furnace doors, before the heavy bucket of molten ore and the conveyors and pulleys and a thousand other ways to lose a finger or opposable thumb, stood staring into the church-like space above them, through the daily firelight of Hell, dreaming they were building a world fit for their children, a place so sturdy and golden in the perfect light of America that God himself must surely envy them, the sons and daughters of the new paradise.

Chanelle calls pigeons sky-rats, vermin with wings, but I suppose they could be mistaken for a kind of dove, a poor man's heavenly omen, and the light through the high windows at the far end, the light that is a tiny puddle by the time it reaches the ground, could be mistaken for some diminished breed of celestial glow. The steel, hot and newborn, a firm handshake between man and God.

More pigeons rise through the light and escape out the hole in the roof, noisy and shitting as they go, and I stand and stamp my feet to get the blood moving, an awkward dance for the frail ghosts of men with dreams, men who woke up one day to discover they were the butt of a cosmic joke, my brothers, not by birth but in

92

destiny, the awful heroic illusion come round to bite us all in the ass.

Chapter Thirteen

When I was ten or so, a couple of friends and I crawled on our bellies through a cement culvert pipe the length of two small-town blocks. We entered where the pipe opened into a ditch, entered on a dare or to escape the heat of Nebraska summer that weighed a ton on our young heads, or merely to explore some ground doubtless no other living soul had ever crawled across.

We hoped the culvert opened into a manhole in the street two blocks away. We hoped it did not end abruptly or open into an abyss. We were adventurers, not drainage designers, more curious than smart.

The pipe was just big enough to inch through, our elbows tight to our sides and our hands under our chests, our toes pushing us along through the interminable dark, an absence of light so total I only knew there was someone ahead of me when I bumped my head on his shoes. I thought of rattlesnakes crawling into culverts to escape the heat. I thought of an earthquake and how it buckles the ground, trapping miners. I thought of the abyss and forced panic back into its tight seed at the center of my soul, that infinitely compacted wholeness like the origin of the universe.

The alley ahead of me is the same absolute dark as the culvert all those years ago. There is no moon, and there haven't been streetlights in this neighborhood for years, or so said Chanelle one night as we walked the streets to get to the Lucky Satyr because our usual path of alleys wending through the neighborhood was too dark for travel. Because this alley curves to the left to match the odd shape of the street that the buildings on my right face, I don't have the advantage of the barely-lit street on the other end that would at least let me see silhouettes. I stand at the entrance for a few minutes, exposed against the vaguely lighter atmosphere to anyone who might be in the alley, waiting for my fate to hit me square in the face. Nothing comes.

I wish I had thought to bring a light, but when one is willfully walking toward death, the mundane details of daily life cease to matter much. I sidle along one wall into the dark, stop and listen, move some more with my back to the brick. I nudge a trashcan and feel my away around it, and then around the pile of garbage bags stacked next to it – higgledy-piggledy my mother would have called the arrangement of this pile of trash – and touch the wall again. I wait some more and listen, but all I hear is a rat tunneling somewhere in the bags. The stench rises in spite of the cold: rotting effluvia amid the inert construction materials of late civilization that spills from the bags, Styrofoam and paper and plastic. Then I inch my way forward.

The culvert in Nebraska had opened into the manhole, but fifteen feet up from anyplace to stand, or so we estimated from the time it took a ball of spit to hit the puddle below. The boy ahead of me said that, by the light coming through the two holes in the manhole cover, the holes we'd watched workmen put pry-bars into to ease the steel up far enough to grab, he could barely make out the rebar rungs of the ladder built into the far wall. The boy behind me began to whimper. His tiny animal sounds echoed in the culvert pipe like a thousand boys whimpering.

I feel my way down this alley to the next trash pile, making sure I don't kick any of it over. Then a light comes on just ahead of me, an ancient steel fixture with a steel shade the color of green only such shades ever achieve. The shade pushes all the light into a pool ten feet across. I freeze just outside the circle and flatten against the wall. The door the light is over has no handle. All the doors in the alleys of this town are without handles. I wait a minute, two, three. Then the door opens and a man in an apron smeared with blood props it open with a cinderblock. He reaches into the doorway and lifts out three bags of garbage and tosses them onto the pile across the alley, higgledy-piggledy. He doesn't see me against the wall, a dark blue man in a dark coat and hat in the hellish dark of the alley. The man takes the cinderblock inside, and the door slams shut behind him, but the light stays on.

This is as good a place as any. I will wait here for the assassin. I spent the day in the empty steel mill plotting, playing out the assassin's death in my mind, like athletes envision the homerun or the field goal before the attempt. I found a piece of flat stock about three feet long among all the other rusting metal, hefty enough to cave the psychopath's skull in with a single good swing.

I have had enough of this ridiculous existence and want nothing to do with this game or with being blue, and the thought of impending death has become a comfort since Justine died, the way out of this sad labyrinth that is my life, a sure thing in the random world, which is both rare and, therefore, precious. But the bastard killed Justine, took her life, her angelic presence, for no other reason than to see her die and to see the pain and terror in my eyes before he does me, a senseless act if one can suppose that other acts in this life are *not* senseless for the sake of comparison. I will rush him, if I can. If he shoots me dead, so be it. If I get to him first, the son of a bitch will have a fight on his hands. I doubt I'll get more than two steps, but I have to try. If on the off chance I take him out, there are 10,000 ways to die. I don't have to rely on this asshole to relieve me of my blueness and my guilt, to bring my fate down like a hammer.

In the steel mill, as the pigeons cooed and shit and flew in and out of the hole in the ceiling, I imagined a glancing blow, the man's ear coming off like he removed Justine's. I imagined an upward thrust, the spike shoved into his pathetic brain. I imagined a Sammy Sosa-like swat that would send his head tumbling up the dark alley, a back-hand smash, a forward thrust through his eye or his throat or his heart, a steal spear sailing through the rank air of the alley to disembowel him ...

The boy behind me in the culvert had whimpered like a thousand boys whimpering, his voice echoing, and the boy in front of me and I both told him to shut the fuck up before he had something to cry about, both of us just as scared of having to back out of the culvert, of the impossibility. I reached up over the boy's back in front of me, scraping my knuckles on the cold concrete. I grabbed his belt and we inched forward until he hung straight out into the void of the manhole in the aberrant light. He was nearly stretched out as far as I could hold him when he grabbed the rung and fell into the opposite wall with a thud of flesh and a sigh of relief ...

"Hello, Agent Blue." The assassin steps to the opposite edge of the circle of light, into the farthest reaches of the light where I can barely make him out, his 9 mm at arm's-length and aimed in my direction. I estimate the steps between us, the possibility of having enough strength to cave his skull in with a couple of 9 mm slugs lodged in my chest because his finger is certainly faster than my legs. But he won't hit me in the chest. One in the center of the forehead, as in the manual, to shut the cerebral cortex off like throwing a light switch, like any predator ensures that his prey will not harm him in its death-thrashing.

"You have me at a disadvantage," I say. The assassin steps closer and I can see that he doesn't have his sunglasses on, that he is smirking and his eyes are a rare shade of green, and I want more than ever to kill him and I count the steps again, the feet per second a 9 mm bullet travels, the weight of the flat stock stuffed up my sleeve, the foot-pounds of torque it takes to crush bone.

"That's not important. Let's just say that we have mutual friends."

"Did our mutual friends tell you to kill the woman?"
"No, of course not, Agent Blue. You know the latitude one has in the field, the need to improvise."

"Technically, improvisation suggests a purpose. You killed Justine because you're a blood-thirsty asshole, because you get a twisted pleasure from the suffering of others, because you're just another cowboy over the edge." The assassin is smiling broadly now, obviously pleased with the results of his work. As I squatted in the steel mill, I planned to deny him the pleasure of knowing he'd hurt me, to show no fear. I've already blown the first objective.

"Why, Agent Blue, I only did what was expedient. I needed your attention, so I turned you blue to let you think about this encounter, who you are dealing with in relative terms, and I killed the woman so you'd know I am serious enough to kill whoever it takes to bring you in."

Now I am confused. Bring me in? He sounds like a movie character, an Old West sheriff offering up story line in the form of code-of-the-West bullshit, or a spy's handler telling him to come home, all is forgiven, which is never the case of course. The assassin's enunciation is mock-perfect, his manner so studied he is just short of effete. "I was sent to recruit you, Agent Blue. The people I work with believe you have skills we can use."

"That makes no sense. I was an operative decades ago. Surely you have people in place who have all of my paltry skill in mayhem. Why go to this trouble after all these years?" I still think he wants to kill me, that this is an elaboration on the game, that the sick bastard wants to put me at ease a little so the look of shock on my face when the slug hits my brain is ten-fold stupid, a thousand-fold, a real laugh riot.

The man smiles again, but the gun is still held at arm's-length and pointed at me. "According to my superior, you are understating your talents. He says you know the Lacandon people quite well, and for my money, the quaint note you left for me seems to prove him right. At least, my superior showed me some Mayan mumbo-jumbo once that sounded a lot like your note."

The *Lacandones* are maybe the most pure tribe of the Mayan lineage remaining, at least they were a couple of decades ago. Then, this tribe lived in a preserve in Chiapas, Mexico. The government only made the preserve, however, to gain some measure of control over the land. The tribals weren't impressed and went about the business of tending their gardens and hunting.

Rudy and I had been sent in to help the local cowboys convince the southern *Lacandones* to move from a chunk of ground the Indians considered ancestral homeland because the government wanted the minerals underneath it. We were only in the area three weeks or so because our help wasn't needed. Some Seventh-Day Adventists and over-priced market goods did the job for us.

The missionaries convinced several of the tribe's

99

leaders that the Christian god made more sense than the ancient ways, and the oldest members of the tribe, who normally would have given the people spiritual guidance, were all killed off a few years earlier by an outbreak of yellow fever. Once converted, the leaders of the tribe were convinced to give up all of their wives except the first, and the results were disastrous. Tribals fought tribals over marriage customs, over the sudden abundance of available women, over drinking, which was also declared taboo by the Adventists along with about half the traditional diet. On top of everything, the government gave the Indians money and opened stores. In short order the tribe was in complete disarray and addicted to store-bought food and clothing. In just a few months, the Indians went from utterly self-sufficient to utterly enslaved because their gardens went to hell and the mining drove off the game.

"I am told you know their mythology and that you have some insight into their way of life, into how they think, knowledge my superior believes may be very valuable to our mission. We have tried our traditional methods to get them to move, but they won't budge. The timber consortium that employs us is getting nervous because our methods are attracting attention. A representative of a human rights organization is in the area and taking notes. We would remove him from the equation, but that would only bring down more of them. We need to close the contract so we can move on to other operations – you know, the old time and money algorithm – and we need to move on before the human rights organization in question begins to put things together."

"You turned me blue and killed someone I care about to hire me on for this … this freelance enterprise, to assist you and a bunch of other former operatives to screw over these Indians," I say, incredulous. "You killed Justine," I say, and my voice quavers with rage, with my desire to kill this son of a bitch. I want to kill him more now than when I thought he was just a psychopath rather than a madman with an actual agenda. I can feel my heart beating at my temples, and I feel strong enough to leap this distance before his finger can pull the trigger, strong enough to cave his skull in before he can say another crooked word. I let the flat stock slide down my arm and into my hand.

"Easy, Agent Blue. My superior warned me that you have a self-destructive streak." I take a step toward the assassin, feeling the heft of the steel and measuring the distance in my mind.

"I promise you, Agent Blue, that I will take you apart a piece at a time, and I will do it very slowly. Then I will do the same to the other one, the sister."

I can't move when he mentions Chanelle, my muscles an ache of hesitation. In that split second, the assassin moves back into the shadows a step, at least one step out of range maybe, but I feel my strength fading anyway. I am old and blue and can't possibly take this son of a bitch down before he shoots me through each thigh, then each arm, then maybe up the ass so it takes me an unimaginable half hour to bleed to death, each second a forever of pain.

"You see, Blue, I didn't kill the first one just for fun. Your nature required that I develop a strategy that would hold your attention and inspire your happy compliance."

I can feel my knees go weak at this assertion of my unwitting complicity, at the thought that I have again caused a death. The great wheel of the universe has spun up death in my wake again, as a kind of karmic insult maybe, if you can believe there is cosmic justice. But I have seen too many men like this one in front of me go unpunished, kill one human being after another with cosmic impunity, so why this punishment for me? There is no such retributive order in the universe, just this seething bad luck. The assassin had exploited my weakness, a woman. And a good agent has no weaknesses. The molecules spin in front of me in their random orbits, flaming blue then sparkling out of existence, and I feel faint and must lean against the wall to keep from falling down.

"Your skills are needed, Agent Blue. The timber consortium can't negotiate with a people who do not understand money, who don't understand the notion of a resource, which is all their trees are, who think the land something sacred, or some such nonsense, and so don't understand the concept of remuneration at all. And we cannot convince them using our traditional means if the world is watching because the world has grown so squeamish.

"Your skills are needed, Blue, and here's the deal. You go to the Lacandon and convince them to move to the new plot of ground the government and the timber companies have designated by whatever means you can devise that keeps attention off our little group. Subtlety is what we expect of you, Blue, some infiltration-earn-their-trust trickery. In return, you will be made unblue and the sister stays alive." He waves the pistol back and forth as he says this last sentence, as if directing it as a minimalist symphony.

"The last time I saw these Indians, they were all but whipped. What can they possibly do to keep the government out of their trees?"

"You worked with the southern faction, or whatever the proper terminology is. The northern Indians have been too far in the bush to even reach until recently, and now the timber people are slavering over their 400-year-old mahogany trees."

"And after I do this job, assuming I can carry it off

102

the way you want, what happens then?" "Frankly, Blue, I don't care. Right now you are to go to the Corinth Hotel," he says and throws me a room key with a plastic ring, the number 206 on the tab. "There are clothes and travel money there, and you can clean up. Take this too," he says, and he tosses me a single capsule in a small vial. "You'll be back in the pink, so to speak, in about forty-five minutes, give or take. Look sharp," he says. "I'm watching." And he backs into the utter dark.

I take the capsule and step into the circle of light. I turn my palms upward and watch as my hands go first a lighter shade of blue, then gray, then return to their Caucasoid norm, a strange metamorphosis that takes nearly an hour – the unbluing of Agent Blue. I can feel my strength returning with my normal color, the first stirrings of deadly purpose, a wave of energy rising from my bowels. *Spleen* they used to call it in old plays, a deadly desire that energizes a man, makes him stronger than his age maybe, than years of drink and lethargy. I catch myself stretching my fingers compulsively as in the old days, and I cannot stop picturing the assassin's death, his blood spread over the ground in a mosaic of gore and retribution, his head a doorstop.

That day in childhood, the first boy had pulled me across to the rebar ladder that ran up the inside of the manhole, and we talked to the other boy for ten minutes before he'd trust us enough to pull him across the abyss and to the safety of the ladder. We told him that he'd die in this culvert if we left him, that he'd starve, or he'd die of fright in the night, or something that lives in culverts would come up behind and eat him, devour him body and soul. He reached and we pulled him across and he clung to us.

We pushed the heavy manhole cover aside and

climbed into the blinding light, into the summer heat, and we never mentioned the boy's fear because we were all equally afraid, because we knew that death lingers in dark places and lays his bony fingers on you, reaches inside and fondles your heart, because we felt like men who have survived a mortal wound as we stood in the hard light of the Nebraska afternoon blinking and laughing nervously and wondering how on earth to go on carrying this new knowledge, this new strength.

Chapter Fourteen

The Corinth is a bathroom-down-the-hall flophouse near the row houses that are home to drug dealers and prostitutes. I had to walk several cold blocks to get here, but there's a noisy radiator under the single window that does an adequate job of heating the place. There are new suits in the closet that fit as if a tailor had pinned the cloth around me, except for a tightness around my middle if I button the coat, and crisp new white shirts and a half dozen blue ties in a dresser drawer. There is also an envelope with twelve thousand dollars in it, a fat pile of crisp one hundreds.

I put on one of the suits, dark blue, pack the rest into the suitcase that is also in the closet and leave it on the bed, stuff the wad of bills in the breast pocket of a new overcoat that was nestled among the suits, and take a cab uptown for a haircut and shave at a place that stays open late, the barber an old Italian guy who talks sports in a soothingly thick accent, as if there were still difference in the world, subtleties of inflection and pronunciation, whole other languages with their own nuance and variations, as if middle-of-the-country TV English wasn't the only dialect.

I had to walk almost as far as the Seven-Eleven where I used to work to hail a cab, and the shiny patent leather shoes that came with the new wardrobe pinch a little at the instep. The taxi drivers won't come much past the Seven-Eleven, into the rundown neighborhood of my old apartment, let alone into the decaying slums where the drug dealers work. Not because of the dealers, who always have money, but because of their customers who never have enough. I go to a Turkish bath to clean up, then I go to a bar out by the interstate, a bar in a hotel with a guy in a tux at a baby grand playing dainty music to drink by. Show tunes minimized yet further to a tinkling right hand and barely audible left.

The place is sparsely populated with hotel guests, all sharply dressed in suits, the women too, all preoccupied with their cell phones or business conversation with fellow travelers in the land of commerce, the upside and the downside and if only we could have bought in sooner. The barmaids wear an upscale version of the skimpy costume Justine wore at the Lucky Satyr, a variation on a maid's outfit, black and low cut with white ruffles to cover their asses. And my throat goes tight and my hands flex and I take a big hit of the upscale whiskey in my glass at the thought of such a wonderful human dead on my pathetic account.

The assassin will certainly contact me soon. I'll need to go along with his directions, so he follows me out of the country in case I miss, so he has to go far out of his way to hit Chanelle, her murder an inconvenience even a psychopath has to reconsider. But I won't miss. I'll find him and his boss and gut them both. The bloody intensity of my thoughts surprises me, and I take another big swallow of whiskey. By the time I was banished, I'd become sick to my core with the killing, with the daily bloodbath in the name of God who is a capitalist, but killed anyway because that is what I was programmed to do, all I knew – the mechanism that runs the world.

I told myself for over a year that I was merely burned out, as Americans called it in those days, my nerves frazzled from all the stress, the anxiety, the ersatz responsibility of being an American hero; but that

106

barely masked an existential sickness, a dread so big it outweighed fat Rudy and his Christian shtick top heavy with two millennia of broken hearts. It was years after my banishment before the nightly nightmares ended: headless corpses, flaming corpses, corpse lovers writhing in their own ghastly light, corpses singing cantatas in the drear light of my dreams so that I awoke sweating and sat up for hours drinking and trying not to remember. Now I am all bloody purpose, again, malevolent intent incarnate. Now I can't think of anything else but this man's carcass rotting into the ground. The thought scares the shit out of me briefly, but then the whiskey starts to take hold.

Fastidious, that's the word. I hear a man down the bar say it, that his wife is fastidious. Buffalo Bill Custer was fastidious, his hair perfectly coifed, his suits tailored to fit him as if he were born in them, his ties all silk and all blue, for luck he said. He was Tom Wolfe with a vengeance and no particular passion for white. Dapper even in the equatorial heat as the streets went dusty, even when rain fell like a plague for days at a time and the streets were rivers of mud. Bill Custer was always as clean and well-kept as a show dog.

And he was Polonius in dapper dress. He liked *one* as a pronoun, stringing together labyrinthine sentences, using the abstract indefinite pronoun ten times in each. He liked Anglicized French. He liked to say *and etc* to hint at a list of options at his disposal, a depth of knowledge that lesser men could only wonder at; and he liked muscular relative clauses stacked shoulder to shoulder to delineate the world in all its nuanced detail, each sentence a collector's log.

But metaphor was beyond him. Even clichés stopped him cold, and he'd get a queer look on his face, a quizzical look, and he'd go quiet as if pondering the juxtaposition of objects or images, trying to make it all cohere. Then he'd ask for an exegesis, but Buffalo Bill Custer was a literalist in the extreme and sometimes even the explanation would require an explanation. Rudy used to say, "Christ, Bill, it's just a goddamn saying," and refuse any further consideration of the matter.

I remember explaining that the first word *look* was intended to be an imperative but was also the reciprocal action, and that the second word, *sharp*, was the modifier, that the first word could mean literally "to look" and the modifier then meant that the one spoken to was to pay close attention; but the term also meant that the hearer was to show all outward sign that everything was in perfect order, in the shape it should be because the speaker expected it to be so.

Bill was delighted with the implications for his management of operatives, and from that day forward ended every conversation on the phone or in person with "Look sharp. I'm watching." The assassin's boss must be none other than Buffalo Bill Custer, former CIA section chief for Mesoamerica, or perhaps he is still the chief and doing side-jobs for the extra cash. The assassin must have picked up Bill's verbal affectation. It's a leap maybe, but Rudy was right. There are no coincidences on the endlessly self-referential stage of covert operations. I also assume the assassin is Mankin, the ghost of central Vietnam, Bill Custer's one-time First Sergeant. Who else would take an ear home to the boss? Buffalo Bill's collection must stretch from the Mexican border to Tierra del Fuego by now, and my dear Justine is just another marker in history as it is told by Custer's macabre string, just another entry in his collector's notebook: black female, half of a more-or-less matched set, age forty-three, one nipple higher than the other, sings like the plucked heartstrings of some enraged god.

A woman down the bar laughs at something the man said who used the word fastidious earlier. The bar takes an abrupt left turn at that end so I can see them clearly. The woman is a little drunk. It's in her eyes that don't completely focus and how she holds her cigarette. The man is hungry in that sexually tense way, smiling too vibrantly, looking as if he might pounce. The two are rubbing elbows, literally, in one of those rituals before closer relations between a man and woman who do not know each other well, as if they need to get used to the idea as well as telegraph their intentions, their receptivity to the other's intentions. She laughs again, and he lays his hand on her forearm, and she lays her other hand on top of his hand. The woman orders another drink, a white zombie, whatever the hell that is.

Rudy used to name his drug cocktails like a bartender names drinks. There was a mixture he called a zombie because that was the effect, a blank-eyed and unblinking stare and the client talked as from a well, pulling up syllables wet and fraught with darkness and terrible difficulty. There was another called a Harvey Wallbanger because, Rudy said, you could tell a guy his name was Harvey and he'd fuck a light socket if you ordered him to. There was the Armageddon, so-called because the client went into a seizure like the final war, the war to end time, raged inside of him just before passing out into tongue-lolling oblivion. There was one called Beatific Vision for the gaga-blissful look on the client's face even if he was broken and bleeding, even if you told him you'd killed his family.

But regardless of the pride Rudy took in his chemical expertise, he preferred electricity – battery cables and the first incarnations of stun guns and the arcane cattle prod. "When drugs fail to fry the obfuscation from a client's mind," Rudy said in his ersatz drawl, his thumbs slung in his red suspenders like a horrific version of Slim Pickens, "nothing like a lightning bolt shoved up his ass to loosen the most recalcitrant tongue. Pain mixed with the deepest possible desire for it never to reoccur, missing teeth and chewed up genitals from the shock and broken fingers all add up to a broken psyche, a bottomless pit of horror the client carries in his or her body as a continual reminder, if they live, that they gotta play ball with ol' Rudy. If I call on 'em in ten years, I guarantee they'll still sit right down and cry and tell me everything I want to know and then some."

I order another whiskey as a man sits down to my right. The Mayan. He orders a rum and Coke and sips on it when it arrives, nonchalantly, like he doesn't know I'm here. Then he asks without looking at me, "*Que soñaste, Señor Azul*?" My fingers flex, but without reason now because I don't have a weapon.

"More riddles after all these years? Why should you care what I have dreamt?"

"It is a traditional greeting my people use, but we mean the question too. We live as much in the other world, that one where dreams come from, as in this one, and so the answer is important if we are to know a person, the dreamer. What did you dream?" The Mayan takes another sip of his drink, stirs it with the little plastic straw, an infinite patience in his voice.

"I dream of dead people, of the Underworld with row upon row of dead people. And why would you want to know me at all?" I have no idea what this Indian has to do with my being blue, with my journey to steal from his people, maybe to enslave them, maybe to kill them. Why wouldn't he kill me when he finds out? Maybe that's why he's here. Or maybe he doesn't care at all, just another sell-out in the interest of *Norte* expansion, just another brutal cowboy like the assassin. Maybe

110

he'll play inscrutable Indian to my white straight man one more time then shoot me through my blue heart just for fun.

"An interesting dream," he says. "Especially for a gringo. But then you are an interesting man, Mr. Blue, at some deep and abiding level I don't understand. You see, I was told years ago that you play a part in the destiny of my people. You, a former CIA operative who killed many of them, or had them killed, or trained the men who killed them – all the same thing. You, by all outward appearances just another Caucasian drinking himself to death because he can't face what his race is guilty of, what he's guilty of." He takes another sip and asks the bartender to bring me a refill.

"An old man who knows things the rest of us don't told me you have this role, a man who carries on conversations with the gods that others in the room hear only as gibberish, a child's rhyme maybe or a madman's ranting. But then he directs you to do things that he says are important, that the future of the world hinges upon because the gods just told him so, and after you've done them you realize that he was right, although you don't know how." The Mayan sips his drink and is silent for a full two minutes. I don't know what to make of this odd prophecy, or even if it is true that some old man has spoken of me, and I decide I don't care. The softness of the whiskey is now washing over me and I could cry for losing the twins, cry for having to kill Mankin, for returning to that life, however briefly, however deserved the retribution. And then I am merely angry, on the doorstep of a mean drunk and looking for any excuse to pummel the shit out of this Indian and his annoying riddles and superior silence that he is using on me now like a club.

"My people call the Underworld *Xibalba*," the Mayan says. "A terrible place ruled by the nine Lords of the

Night, one king over them all. Only those earthly kings who will be gods ever escape *Xibalba*, and only Jaguar can travel back and forth with impunity carrying messages between the living and the dead."

"Forgive me, Indian, but the last few days have been taxing, so we need to cut to the fucking chase. I know you were watching my apartment. I know Mankin's intentions and yours probably aren't the same, or at least that they are not ... what ... covalent? You may have mayhem in mind too. You may even work for the timber consortium too. Maybe you're the competition. But you get in my way, and I'll tear your fucking throat out."

The Mayan is amused by this outburst. He smiles, an incongruous addition to those dark eyes and his quiet intensity, like he could pull his gun and off me here and disappear into the rust stain of this town in the space of a single heartbeat. The man and woman at the end of the bar are nuzzling each other now, talking in whispers, focused on this moment as the prelude to what will follow.

"So you recognized Mankin," says the Mayan. "I didn't think you knew he existed."

"I didn't know for sure until just now. I had never seen the bastard before the first time he staked out my apartment."

"Ah," says the Mayan, and he reaches into his coat. I go tense, knowing he must be here to make sure I follow some kind of rules of decorum, some assassin's code whereby I don't let on I know anything beyond what I am to do in the name of greed, and the consequences if I don't do what I'm told. He pulls out a handkerchief, actually a night-black bandanna folded neatly, that he lays on the bar in front of me.

"Mankin was your handler when you were in the Agency."

112

"No. My section chief was Custer."

"Yes, but Mankin followed you everywhere. I noticed this about your kind, the agent in the service of capitalism, that you all think you stand nearest the center of power, a grand delusion that means operatives look right through other operatives. The truth is, there are circles within circles. It's an ancient Chinese model of government: the ruler lets agents believe they are the last line of defense against the dark forces of his enemies, when in reality the agents are watched and those watchers are watched and those watchers too. Somewhere in the inner rings, there is the realization that the circles might as well be infinite, and in some sense they are, as a certain picture of steps by M.C. Escher is a picture of an infinite staircase because it is an illusion, steps that go impossibly on and on without end because you think they do – and so these enlightened operatives are hyper-vigilant. These operatives have no illusions as to their status as the last defense, quite the opposite. But in protecting themselves they also protect the ruler because absolutely everyone is a potential rival, a potential killer. They destroy all perceived threats as an act of self-defense without a single qualm, and by so doing, are the perfect agents – paranoids under the ruler's control who see the enemy in every face."

The Mayan takes another sip of his drink, and the man and woman at the end of the bar taste each other for the first time, a lingering kiss that smells of jism even from here. I am not sure what to make of the Mayan's explanation. The Mayan seems to sense my doubts.

"Mankin was at the dump the day you killed your partner. He stepped among the rag pickers disguised as one of them as you got out of the cab. You walked right by him. He was there because your partner was a

113

hazard, because he was losing his mind, but you did them all the favor of putting a bullet through him before Mankin could do it himself."

"So why banish me then? Why not give me a fucking medal?"

"Because they discovered who you really are when they debriefed you. You let them know you weren't one of them. You have these tendencies that are not the tendencies of an agent. For one thing, you want the world to make sense beyond the job you're assigned."

"So why not just kill me?"

"Because Buffalo Bill Custer might need to recruit you one day," says the Mayan, and he pays the bartender for my drink. "Custer has done this same thing to others, but mostly retired men with hearts as dark as the day they left the Agency, men who skimmed a little or shot their wife's lover and made it look like suicide or a foiled robbery or who had habits they didn't want the family to know about – a sexual taste for children or for blood."

"How do you know any of this? I was questioned in an airtight CIA safe house. I know you didn't have it bugged because they swept for surveillance devices all the time," I say, and then it dawns on me. "So I'm guessing you occupied the circle inside Mankin's circle."

"Yes and no, Mr. Blue. I was assigned to keep track of Mankin because his methods were, well, a bit over the top, as they still are, as you have discovered. He likes hurting people, and Custer knew that fetish could get in the way. I watched the day you shot your partner too. I could almost feel Mankin's disappointment from where I was parked on a bridge overlooking the dump."

"So, what's this? A follow-up interview? Just making sure your agent did his job right, a kind of employee evaluation?"

114

"I also had my own reasons for watching Mankin all those years ago, for appearing to work for the Agency, for going through the training and the School of the Americas, for becoming an assassin and then accepting Custer's offer to work for him. Didn't you wonder why you were naked in that alley, naked when you woke up blue?"

"Yea, but I was afraid to ask Mankin for fear of the answer, what the sick bastard might have had on his bleakly conniving mind."

"The bluing agent was in your clothes. I saw him put it there, but I thought it was poison. I have seen him use such a tactic before, insert toxins of varying strength into a person's clothing and then watch them die, by degrees if he felt he had time, or all at once if not. I hoped to save you from such a fate, but then I watched as you turned blue before my eyes. You've got to admit, some of these killers have a sense of humor."

"Why would you want to save me? Custer can't have such a great need for my services that you would put yourself at risk of being discovered."

"I don't work for Custer. As I told you, I only nominally worked for him all those years ago. He has a small army of men, all sociopaths like Mankin, trying to find me because we are the truest of sworn enemies. I serve one half of the universe and Custer the other. I serve the light and he the dark."

Just as years ago amid the ruins when he made like assertions, the Mayan says this without a hint of grandiosity, without irony, without any sign that what he has just said is anything less than verifiable fact, as if he'd said it's cold or it's dark or the man and woman at the end of the bar will be screwing in the next ten minutes. The couple heads for the exit, leaning on each other like honeymooners, and they will screw like honeymooners too, then dream of their separate lives and take separate flights and never see each other again in this lifetime.

"Besides, *Señor* Blue, I told you that an old man says you have a role to play in the destiny of my people. I will make sure you fulfill your role, whatever that may be, and I will kill you myself rather than let you fail, rather than let you defy the prophecy." He stands to leave, and as if to prove his point, his suit coat swings open far enough for me to see his shoulder holster tucked away in the dark like a promise.

"You should know, Agent Blue, that the old man says that it was the Lord of the Underworld, the King of Everything ultimately, *Kisin* in my language, he who eats maggots instead of beans and moldering human flesh instead of *piñole* – it was Lord Death himself who told the old man about you. He assures me this is a sign unlike any other in his lifetime, and it's rumored that he's over a hundred years old." The Mayan straightens his tie and looks straight into my eyes, a hard, cold look as if he were trying to discern something hidden there.

"I think the old one believes you are the harbinger of a new epoch, an epoch of ascendancy for my people and of the final decay of all this, which is crumbling into the ground before our eyes, if you only knew how to look." He sweeps his hand over the bar and its dwindling occupants in their suits and talking on their cell phones, over the television in the corner of the ceiling playing CNN coverage of some disaster or other as just one more form of entertainment, over the piano and the pianist who is now drinking a margarita at the end of the bar where the lovers had been a moment before, the look of constant boredom, boredom raised to ideology, on his face.

"We've watched it all sliding toward some ending for

116

a long time, and now the old man sees your association with the King of the Underworld as final proof of the end of all this strangeness you call your world. History you call it. He says this is a sign my people must act if we are to ensure our destiny and once again build altars to the Sun God greater than the altar at Palenque."

The Mayan walks toward the door a few steps, stops and turns toward me. I have spun around on my barstool to make sure he goes, to search the room for other cowboys. "The old man calls you the Blue Man Who Will End Time," he says, "and thus my shock when you turned actually, truly blue before my eyes. If he's right, you are the most powerful man on earth. Walk lightly, Agent Blue, so you will know which path is your path. Fail and I will spread your viscera over the ground for the pigs and dogs to eat."

Part II

Behind each name lies that which has no name.
Today I felt its nameless shadow tremble
in the blue clarity of the compass needle

whose rule extends as far as the far seas,
something like a clock glimpsed in a dream
or a bird that stirs suddenly in its sleep.

Jorge Luis Borges

Chapter Fifteen

Mexico City is hot as hell, and the air is so thick people walk around with kerchiefs over their faces like a whole population of TV bandits. The air was bad when I was here decades ago. Now it isn't even air but something palpable, a stain we all walk through that permeates us, that undoubtedly kills the equivalent of the population of the state of Maine every year.

This morning, I paid a cab driver a hundred dollars to take me from the hotel where I met the Mayan to the Hotel Corinth, and I had to promise him an extra hundred to wait while I grabbed the bag of suits and checked for instructions. There was a plane ticket and a Mexico City address on top of the suitcase. Then I had the cabby take me to see Liebowitz. I gave the old man a couple hundred bucks for having to dispose of my few belongings and asked that he deliver an envelope of cash to Chanelle when she came back, a brief note of farewell and vague promises of retribution yet to come.

The old man just grabbed me by the lapels of the deep blue herringbone suit I'm wearing and said, "Very nice. Good cloth. Good workmanship." Then he slapped me on the chest and went back to his press to work until he drops dead.

Buffalo Bill's house is on the outskirts of Mexico City, on a high plateau where the Aztecs built a palace a thousand years ago, that Cortez lived in for a time after he kicked the Indians out, or so says the driver in colloquial Spanish. At first I had to strain to understand the words after so many years, but after a half hour of

121

creeping through the crowded streets, I can understand him like I never left. He tells me the palace fell into the earth maybe 300 years ago, and now a few rich Mexicans live on the plateau above the brown cloud like heavenly beings in the pure sunlight.

Custer's house is classically Mexican, with barred windows and plastered outer walls as white as alabaster, red slate shingles on the roof. A gardener wearing a tattered straw sombrero is pruning and watering hanging plants just inside the courtyard. A young Mexican girl of fifteen or sixteen dressed in a sky-blue dress and huaraches lets me in the door. She bows to me, then leads me through a dark hallway to a brightly lit room she calls the library, but there are only a few books on the shelves that run floor to ceiling on every wall but the outer, which is all glass. The toxic cloud over the city to the north looks likes a roiling brown lake, like the headwaters of the River Styx maybe.

The shelves hold Custer's artifacts, and I can see immediately that most are closer to the trashy souvenirs tourists buy than to anything of cultural value. I look over a few stone artifacts and a Spanish helmet, an ancient musket and a couple of stone tablets with Mayan alphabet figures running across them, but the rest are tacky baubles, garish and aberrant, the detritus of no known civilization but of every civilization too. These artifacts are the result when cultural production is enjambed and convoluted as a singular culture swallows the globe one big bite at a time, the stuff of the market: a gaudily painted and heavily lacquered wooden spoon with a picture of Zapata in profile, a felt sombrero with sequins around the brim, badly made stone bowls, unidentifiable gewgaws carved of wood or rock meant to imitate something old, to intimate strangeness, something for gullible tourists to send

122

their gullible relatives back home with a note that says "a piece of history." Maybe they hope this thing, this false relic, counterfeit artifact, is an amulet against their daily sameness, against McDonalds and Reebok and Toyota and all the major and minor manifestations of banality in their lives.

I sit down in an overstuffed leather chair to wait. On the mahogany table next to the chair is a porcelain ashtray in the shape of a naked woman lying on her back with her legs spread and in the air, her large pert breasts pointing unnaturally upward. The ashes go in her oversized vulva, which is not so much labial pink as torrid pink, her gaping hole a slash of color that is both beautiful and grotesque at once. The features of her pudendum are so exaggerated that at first I thought the figure had a hungry flower sprouting from between her thighs.

"So good of you to come, Agent Blue," Custer says just as I hear his heels clicking on the expensive tiles.

Custer is dressed in a deep blue linen suit, a white shirt, and a tie that is a few shades less blue than the suit. He looks little older than when I saw him last, a boy in a man's body even as he approaches sixty. He crosses the room to a small cabinet with booze on it and pours two glasses of brandy. Henry Bagby enters the room and nods in my direction. Then he stands off to the side, watching his boss with his arms folded as if in a trance. Bagby is in his shirtsleeves and wearing an ornately tooled shoulder holster with a gleaming chrome semiautomatic like the handle to some monstrous machine.

"It's not like Mankin gave me much choice." Custer stops before me and extends a glass. He smiles as if we are old friends, as if his man did not kill Justine and threaten Chanelle to get me here. I'm sure he is disappointed that I am not surprised the address left for

123

me at the Corinth is his.

"I must admit, I didn't think your skills were still intact enough to figure out your handler's name, Agent Blue, or who you were coming to see for that matter, but you certainly don't seem at all surprised. I didn't think you'd put things together this soon anyway. Bravo." He raises his glass in mock salute.

"Let's get to the point, Custer. I was recruited for a job, and you need to give me the particulars so I can move along and get it over with ..."

"And go back to what, Blue? It doesn't sound like you've done all that well for yourself since your departure from the Agency." Custer moves across the room to a stone incense burner on a shelf and picks it up. There are figures from the massive Mayan alphabet, which is actually some 800 ideograms and symbols for pronunciation, carved into it in bas-relief. "Maybe you should work for me. I'll make sure you're back in fighting trim in no time, your muscles and your mind taut, that you remember all you've forgotten of the craft, and etc, and I'll make you rich."

"Freelancing has obviously been lucrative for you, but I'm not interested. Being poor white trash suits me fine."

Custer lets out a faked guffaw. "And where's the excitement in that, Blue? How un-American of you, how inhuman to *not* aspire to rise, to *not* desire wealth and prestige." He pours himself more brandy and brings the bottle over to add to mine. Bagby hasn't budged but watches every gesture as if in training to be just like Custer, as if so many years of sycophancy were not enough for him to know the boss like other men might know a wife – all the possible permutations of facial expression and gesticulation, each nuance of inflection. "Besides, don't think for a minute that I quit the

124

Agency ten years ago because of the money in freelancing alone, although that was certainly an incentive. The job just no longer appealed to me like it once did. Things changed. The world changed. Methods changed. Now there is voice print analysis, surveillance of everything a man utters, pictures from outer space of the lapel pin on his coat, a thousand toxins that can transliterate to the bloodstream through a feather touch, a light brush of the skin, and etc. A man can appear to asphyxiate on his own vomit after a heart attack, to sputter his last because of a mysterious virus, to die in his sleep because of some extraordinary violence inside his liver or his spleen, etc. Where is the sport in that, Blue?"

Custer walks to the wall of glass and talks to me with his back turned as he looks at the sea of brown roiling in the distance. "Did you know I helped start the School of the Americas, Blue, or rather helped move it to the States in '72? I was still working for the Army and took it as a side gig at the request of the CIA Director himself. Those were glory days. The course list read like poetry: 97 Toxins Difficult to Identify in the Bloodstream; How to Kill a Fat Man and Leave No Mark; a Thin man; a Woman; Poisoning a Village; Knife Wounds That Will Not Close; Sexual Protection as Toxic Medium; Controlling an Agrarian Society through Terror; Electric Shock and the Truth; Serums; Vasodilatation unto Death; The Virtues of Evisceration in Winning the Hearts and Minds of the Survivors; Landmines in Perpetuity; Cattle Prods, Rape and Politics; Pain and the Various Orifices; Insurrection as Biblical Metaphor; Overthrow; Subterfuge; Riot; Drain-o; Starvation; Induced Poverty; and my favorite: What Does a Burning Bus Filled with Civilians Have to do with Freedom?" Custer ends his Professor of Death Emeritus lament with a sigh and turns again to face me.

"Oh, the Agency still breaks legs, and even cuts off fingers and genitalia on rare occasion. Sometimes they even shoot somebody, especially in this theater, Mesoamerica, where the drug war is a way to control the populace, a way to make all damage appear collateral or somebody else's doing altogether. But mostly agents are Peeping Toms with an electronic hard-on poisoning the enemies of America with a long distance kiss."

I am tempted to compliment Custer on his newfound ability to use metaphors but don't. I just want him to finish.

"All the bloody art is gone, Blue. It was always about the money anyway, but now the middleman is irrelevant and foreign governments or, more often, corporations pay us, those who have always done the real work of history – moving nations along into the next era via any necessary means – for what our services are actually worth."

I drink my brandy in a single gulp. "To the point please. I need to know why I'm here so you can get your payday and I can get the hell out of this country."

Custer swirls his brandy and looks at me as if he knew this would be my answer to his offer, a foregone conclusion and the speech a pro-forma recruiting spiel he gives to all former agents pressed violently into service. He is smug and feigns a studious concentration on the middle distance between us, the Professor of Death in thought.

"Very well. This incense burner is not antique, not very old at all, less than ten years probably. I had Mr. Bagby filch it for me from the Mayan altar at the community in question. They make and anoint new burners every eight years or so. That's how I know this thing's age more-or-less, because that's the cycle. The burners take that long to get full of ash, then rather than

126

empty them, the Mayans spend forty-five days engaged in rituals to sanctify new ones, fasting and otherwise abstaining and praying and chanting. As far as anyone knows, this ceremony is several hundred years old at least, dating back in direct descent to the ancient people on the Yucatan Peninsula maybe thousands of years ago, at least to the people who built the temple at Palenque."

Custer holds the burner, balanced on his fingertips, at eye-level, staring into the runes as if he could read them, like a child pretending to read *War and Peace*.

"That's what we are up against, Agent. The Christians have been pretty good at taming the rest of the tribals all over the world, even other Mayan groups, but these people still practice a religion that is older than the occupation, older maybe than the white race, and they practice their religion with only a modicum of Christian inflection, unlike the southern group that has integrated everything the missionaries ever threw at them, from Seventh-Day Adventist silliness about their diets to Catholic saints. So this group, the northern *Lacandones,* doesn't feel at all inclined to see the world any way other than the old way. The trees they have are rare and therefore precious. The timber consortium expects to get at those trees by the time they finish building a road to the area, and all our more direct methods have failed."

Custer puts the burner back on the shelf. He swirls the brandy in his glass again and stares into it, a pose of thought by an automaton who plots and plans but does not think in the truest sense of the word, a man who is at the correct low rung of the evolutionary ladder for his times and so gets rich.

"So what the hell am I here for?" I ask, unable to keep the hatred out of my voice.

"Because you are, Agent Blue, for lack of a better
127

word, sensitive. You always saw the world through the eyes of your clients, even when you were new at this game, even when you weren't and tried hard to pretend that what we do has a higher purpose. That's why we hired you all those years ago, why we let you stay as long as we did, and why you are here now. You can, by some trick the rest of us can't seem to pull off, be one of them, a Mexican peasant or a Guatemalan singer with a battered guitar or an Indian, a goddamn Mayan with a hundred gods and a penchant for jungles left untouched except when they need to burn a plot big enough to grow a few ears of corn, a few beans and tomatoes and etc." Custer stands before me now, his hand on his hip to hold back his coat, to display a silver colt with a pearl handle stuck in his pants like a Hollywood wet dream of a cowboy riding the silver screen to keep the heathens under control.

"You are guilty of empathy, Blue, a damned strange trait in a killer, but one I intend to put to good use. The ceremony to anoint the new incense burners is ending in a few days, so the members of the tribe who participate, the powerful ones, especially an old shaman named Olvidero, will be done fasting and chanting so you can get at them. I have no clue how you will proceed, but I trust that you'll think of something when you get there."

"What about the Mayan agent, the one who used to keep an eye on Mankin?" I ask, and Bill Custer stops swirling his brandy and immediately looks more angry than I've ever seen him. He was always the calm killer, the calculating giver of orders, but now the practiced look of intellectual assassin has disappeared completely. He casts a sidelong glance at Bagby, who is also distraught, but whether mirroring his boss's mood or truly depicting his own is beyond telling.

"You've met former agent Valasquez?"

128

"If that's his name, yes."

"I should have known he'd show up on this one, but I thought he was in Guatemala hiding out in the mountains. That's the last place the men I have looking for him said they encountered him. He killed four while they slept and three more when they caught up to him, and then he lost the remaining two, or rather let them go so they could tell me about the others, I suppose. How he cut off the heads of the first four he killed and stacked them up for the others to find."

"How is it that you are still alive, Blue?" Bagby asks, and there is accusation in his slightly falsetto voice, more energy than I thought him capable.

"I don't know. Maybe he doesn't know why you've recruited me exactly, or maybe he does and is waiting until your aims are more clear, waiting to see your hand because he thinks you have a better plan than assuming I'll come up with something when I get to the Indian enclave." If Custer recognizes the sarcasm, he does not let on. He is the calm killer again, his voice a calculated smooth, a tiny smirk of a smile on his face.

"Treat Valasquez as a serious threat, Blue. His code name was Jaguar, and he deserved it. He's the most dangerous man I know, and he has taken it upon himself to avenge all violations of what he calls 'native sovereignty'. This job certainly qualifies. He's been a major pain in the ass, to say the least, and has killed more than twenty of my men to this point. He won't think twice about slitting your throat if he gets a chance, Agent Blue."

The same young woman who led me to Custer's library shows me to the door and swings it shut behind me with a bang like a coffin lid of heavy walnut, dark and medieval. Custer and Bagby, Hank Butterbuns, were whispering together even as I left. "Look sharp,

Blue. I'm watching," Custer said over Bagby's shoulder as I entered the hall and the door closed behind me.

I catch a glimpse of one of Custer's men looking at me from a garage window and another from a window in the monstrosity Custer calls home – houseboys in dark glasses and armed to the teeth. They will be hard to slip by if I get the chance to come back for Custer, and maybe for Bagby too, the obsequious weasel.

The drive to a tiny airstrip on the eastern-most edge of Mexico City is interminable. The same cab that brought me to Custer's house takes me through the sweltering streets, past the multitudes in their white kerchiefs walking or riding bikes, wending among the buses stuffed to overflowing with people, among the trucks strung along the road with livestock aboard or boxes of eggs or sacks of beans and flour, through the heat that weighs a million pounds on my head and heart after dealing with Custer the inveterate collector. I make yet one more silent vow to come back for him if I succeed in killing Mankin, then I make a silent vow to succeed.

The same cabby talks nonstop about how Cortez saved Mexico from its savage inhabitants as a rosary sways from the rearview mirror, Christ writhing in his famous agony to save the race entire. He tells me that the blood of these people around us stretches back to Spanish kings and Spanish generals. He tells me that his Spanish blood is in the process of dominating his Indian blood until one day, in a generation or two, the race will be pure, all Spanish, the Indian blood purged by some hitherto undiscovered legerdemain of biology and time.

The taxi is a Chevy that would have been new when I was here last, big and roomy and without air conditioning. On the dash beneath the rosary is a plastic hula dancer with hips made of springs so she jiggles mechanically with every bump in the road. Next to the dancer is a wooden figure, a Mexican man in a sombrero with a barrel for clothes, which the driver lifts over the figure's head and a huge erect penis springs up. The cabby laughs. Now with every bump in the road the erection bounces in unison with the hula dancer's hips.

The seats of the cab are covered in plastic with raised bubbles in it. I remember the stuff from an ancient Chrysler my old man owned when I was a kid. The bubbles don't add any cushion, but they keep the back and ass raised off the seat in roughly one inch intervals so you stick to the plastic in a checkerboard pattern.

The heat is monstrous. The heat has teeth of vernacular steel. The heat is unremitting and remorseless and a thousand other multi-syllabic descriptors. The Inuit may have several hundred words for snow, but Mexicans know the heat is a god, unambivalent and voluptuous as the universe compacted to fit the street you walk, the road you drive like a zombie because your blood is congealed syrup and your brain weighs several slow tons, and they do not speak of the heat for fear it will grow angry and set the world alight one last time, cook us all like chickens in a pot.

The driver has an Elvis pompadour and sideburns so thick and perfect that he looks like he's wearing a bad disguise because no one could trim facial hair so exactly before the morning mirror. He wears Elvis's over-big sunglasses too and smiles with Elvis's half-sneer, but he could never pass for Elvis-pale. He's stridently Mexican. Coffee-bean brown with high Indian cheekbones and, when he lifts his dark glasses to wink at me after a joke about his wife, her fat ass and the sound of thunder it makes in the morning, the hint of an epicanthic eye fold inherited from his ancestors who crossed the Bering Strait fifty thousand years ago. He calls Indians niggers when we pass them, and I almost ask him not to use the word, thinking of Justine's and Chanelle's perfect black skin and feeling offended and sad and guilty and raw from the drink at Custer's and the heat and lack of sleep. But I don't say anything. I just let him ramble on about his despoiled race that will one day be pure, his grandchildren's blood as clean as the blood of the kings and queens of Spain, which he repeats like a mantra. Kings and queens who were inbred and thus pure in his estimation.

If the heat mixing with the brandy weren't making me sick, if the detail I am on were not making me sick, if dealing with Custer and dreaming his death and the assassin's death were not making me sick, I might find the energy to tell him he has it backward. The kings and queens were despoilers and the only pure thing that remains in him is his Indian blood, that last remnant of this ancient land that is being turned into a source of cheap labor for the *Norteños* before his eyes. But I don't say anything. I just listen to his machinegun Spanish and try not to puke all over the plastic-covered backseat of the cab as the hula girl hulas and the wooden man's oversized dick bounces up and down, as we drive past the poor and the poorer, the ragged and the nearly naked, the children begging for pesos on the corner with the one-legged and the one-eyed and the too-old-to-work.

The further east we go, the more squalid the landscape, the more like a wasteland after the apocalypse. The people wander through the haze of dust and smoke as ghosts, their raiment increasingly tattered, their burros thinner and more sickly by the mile. There are a few automobiles, which are older and more ramshackle than those we passed thus far, held

132

together with wire and duct tape. The taxi looks new by comparison.

I glance out the rear window and catch a glimpse of a tawny Mercedes so out of place amid the tattered trucks and corrugated metal houses that it is obvious Mankin doesn't care at all that I know he's behind me. The car is a sensuous grotesquerie in this place, a wave of steel and chrome and leather that may or may not be real to those it passes. The car is maybe a vision to inspire prayer in a barefoot man riding a sweltering burro, in a one-eyed woman begging, her legs white with dust, in a man driving an ancient cab doing Elvis in Spanish and dreaming his gene pool the once-and-future sea of chromosomal banality as the out of place hula dancer hulas and the peasant swings his gargantuan cock incongruously over the dashboard like a magic wand.

I look around for the Mayan, Valasquez the Jaguar, who travels between the light of day and the Underworld bearing messages. I do not see him among the sad wayfarers in the heat and deadly air, but maybe I am looking right through him, like he said I had done previously, as if he were just another poor Indian dying for lack of everything.

I take the black bandanna he left on the bar out of my breast pocket as the driver talks endlessly about the Indians and how he hates them because they are stupid farmers and don't embrace the new Mexico of Big Macs and the *machiladores*. I unfold the handkerchief and lay it on my lap to try to decipher the glyphs in white running across it from corner to corner. I have not bothered to look at the thing until now. The Mayan had left it for me like an odd gift. There is a powerful sword-wielding creature on the bandanna, like the figure on that first stone piece the Mayan and I

133

stood in front of in the museum in Mexico City all those years ago, half-man and half-monster with a big Mayan head in caricature and a misshapen body. That would be *Kisin,* Lord Death as Valasquez called him.

There are two other figures running ahead of *Kisin,* identical smaller figures in the shape of men. I thought at first the men were running from death, but that fits nothing I know about the Mayan religion, which is admittedly not much. They are ostensibly the Twins who fought the rulers of Hell, who defeated the black forces of the Underworld, but these Twins seem to be working in the service of the Lord of the Underworld. At least, they are engaged in the same grisly business.

The running men carry swords too, and the expression on their identical faces is not fear as if fleeing the Lord of Death but a scowl, and they are running toward a city with towers that appear to glow in the sunlight. The towers are somehow malevolent, but I can't tell why they make me feel this way. And there are headless corpses everywhere with flowers coming out of the wounds where their heads used to be. The flowers also grow out of their heads, which are scattered over the ground away from their bodies. Corpses stretch all the way to the horizon and, somehow I know, far beyond.

Then I notice that the figures on the cloth make a larger pattern. I notice because I can't keep my eyes focused in this condition, sweating and straining to keep the contents of my stomach from backing up. If I look at the entire bandanna and don't look at any single element, I can make out a face peering through the carnage but made of it too. The great face of Lord Death is one eye, and the head of one of the Twins in combination with a flower-strewn corpse in the background make up the other. The great knife of *Kisin* forms the outline of one pert ear, and the furthest tower, shaded just so, is the other ear. There is a mouth among the corpses and the daisies, a whisker that stretches into the towered city.

The face is a jaguar's, and the wild cat stares out through the human and mythic world of the picture and *is* the human and mythic world at the same time. The image is both made of the reality and the mythology of death and transcendent. The face is neither stern nor remorseful, not malevolent and not kindly, but decidedly unmoved, as if the terrible vision that is the rest of the picture were just everyday carnage of the everyday world. Jaguar is simply there, behind it all and made of it all, the fallen and the bleeding, killers and killed, sacrificers and sacrificed, the supreme executioner and the Twins, who are somehow implicated in his plan, and their victims. Just there and watching, but not watching the action – the jaguar is watching me: The Blue Man Who Will End Time, as an old man I have never met has deemed me, according to the Mayan – whatever that name can possibly mean.

Chapter Sixteen

"A Nigra, a Jew, and a Mick walk into a bar ..."

The set up was always the same, and these three characters always *in* character, the virtual racial clichés of jokedom: the first an idiot or filled with lascivious need, the second a thief and a liar, the last the unwitting observer doing penance for hanging out with the other two, always the receiver of some gift of wisdom that grew out of the antics of his companions. It took me a year to figure out that Rudy was telling me parables, that I was the Mick, or rather that he expected me to have some understanding after the parable to match the Mick's understanding, some insight into geopolitical reality as filtered through Rudy's narrow Baptist sensibilities.

"A Nigra, a Jew, and a Mick are drinking shots of cheap scotch and talking about women. The Nigra says he's not had any since ... well he can't even remember, but then he can't remember the last ten minutes without a prompt from the Jew. The Jew, he says he hasn't had a woman for exactly thirty-seven days, and he knows this because he doesn't forget anything. Hell, a Jew's memory is thousands of years long, and everything he does is related to those thousands of years and so takes on a mythic quality, but the Jew is always the center of his own mythology of course, and thus a model for us all – even though the bastards killed Jesus. Anyway, the Mick, he says he just had a woman in the parking lot and she is waiting for him now out there in the backseat with her panties around one ankle and her legs spread while he quenches his thirst."

Rudy then hit a flaming-red golf ball with his sand wedge out into the jungle as it moved slowly by us. We were hitting balls from an ancient train, from the top of our car, as it crawled through Guatemala from the coast where we met up with an anthropologist who was certain he knew exactly how to convince a particular group of tribals to migrate to the slums of Guatemala City, where the government could keep closer tabs on them, so the government could seize their land more easily.

Rudy said the red balls – designer balls manufactured this hyper-red, a color both brilliant and deep, to Rudy's specification – were like chunks of anomalous Arkansas chert the locals would one day think a calling card of the white gods who rode the rails. He said that they'd spend years investing those little spheres with meaning, building tales around them, figuring a purpose that exceeds the mundane reality of the balls' existence, and then some bright missionary would come along and use the truth to debunk the local religion and convince them of the absurdity of their ways, then lay on "the truth that is Jesus H. Christ and thereby save the locals from their pagan ways. Christ, Blue, we are doing a service here, just by hitting these damn red balls into this unforgiving jungle, just by being here," he said.

The bottom half of the wall across the road from the outdoor café where I sit on a stiff wooden chair at a spindly wooden table is the same red as Rudy's designer golf balls all those years ago, a flamboyant orange-red like flames mixed with the earth-red of decaying blood to make a color that is spiritual. The top half of the wall is Gauguin-green, the immaculate tint of the rainforest in a dream of the rainforest, a green two shades deeper than real trees and warm-weather

137

foliage in tropical light. The color of the souls of trees and plants maybe.

A man carries a basketful of coffee beans up the street on his back, the basket suspended from a tumpline that wraps around his forehead. He is bent slightly forward under the weight, the cords of his neck standing out with the strain, and his straw cowboy hat sits absurdly thrust up into the air because of the tumpline's leather strap underneath. The man smiles and says something I'm too far away to hear, says it downward to a girl of ten or twelve as she fills an unglazed jug at a water spigot that comes out of the extraordinarily red and green wall, her brilliantly red dress nearly glowing against the backdrop of the flames-and-dead-blood-red of the lower wall, her raven-black hair a gorgeous silhouette against the green of the upper wall. The man is walking toward the town square where the open-air market is set up.

The air is as warm and thick as I remember, my back drenched with sweat. I have taken off the jacket and tie, but I haven't had a chance to change into the khakis that the young woman who showed me to the door at Custer's house handed to me in a large paper bag. She handed me bush boots and a billed hat too.

I puked a hundred times, or so my stomach muscles feel, on the flight in the tiny plane from Mexico City to this town, San Cristos de Silva, the closest town to the Mayan enclave deep in the forests to the north. I puked into a bag the Mexican pilot handed to me, which he dropped out the window. Then he handed me another without comment as if all of his gringo passengers puke and threaten to pass out with every bounce on the air currents, as if they all feel only barely human in their reeking skin. Then he dropped that one, another puke bomb, to the unbroken forest below, and handed me

138

another empty bag and another.

The mescal that the waiter in his peasant uniform – white smock and high-water pants and vine sandals – just put in front of me does nothing for my stomach, but it eases my head and makes my flesh feel slightly less electric. The warm tortillas and beans on the table smell good, like the most articulate food imaginable because it is so basic, so true to the constituent ingredients, like a great poem, but the smell only rouses another rumble from down deep in my body, from my intestines now as if the army of chaos that had set up camp in my stomach has moved south. The girl at the water spigot hoists the full jug to her shoulder and makes her way briskly up the dirt street in the opposite direction from the town square without spilling a drop, as if the jar weighed nothing at all.

I am surrounded by a field of static and I hum when I move in this high-pitched resonance of nerves seasoned with a touch of fear. I am not afraid to die. In fact, I am so sick to my soul that I hunger for it, for the end of this mission and the final rest I have promised myself, but I don't know if I can pull off what I am really here to do. I don't know if I can save Chanelle and avenge Justine by killing Mankin and Custer, and probably Bagby for good measure, like you might shoot a loyal dog whose master has passed away so the creature won't starve to death lying on the grave, so he doesn't have to pine himself to death. These killers have been in the trade all these years that I've been drinking booze and sinking toward an ignominious death, toward my fate of wide open stomach ulcers and an exploded liver. They've grown stronger with every drop of blood they shed, like vampires, and I've grown old. The long odds of success threaten to overwhelm me with despair.

I don't even know what my next move is, but I have

139

to appear to be working on the assignment Custer recruited me to fulfill, the reason Mankin killed Justine, because someone is certainly here and watching, hopefully the assassin so I will not have to hunt him. Right now, I have to get control of myself, to think.

The anthropologist's plan all those years ago in Guatemala was premised upon tribal superstitions regarding the dead. He had devised an ornate ruse involving hallucinogens and auto-instruction. He sat in on rituals after gaining the holy men's trust, rituals in which the long lost souls of loved ones would appear in the shamans' visions and demand that the people move to the city because the anthropologist set the shamans up for this little disclosure through a kind of psychological legerdemain. Even Rudy, who has no particular respect for anyone not white and not from the "good ol' US of A," thought the guy an idiot when he told us his plan because the Indians would not be so easily misled, but the anthropologist pulled it all off with amazing ease.

The Mayan worldview is both their strength and their weakness, it would seem. It helps them survive in an inhospitable environment because they can explain it in mythological terms. Their mythopoeic talent is a means to get their minds around the enormity of the wilderness in this part of the world as it were. But what they believe – in combination with what they don't know of the larger world – can also be the means by which outsiders take advantage of them. That was the message in Rudy's parable in Guatemala. And that there are forces at large in history to equal any god of hellfire and damnation stalking these jungles, and vastly more invidious.

"The Jew says to the Nigra, just how d'you expect to get along in this world, to have women in the biblical sense, if you have no sense of time, of the weight of the

140

moments passing? And the Nigra, he says without a hint of irony, I don't know how you stand up at all under the weight of all those minutes and hours and years and centuries piled on you, all that suffering. My people suffered enough for ten races, and we just as soon forget. And the Mick, he just smiles to himself because he knows we all have pieces of history stuck in our teeth, the embarrassing remnants of a former meal we just as soon deny we ate, even the sufferers-at-the-hands-of-others who emphasize their own suffering so they don't have to own up to the rest. The Jews have the Mossad, and what do the Nigras have but preachers and ACLU lawyers and the like, but don't the Nigras *wish* they had evolved sufficiently to have this same sense of history and so utilize a secret police force to protect their interests? It just makes sense, Blue."

Rudy was a redneck with little sense of remorse for anything he was guilty of personally let alone any glimmer of racial conscience, but he was right in his way, that the killers this time around might have been the oppressed previously, as if the confluence of power and violence was the human birthright, what we stumble toward unconsciously, and we name that stumbling in and out of power *history*. The Maya were famous sacrificers of human flesh in centuries past, sacrificers of slaves, and perhaps it is that power over the other that the Jaguar pines for now.

My way into their good graces can't be the same as the anthropologist's all those years ago. I lack his skill for cultural subterfuge, but power I know, the way men will do anything to gain it, especially if they know they had it once, that it is possible to hold sway over others. And these people, if the Jaguar is to be believed, think it their destiny to rise again. So I will incite them, unto self-destruction if need be, because my show of

141

complicity in this enterprise to steal their trees must be real enough to fool Mankin and Custer. They have to believe so I can get close enough to gut them. Mankin is probably watching now, this very minute maybe, but he won't let me see him until the bloody end, and then, my purpose in their plan ultimately served, he will probably be stalking me to kill me.

I swallow the last of the mescal and look around for the waiter to order another, but when I lift my eyes from the glass, there is an Anglo woman with shortish red hair and long, slender fingers with blood-red polish on perfect nails standing at my table. She has a duffle bag in one hand and looks lost. Her sunglasses are high-end shades like rock stars wear, and her khaki outfit is straight out of L.L. Bean, complete with a paisley print silk scarf around her thin, pale neck in this terrible heat. A brassy eco-tourist maybe, unafraid to hit the spots her fellow socialites haven't even heard of, so she can tell them tales that make her the bravest among them, the most adventurous person they know in a late-capitalist bourgeois kind of way. Who else would traipse about Chiapas in such clothing but someone who gets her idea of what the third world is like from a catalog that caters to her ilk – another culture just another marketing gimmick?

"Lost?" I ask when she just stands there looking perplexed.

"No, actually. I was just a little taken aback when I saw an American here at all, let alone one dressed in a suit." She sounds haughtily amused like rich people affect, at least the few I've known. I hate the rich like everyone else, because I'm not and because they hold it against the rest of us as a failure of both breeding and will. I hate this woman and I don't even know her name yet.

"The only hotel in town is up this street several

142

blocks. I would show you where it is myself, but I intend to drink until the sun goes down and wander there in the dark."

"I know where the hotel is," she says, the hint of indignation in her voice like a garnish for the haughty amusement of before. "I have been staying there for two weeks waiting for my guide to clear things up with the *Lacandones*, which he claimed he had done, but now I can't find the son of a bitch. Maybe you've seen him. He's a one-eyed Mexican of about five feet and he smells like lilacs."

I have seen him. The man gave me a lift on his white burro from the airport to the hotel and then waited for me to sign in so he could give me a bony-backed ride to this very seat. I tell her so, and she goes off at me like I'd stolen the man from her. She uses the word *proprietary* several times, and then she turns up the street toward the hotel, lugging her duffle bag and cursing. I can hear her for a block.

Her so-called guide needed the lilac to overcome the smell of his beast-of-burden. The thing stunk of shit and something worse. I asked why the animal smelled so badly, and the man told me the donkey had a disease and would be dead in a few days, that its guts were rotting even as it walked. The man said he was merely getting what he could from the animal by hauling cargo and a few people until it dropped and didn't get up again. I deemed him a staunchly pragmatic capitalist, making money where death and suffering loom, at which he smiled proudly and hit the animal on the flanks to make it suffer along more quickly.

The woman and her hollering did me a favor. The restaurant owner, unsure of the commotion, shows up looking sheepish. I order the whole bottle of mescal and

143

leave the man a twenty, the smallest I have, change from the hotel bar in the Ohio Valley a day and a lifetime ago. The man looks puzzled at first. He probably doesn't see much gringo money in this little town on the edge of a wilderness so vast the greed-heads of the world are only now getting around to despoiling it. But after an awkward minute he recognizes the bill's worth, *Americano* money being the most hotly sought after tender in all places on earth because of the strength of the illusion that it is actually worth something. He smiles and hammers me with thanks in rapid Spanish. Then he disappears inside and sends out his wife and daughter with plates of roasted chicken and roasted tomatoes and squash.

This is probably their own dinner, and I ask the daughter to retrieve her father and invite them all to sit with me when he arrives. I am still squeamish but eat a little to show my gratitude for the food and drink. The food is delicious, but I have to stop after a few bites of everything to still the rumbling in my guts. The man and I then proceed to get drunk on the mescal as the women clear the table and sing a song that Miguel Santiago used to sing: *Death rides to town on a white burro and we drink to his health, Death is the white burro and we drink to his health, Death takes the white burro and we drink to his health, the long night through.* The waiter and I drain the bottle and he brings out another. I stumble to the hotel, up a street as dark as the alley where I met Mankin, dark as hell, and I'm singing at the top of my lungs: *Death rides to town on a white burro ...*

Chapter Seventeen

The town square is filled with people selling their wares. Along one edge of the square are stalls made of corrugated steel and rough-cut timber, but mostly the vendors are aligned in rows with room to walk up and down the length of the town square in front of and behind them, and their goods are spread over the ground: big loosely woven cotton sacks of corn and beans, fresh potatoes and tomatoes and squash and cauliflower and radishes and slender green onions and green beans and green leaves of raw tobacco, and there are red-brown chickens in cages of unhewn sticks or the chickens are held tenderly in a woman's arms as if she offers a child for sale, and there are little noisome pigs tethered to a post and scarlet macaws sitting on burlap bags of coffee and cocoa beans, and there are straw sandals and striped serapes and white smocks and *pantalones* and vividly blue and red and green rolls of cloth.

And the people are trading. A grizzled man gets four pairs of huaraches for a mature spotted pig, a woman gets a smallish black pig for five chickens, another gets a chicken for a pile of potatoes.

"My people call money *takin,* shit-of-the-sun, which says something of how we feel about it. It is an object of curiosity because it commands so much attention, especially by gringos, but it is also pretty worthless. You can't eat it or wear it."

The Mayan, Valasquez the Jaguar, has stepped up beside me. I hadn't noticed him among the crowd because he is dressed like the rest, in peasant white that is sweat-stained and fading to gray, with a broad-brimmed, high-crowned straw cowboy hat, also dirty white. His visage is incongruous given my previous run-ins with the man. He always wore high priced suits and shoes so shiny they reflect light.

"Mankin must be elsewhere, I assume." We are standing in front of an unlikely sight, a booth at the end of the square filled with plastic goods: plates and utensils, gas cans, bottles with cork stoppers that could hold water, even fake fruit and corn hanging from a post amid all the real fruit and corn in the other booths or spread over the square. And the colors are astounding, reds and blues and yellows that are deep and dark –Tupperware done by Kandinsky.

"Yes. He is staking out the trail you will have to take to the enclave. He's about twenty miles from here by now. He'll be to the Usumacinta River by nightfall."

"He must be happy as a pig in shit to be in the bush again and plotting mayhem, the scent of blood on the thin air of his bleak imagination," I say. The vendor of the plastic goods is proudly showing us a gas can, how the lid hides a long nozzle that you turn upside down and shove back through the lid.

"The scent of blood is on the actual air, Agent Blue. I have people watching Mankin, but I'm here to tell you that you must get to the village as quickly as you can. The man who brought you to the café on his burro, Mendoza, can lead you. He's leaving to take a woman from the Committee for Peace, a *Norteño* human rights organization, to the village at first light."

"Yes, the woman and I have met." The vendor is now showing us a set of red plates and metallic-blue plastic spoons and knives. "So, if your people are so averse to money, how come you wear thousand dollar suits and carry that flashy German automatic?" I look

146

sidelong at Valasquez to see if I can determine where he carries the gun now, an old habit only, because it really doesn't matter much. I'm unarmed and on his ground, at his mercy, to put it mildly.

Valasquez thanks the man for his time in Spanish but says we must pass on his goods for now. We walk together along the edge of the square where the width of the aisle is enough for the two of us abreast because most of the people in the square are actively looking at each other's trade goods. Their faces hovering over each other's goods wear expressions of intense study. The air is filled with the noise of barter and the smell of beasts, a good smell for some reason.

"The old man, Chan Lin, the man who told me that you have a role to play in the destiny of my people, told me the same thing when I was still a boy – that I have an important role to play in the people's future. He said he had a vision of me picking up the shit-of-the-sun from all over the world and using it to defeat the people whose money I took. So the village sent me away to school, first to Mexican grammar school and then to a preparatory school in Mexico City on scholarship, and ultimately to Harvard. I studied how your people use money, how they have diminished all of life to this abstraction, and I learned how money moves invisibly through the air from one place to another.

"Eventually, I figured out how to take money via intervention in those ethereal transactions, and I learned to use money to my people's advantage, because our enemies are so overwhelmed in its presence, so hungry like pigs that never stop eating until they are butchered to be eaten themselves. The expensive suits are just part of the act, a disguise that works pretty well, don't you think? No one expects an Indian to be thus outfitted, and so they do not look at me for what I am but for what they believe me to be,

147

usually a Mexican banker or some other professional. The German automatic is simply part of the disguise too, but also a tool of the trade. One should use only the best tool available, don't you agree?"

"And exactly how do you use money in the service of your people? These folks look pretty poor, and they seem to be trading for everything. I haven't seen a single peso."

"And you won't see money in this market," says Valasquez. "Currency is *not* used by tacit consensus, because it has *never* been used here and the people see no need to start now. My work, the money business, is all outside of this place, away from the people, in North and South America where our enemies live," says the Mayan, and for a split second I think that he may have looked sad, that his exterior of utter restraint cracked just a little to let out some of the man underneath; but he returns to his stoic self so quickly that I may have projected that look onto him, imagined him a real person for an instant, a man who loves his people and misses them when away "on business" rather than the cold-blooded killer who walks unmoved with me now, talking of fraud and God-knows-what other offenses he is hinting he performs in the name of his cause. Bribery and extortion at the least, maybe worse. According to Custer, the Jaguar has killed men who work for the former section chief, but if true – and the concept is pretty slippery given the source and the context – the line between murder and self-defense, between murder and vermin extermination, seems pretty slim.

"And you want me to ride with that little Mexican flower, Mendoza, to the enclave immediately for what reason exactly?"

Valasquez stops before a stall with pigs and chickens hanging from hooks. A pretty young woman

148

smiles and offers us the finest pig in the world, or so she calls it in Spanish. Valasquez speaks to her in a language I don't understand at all, Quiché I presume, although there are many dialects of the Mayan language and this could be any of them; then he waits while she untrusses two live chickens from a fly-covered group hanging upside down like a bunch of bananas. The place smells of blood and aging animal flesh, which is not the good smell of animals from before, the smell of the earth made flesh. This is the smell of death, and the stench awakens the storm in my guts that is worse than ever because of last night's mescal.

The girl twists the necks of the chickens in two quick yanks, and I feel myself jerk back involuntarily, like every death spasm I have ever witnessed was in the swift, nonchalant movement of her hands. She presents the birds to Valasquez. He whispers something to her, and she smiles and bows slightly as we walk out the door.

"Why do you call Mendoza a Mexican flower?" Valasquez asks as we walk back the direction we came.

"It is a joke. I guess you had to be there, as we say in the USA. But then I assume a guy like you, a man who cuts off heads and stacks them like fucking bricks for some kind of macabre effect, probably has an enemy's-blood-on-his-shirt kind of sense of humor – all gore and splattered brains and ha, ha, ha."

"Death is never funny, Blue, nor human suffering, even if the sufferer is your enemy and your destiny is to cut his throat and watch him bleed to death before you stack his head on top of another enemy's head, so his companions who remain will feel the weight of your resolve tearing at their hearts."

We stop before a stall filled with fresh vegetables.

Valasquez points to corn and potatoes, which a young man puts into a cloth bag. Velazquez whispers again and we leave with the young man bowing like the girl in the stall of dead animals.

"More blithe conversation about murder," I say. "You assholes are amazing, how you rationalize this bloody damned business. Custer waxes Professor Emeritus on me over the old days at the School of the Assassins, and you wax Philosopher of Mayhem, as if this purpose of yours was more important than human life."

"It is, Blue, because it is the life of an entire people, and because they are my people, a culture that has attributes your own people do not even dream exist. Did you know that the enclave you are going to enter now has nearly 500 people associated with it? That same enclave was but half that number when you were in Mesoamerica plotting their ruin years ago. My people were on their way to extinction. The dark forces you served had nearly won before I started this campaign that you know nothing about, and now the old man seems to think our time to flourish again – for the rebirth of our civilization which first requires the eclipse of your own – is at hand. At least he hints this is the case."

A child runs from the crowd in front of us and hugs Valasquez around his thighs. The boy is grinning and talking Spanish too quickly for me to catch everything, but I understand when he calls Valasquez "uncle" and says he is old enough to hunt now and will his uncle take him. Valasquez pats the boy with his empty hand and says he will take him one day soon if his mother consents, and the boy disappears into the crowd behind us as quickly as he appeared.

"So what makes your murder of others any different than a CIA wonk's murders in the name of God and country? An agent goes home to his nephews and the

150

rest too. He is just as adamant a believer in his divine right to take your life and the life of everyone you love as you are a believer in your right to kill him and his kin."

Valasquez is looking across the square intently. Then he takes my arm with his free hand and turns my back to that direction and steps in front of me. We are standing nearly nose to nose, as if we were dancing, but slightly off square so the Mayan can look over my shoulder.

"Two of Mankin's men have just entered the plaza. They are former Mexican Secret Police dressed as *campasinos*, and they are here to find you, to watch you in Mankin's absence. I must be going, but first your explanation," says Valasquez with only a hint of urgency in his voice.

"We are aligned with different forces in the universe, Blue. A CIA operative, whether present or former, is aligned with the dark forces that would burn the world for fun and profit, and I am aligned with the forces of the light, with gods so ancient they make the god of the Old Testament look like an errant child. Although our means may look the same to you, the truth is that our goals are utterly antithetical. The good old boy in the CIA wants to destroy all difference in the world, wants his god and his culture to eat all the rest and make the human race slaves to an epidemic sameness, which is also called death, the absolute absence of vitality, which is any totalized system, or at least he wants these things intuitively because this is what he is indoctrinated to desire, if one can even use that word. I am a killer for the sake of variety, in nature and cultures and peoples, for the sake of a vital existence, though my methods seem barbaric to someone like you, someone so steeped in that other way that you can't see the inversion, can't see that what you think is life is

151

really death and vice versa." Valasquez is quiet for a moment and looks down at his shoes as if avoiding someone's glance. Then he looks up again, peering over my shoulder, his eyes following Mankin's men.

"You must get to the enclave as quickly as you can. The old man is ill and he is very old, so this may be his natural end, and if he dies, that will change everything in ways I can't predict. At the very least, I may have to kill you for want of knowing what your purpose is in our struggle, so you should make every effort to make haste, so the old man can put you on the path, if indeed that is his aim in wanting to see you. The bandanna I left at the bar is your calling card. The old man painted the image himself."

"So much for my fate being cosmically entwined with your people's fate. If you can't figure it all out, you'll off me, like any agent in the service of the State I ever met. I guess our conception of fate is not so different after all. Humans write it and enforce it. I am living proof – all you assholes pushing me hither and yon."

Valasquez is still peering intently over my shoulder but he smiles at this. "Actually, fate is very strong, like a story that is already written but that contains multiple potentialities everywhere and all the time, all a function of human volition that can alter the details of the story; and if enough details change, then the story is no longer what it was, but a new story. Most people in your experience have no volition, no will, so their lives unfold as if scripted. They just stumble through their days toward whatever awaits them, heaven or hell, and almost always the latter, like you've done yourself for several years."

"So the only thing keeping me from stumbling out of this little passion play of yours, out of which I get nothing but Mankin hunting me regardless of how it ends, is your promise to kill me if I do."

Valasquez looks as if he might laugh. "You don't look very closely at what is right in front of you, let alone up the trail, do you? The story in which you play a part is complicated, and the complicated details are unfolding so even you can read them, and the details are so complex that very soon you will be totally without choices. It won't be long before I won't have to threaten you to do anything. You will simply do what you must in order to survive. My offer to kill you was for my own peace of mind, of course, but almost a gift, so you can escape what lies ahead, whatever it may be. I know you are here for reasons that have nothing to do with the organization's plans for you, to kill all of them if you can to save the one sister from your previous life as a convenience store clerk and to avenge the other. That much I've guessed, and even a cold-blooded dolt like Mankin, who has more instinct than reason, can figure this out.

"That your being here has something to do with Chan Lin's vision – and maybe you're here at the behest of Lord Death himself, I can't tell – Custer and Mankin and the man who is really running the organization can't possibly know. Only you and I and the old man know these facts.

"Which means that Custer and the others will figure out that something is amiss soon. If you were merely their functionary in this plot to get the mahogany trees, I'd have killed you in the hotel bar and they know it. They know by now I'm here and working against them. They will wonder if you are working both sides, and they know I have access to money to entice you, money beyond even their very substantial resources – although they have only a hint as to one of its sources and none as to its multiple locations. Or they'll wonder if you are freelancing maybe, working the contract yourself under the auspices of the timber consortium, circumventing the middleman as it were."

I am growing more ill by the minute as I realize that my fate really is closing in on me, as all choices become a null set, replaced by the absolute certainty of death. Valasquez is right, of course, and I should have figured this out myself, and would have twenty years ago when I still rose to the smell of blood on the proverbial air and the game afoot, or some such diminished euphemism for the evil that men like Custer and Mankin perpetrate upon the world. Custer and the rest will be suspicious, and that will do for surety, as Shakespeare says somewhere. Terminal impasse yields my blood spilled over the ground as the only viable option, the answer to all their uncertainty, just as it is for Valasquez when he tires of waiting for me to play some role in the passion play of his people's extinction that neither he nor I can even imagine.

"Custer's men have seen you and are working their way through the crowd. They'll only follow you to the enclave, then keep an eye on you for any sign you aren't living up to your end of the bargain. If they suspect anything, they'll gut you in the night. Unless I want to kill them here, I must leave now, but you should know what you are up against. You seem to know that Mankin is good in the bush, but so are all of the operatives working this one, former elite paratroopers and the like. Far better than you at your best, which was some time ago."

"What did you mean that someone besides Custer runs this show, and what about the woman from the US? She looks like she'd rather fly first class back to New York or LA and catch a late dinner and a ridiculous play about her ilk, other insipid rich people, than follow Mendoza the Mexican flower deeper into the trees."

"The woman is a lawyer for the human rights

organization I summoned to fight the timber consortium, to cover my people's interests on multiple fronts so to speak. She's smart in the vagaries of international law and has done much good for the rights of indigenous peoples, but that's all I know of her. She's meeting her colleague, a man named Jack France, who is already at the encampment, to discuss strategy."

"You summoned her?"

"Who do you think funds the organization?"

Valasquez's eyes narrow and he moves his head more into line with mine. "I must go and you must hurry," he says. There have also been attacks on a group of Christianized Maya moving in to start up farms, Christianized Maya slashing and burning who don't know what they're doing. They are being attacked by traditional Maya like those at the enclave you are going to visit but living further to the west and not under Chan Lin's control. The government is sending troops at the Christians' behest, which will complicate everything, and maybe move up the agenda for the timber consortium, which has friends in the military they don't want to put into jeopardy over a few trees, or so my sources say. It appears the timber men have bigger plans ultimately than ousting a few Indians to get their land."

Valasquez lowers his cowboy hat over his eyes and moves a step sideways toward a stall with bags of corn stacked in front. I step sideways too, to stay between him and Mankin's men, a pas de deux for killers. "I am not sure of the degree to which this information will serve you, Blue," he says, "but Custer is only a functionary who *thinks* he runs the organization that brought you here. Bagby is really in charge and always has been, in the CIA days too, when you were sent down here to kill my people last. And Bagby is far smarter than he ever let on to you, and certainly

155

smarter than Custer, so you must be careful. Everything will move quickly now, and I think you will have to be very alert and very lucky to survive for long at all, for even the next few days."

Velazquez then disappears into the milling crowd, the boy who hugged him earlier appearing long enough to wink at me, then following the Jaguar at a run.

Chapter Eighteen

We rode west on burros from sunup to sundown through ever-thicker jungle to the Usumacinta River, and I gained much respect for Mendoza the last mile and a half. The trail was overgrown with vines and a layer of forest that would not allow passage on the burros or on foot, and the man, who is roughly five feet even and about my age, cut our way through with a machete, a thousand swarthy whacks at least as the setting sun beat the sweat out of us and biting flies swarmed.

The woman, whose name I learned from Mendoza is Katie Jenson, and I wait on the banks of the river with our feet dangling in the water to cool them after the long march, and Mendoza goes back for the burros that are tethered where he began his work with the machete. He will have to chop some more vegetation from the trail to fit the fat-assed little beasts, and I expect we'll have to wait a few hours at least for the tent and the food. I make a fire when my feet feel better, as much to keep the bugs at bay a little as to ward off the dark, which is now, except for the gnawed chunk of a moon riding in the east, nearly total. The jungle around us seems to breathe, and the noises are obviously quite disturbing to Katie. Monkeys maybe, and macaws. Perhaps the quetzal that the ancient Mayans revered, plucking their tail feathers gently to make headdresses and capes and killing anyone accused of harming the bird. Or maybe those birds are only legend now and the noisemakers are another of a

157

thousand species in the night, the last thousand. The sounds come in bunches, first from across the river, then behind us, as the various populations of the forest make their contribution to the night's revelry.

The lawyer and I do not speak as we wait. I sought her out the night before to tell her I had some business in the village that I did not specify and that Valasquez had told me to go with her and Mendoza. She looked at me with suspicion in her eyes, said she'd clear it with Mendoza, and took off to look for him. I didn't see her again until we met on the veranda of the hotel this morning.

Mendoza had apparently already heard from Valasquez because there was a burro for each of us and one to haul our baggage, and Katie never talked to the burro man about me. The only thing Katie said to me before we left, or since, was that she'd come upon Mendoza with his dying white burro lying at his feet and unable to get up and watched as he hit the animal between the eyes with an ax and then towed it away into the forest with another burro, the one she rides now. She said that the specter so discomfited her that she left without speaking to the little Mexican guide and stopped at the sidewalk café for mescal, stumbling to the hotel in the dark.

Now, she sits stone-still on a stump across the fire from me, her eyes wide with apprehension at every noise in the darkness, the firelight reflecting unnaturally in the wide pools of her pupils. I am watching her for signs she is something more than my initial determination, rich and thrashing about out here on a lark. Lawyer for the indigenous or no, I am trying to see some sign of human worth in her outward appearance. Then, suddenly, there is a man standing behind her. He is wearing fatigues and has a red bandanna over his lower face like a bandit. He carries an M-16 that looks

158

like it has been used to break rocks, but I assume it still works just fine. Then another man steps out behind him, and another, all with small packs on their backs and M-16 rifles. All with bandannas on their faces. All without making a noise.

Katie hasn't noticed and is swatting at the bugs swarming in front of her face, but when the first man steps in front of her, she jumps all the way over the fire to stand next to me. Her eyes are even wider with fear than before, her mouth agape. I wonder if these are Mankin's men, and for a second prepare to die right here. Then one of them asks us in colloquial Spanish what our business is at the river and where our gear is stashed.

I start to tell them we are headed for the Mayan enclave down river, but Katie speaks first. She tells him the name of the group she works for, and in a tone that is all offense, demands to know who is addressing her. I can almost see the man's smile through his bandanna. He could shoot us both dead in half a second, throw us into the river to be eaten by fish, and then disappear into the jungle as if none of us had ever been at this place on the river at all – and this uppity *Norteña* is making demands.

He says he is Chula, a member of the *Fuerzas Armadas Rebeldes*. Katie claps with glee like a child, and in a few minutes she is conversing with all these men as if they were old friends. Mendoza steps into the firelight with the burros behind him. He is wary and obviously afraid, but one of the guerillas, a mere boy by the look of his slender form and wrinkleless forehead, slaps his back and offers Mendoza a cigarette, and then he removes his bandanna to reveal an adolescent face and they smoke together like old friends too.

The boy is so obviously a boy, his skin blemished and soft with a peach-fuzz mustache, but he is not what

159

most Americans would think of when they picture an adolescent either. He should be a collector of baseball cards, soccer memorabilia. He should be at home jacking off as he thinks about the neighbor girl's recently blossomed tits. He should be carrying books and not this battered automatic rifle. But more than this incongruence, he carries his gun like a seasoned killer, a soldier whose constant companion is this tool of death, which he has carried for miles, slept with, depended upon. He smiles and laughs like a boy, but he wields the weapon like an extension of his being, like he has lowered it to fire many times without ever looking in the person's eyes he is trying to snuff out, as a trained killer is always taught to kill, so the victim never has a chance to register as a person. The dead one just flesh going thump as he hits the ground, gore spread over the earth like a nondescript stain.

Even the tough black and Hispanic kids I've seen in the bleakest ghettos in the US, who carry guns as some others accessorize, can't match the cold and deadly perfection that lurks in this manchild's movements. These US children are products of poverty and their culture's cult of the gun, the gun as hyper-stylized means to success and honor, both illusions at so many levels of course, strutting like some suave bastard they've seen on TV who holds a weapon like a perverse combination of his own cock and the Bible, as the magic key to money and fame and sex and the American dream simultaneously reduced to simple mayhem and writ large as myth; but they do not have this kid's calm facility with the machine, his ease with the destruction, the power he commands. I watch him unsling the gun from his shoulder and lean it against a tree as if unsheathing a holy sword, as if this honed steel and wood were a sacred altar he carries and a means of sacrifice simultaneously. He does not move more than a step from the tree that holds the gun, and he keeps his eye on the weapon as if it might wander off to graze on flesh at which he has not aimed, to feed randomly on any breathing creature it can find.

The guerillas help us set up the single big side-wall tent like movie hunters use on safari, part of Katie's gear I assume. Probably came with her khakis as part of a package deal. All the while the men, except the young one, wear their masks, taking their leave when Katie invites them to dinner, demurring politely and slipping into the dark with a synchronized wave good bye.

"Friends of yours?" I ask Katie.

"Something like that. I helped get their leader better prison accommodations in Guatemala a few years ago. They are members of a Marxist group fighting for freedom in that country. We are pretty close to the border, and I don't imagine that national boundaries make much sense to them out here, or maybe they have business in Mexico now. These movements have spread and conjoined, and often been reborn as something new in Mesoamerica, in recent years." She swats an engorged mosquito on her forearm, leaving a splotch of blood and bug parts she doesn't bother to wipe away.

"Such groups were around when I was here last, two decades plus ago, and it doesn't seem that much has changed for them or the masses they claim to fight for ..."

"On the contrary, Mr. Blue," she says, calling me by the name I used to introduce myself last night, by the name on my passport: Sonny Blue. She had been too annoyed to offer me her name, and so I asked Mendoza as we waited for her in the early morning dark outside the hotel. "The governments down here are monoliths of corruption and self-serving nastiness in the name of corporate profit, and that has changed little, but the people are more likely to defend themselves than they were twenty years ago, more likely to be sympathetic to groups like the FAR."

Mendoza hands us cold roast chicken and tortillas and a green fruit I don't recognize, the same fare we had on the trail for lunch but no less tasty. I haven't eaten enough in the last few days to be trekking through the jungle, and I'm feeling weak and even older than usual.

"In fact," Katie says between bites, "much has changed in this particular area, in Chiapas. Right now there is a lull because the President of Mexico has started taking land issues more seriously, and even used to talk to *Subcomandante* Marcos from time to time I hear, before his group became just one among many, which mostly bicker among themselves these days. But there was a full-fledged war down here not that long ago that most *Norteños* never heard about, although the killers the Mexican government used were CIA trained, which the US government denies of course, and in the end the war was almost funny – except for the killing." She swats another mosquito, then another, leaving more splotches of blood and bug she doesn't wipe away.

"It was funny because the war in Chiapas turned into a damned media campaign in the end, which is perhaps why things have turned out the way they have. At least on the surface it was a media campaign, although many died and I don't doubt that the killing goes on still, if perhaps at a more staid rate of slaughter. Soldiers were shown on TV handing out food and vaccinating poor Mayans, which is everybody but the handful of rich landowners, who are all non-tribals, and their private militias. And there were pictures like this on billboards and the front page too. But this generosity was a trick, of course, on top of being a photo-op. The women were given food a few times, then told they had to bring their husbands if they wanted more. The idea was to identify the rebels so their families could be visited in the night, but there was no way to tell who belonged to what faction, if any, unless one group was shooting at the other, so the trick failed miserably."

Mendoza hands a bottle of mescal to Katie and she takes a swig and coughs and goes back to work on the tortillas and chicken. Then he hands the bottle to me, but I pass. The sun beating on me all day, in concert with the lack of food for the last few days and my heavy alcohol consumption last night, has me feeling thin and in danger of disappearing into the darkness around us like an anemic ghost.

"On the other side, the Zapatistas put their namesake's face on coffee mugs and t-shirts like this is Disneyland," Katie says with her mouth full. "And they gained a certain cachet this way, in the cities, among college students and the middle class. It became stylish to wear a t-shirt with Zapata's face on it, and the hearts and minds of the people belonged to the movement, albeit in a very strange and tenuous way. They bought into the movement by buying the product. How the hell does that work?"

Katie wipes her mouth on the back of her hand and takes another hit from the mescal.

"I know this PR crap happens in all wars, declared and un-, but this seems a bit tawdry, somehow sinister because it is so vacuous when the issue is this important, land reform to free these people from the virtual slavery of working for the big ranches. Hell there isn't even a snappy martial song to hang your convenient patriotism on, not a flag to salute or living heroes to cheer on to bloodlust and destruction. No

163

reference to ideology at all for the most part, which is somehow passé all over the world, except for some famously religious zealots, of course, who blow the hell out of everybody, even their own, like they can't control their rage. But otherwise ideology seems dead, even here, where the roots of a Marxist movement have been growing for generations and where the ideas in that canon should still make sense given the vicious class divisions. But there are believers, like those guys with the M-16s, and there are the rest, drinking coffee from a mug with a dead revolutionary emblazoned on it."

I finish my food and ask Mendoza if there is anything more. He fishes homemade chocolate bars from his pack that he says his wife always puts in his gear for a treat around the fire. I feel almost human again, and the chocolate is the most powerful chocolate taste imaginable, just right to top off a good meal, like a big-shouldered port and a cigar, but sweet.

The chocolate brings to mind a cliché, and I remember that Chanelle and Justine were also strong and sweet at once, and not for the meek or the weak willed. I remember how they were just what I needed so many times I can't count, and that, because of them, I was just beginning to feel something for the first time in my life maybe, to feel something for those women via the jolt of life they delivered to my nervous system by way of my limbic system – and to my equally clichéd heart.

Amazing how memory is more true than the real events, the real people that memory stands in lieu of; amazing how, simultaneously, meaning becomes clearer as the mundane inequities slip into the dark and the subtler tastes and smells and feelings that were the real reason one stayed on in the first place step into the spotlight to become, first, the stuff of longing, then the dull ache of remorse, of grief for what one had but didn't completely recognize. I have the added pangs of knowing that Justine was destroyed because of me, her chocolate-sweet life taken only to entice me here, to the evil task ahead and the end of my life when it's done – or hell maybe in the process. The thought of my possible failure to carry out my real mission deepens my depression.

Katie is just getting warmed up. She is talking to herself now, to the stars. "If you ask a Mexican *campasino* what he believes, the answer will be a sermon, at least a long story with meaning wrapped in meaning wrapped in history wrapped in mythology, big meaning hidden there and waiting for you to dare to peek at it. Ask a student in Mexico City and you will get sound bites and platitudes, regardless if he calls himself a Zapatista or a New World Order capitalist or a fucking monkey."

"You mean," I say, and I can't keep the sarcasm out of my voice because Katie is another smartass liberal of means whose sense of injustice, whose Marxism, is armchair Monday morning bullshit, who only knows which are the peasants by their quaint dress. "You mean that they are now merely like us, nothing but surfaces reflecting light off of each other to make it appear as if we are something special, all glitter and well-oiled machines we work our asses off to buy because they give us an identity, however false and temporary the notion?" Then I step in it completely. "You mean they wear L.L. Bean khaki with paisley accouterments that make some sort of fashion statement for the monkeys and endangered birds in the third world, and they eat at nice restaurants and listen to the crap pumped over the airwaves nonstop and believe it to be art rather than the constant commercial message it really is, and go to innocuous plays about themselves, and fuck other vacuous morons like dead people ..."

"I do not fuck like a dead person, Mr. Blue, and the clothes belong to a friend because I have never had call to dress for the wilderness, and beyond that I refuse to answer your accusations because you don't know me but have obviously jumped to erroneous conclusions." And with that lawyerly response, Katie enters the tent with all the grace of the wind, the tent flaps flying. I can hear her cursing me, throwing gear against the tent's walls that shake as if in a gale.

Mendoza is grinning and drinking from the mescal bottle, amused at white people acting in a way a Mexican or an Indian would never dream, I suppose, because they have no time for trumped-up drama – existence is drama enough. And he is humming yet another song I heard Miguel Santiago sing a lifetime ago, about beautiful women and death. Always death, no matter what else.

Chapter Nineteen

Hope is the most merciless of weapons, and these are the days of hope. It is perhaps Rudy's most miraculous insight, gained from his hours and days and years torturing human beings.

"You tell them that this will be the last jolt if they give you just one more name, one more address, one more date, if just one more guerilla is caught and killed because of the words that come out of their mouth, the same mouth that weeps and pleads and asks for death.

"And I say, what kind of barbarian do you take me for? I don't want to kill you. Hell, I don't want to hurt you. I'm just doing my job, just getting you to talk. That is all I'm here for. You tell me all the answers to all the questions and I can stop hurting you.

"And it is that, hope, that makes them talk, that makes many of them actually like me, the man with the juice who is fucking up their central nervous systems. They like me and they pity me because I really can't stand to see them suffer, and so they give me all they know, make it up sometimes just to please me."

But then came Rudy's stroke of genius: "So one day it occurs to me that hope is a marvelous tool, a way to enter the subconscious of the masses and make them give us the answers we want without having to seize them in the night and tie them to a chair and hit them with the big fat fist of voltage.

"One day it occurs to me that, if we just take their loved ones, make them vanish without a trace, and if we have left other loved ones by the road to town with

167

their heads cut off and their balls in their mouths, then they will wonder all the time if the disappeared are still alive, if they have been tortured, if they are suffering, if they will return, if they will be whole if they return.

"They hope, you see, and hope is a poison that works on their guts, that works in their dreams, that makes them plead with the authorities for the return of the disappeared loved ones, for any scrap of information regarding their whereabouts. And this is power. A power that exceeds putting juice to their pudenda, exceeds the drugs and the missing fingers.

"Hope, the great evoker of terror. Hope, the toxin that makes them tell us everything they know, makes them want to find out what they don't know and bring the truth back to us like a game of fetch the stick to the master. Hope, the worm that eats into their lives where it will blossom as nightmares. Hope, the hobgoblin that will do all our work for us, that will drive them all mad with a desire to know, to tell us the truth so they *can* know for certain, for sure, that their loved ones are dead or not, whole or broken.

"But they will die hoping because there is really nothing to tell them. The disappeared loved ones have become merely a myth, ascended like believers at the rapture but really dropped from a helicopter into the sea or a lake where the fishes eat them utterly, and it is as if they never existed at all, gone without a trace. And we couldn't tell them the truth, of course, because they wouldn't ever believe it with only this glowering absence as evidence, this blank space where their loved ones used to be, this vacancy, which can never refute their hope because it is precisely the space their hope has grown to fill."

These are the days of the disappeared, and I am orchestrating this horrible tactic. Rudy is off somewhere, beginning to see Jesus in his corn flakes,

168

reciting whole commercials as if they were biblical revelation, and drinking Jack Daniels he has flown in weekly from the States. Rudy is off somewhere going mad, and I am now the maestro of mayhem, the gringo with the plan, the one who says which men and women will be hauled off in the night so their loved ones will mourn the rest of their days, so they will hope and so tell the authorities all they want to know.

These are the nights of the disappeared, and the streets of Guatemala City are empty except for the black jeeps that move in a row through this impoverished neighborhood, except for the men in black fatigues and black bandannas. We stop in front of a hovel where the editor of an underground newspaper lives with his wife and kids. We kick in the door and tie up the wife and haul her away as the man sleeps, drugged by one of the men in black with a syringe. The children are crying, and one, a girl of twelve, tries to hold her mother here. She latches on and will not let go, and she is weeping-mad with terror. She is in her nightgown, and she is a child, a girl of twelve, a girl of twelve, a girl of twelve ...

One of the men in black hits her, punches her full in the face, and she stops crying. She becomes as still as anyone living and awake can be, and her eyes turn hard as she stares at us, at her mother bound and weeping, and she becomes something other than a child in her nightgown with her nose broken and bleeding. She curses us calmly, with the power of one who is not afraid to die, who knows she will never see her mother again. She says that we are demons but she will find us and kill us, that she will never stop hunting until all the demons are dead. Until all of the demons on earth are dead.

I am awake now, in the jungle more than twenty years later, soaked with night sweats and willing the girl

169

to silence, as the waxing gibbous moon peeps through the gap between the tent flaps above one of the canvas ties, as Mendoza and Katie breathe deeply in the Mexican night, as the insects buzz, and the girl, this innocent with her nose shattered, will not stop cursing me, will not stop staring at me, will not stop wishing me dead no matter that I am awake, no matter that I wish the same.

I concentrate hard on the improbable sounds of human breathing: Katie's soughing like a breeze through aspen leaves, the tough little Mexican *vaquero's* breathing, the burro master's steady in and out like a stream over rocks, much like the river a hundred feet away but more varied, the blue man's breath stuttering as if it might fail. Then I listen to the river, to the few night birds calling, to the wings of large bats as they swerve into another and another miniscule bite of bug flesh, drinking our blood that the mosquitoes collected as we sat around the fire. I think I hear a high scream away in the dark, and then I am dreaming of the long ranks of the dead who are chastising me with their blank eyes. Then it is light.

Chapter Twenty

Katie and I bid Mendoza, the Mexican flower, farewell at midmorning. The encampment had sent two canoes for us that landed an hour before our departure. The four rowers drank strong Mexican coffee, four pots, ate tortillas with *piñole* spread on them, and laughed with Mendoza, then hurried us aboard. Now I am perched in the middle of a mahogany dugout made by burning away layers that craftsmen then remove with a chisel, which one of the paddlers, the man behind me with two missing front teeth and half-crossed eyes, explained to me as he stroked hard against the current to work the canoe around a boulder.

I can see the muscles shudder and strain in the back and shoulders of the front man in my canoe, as do the muscles in the backs and shoulders of the men in the canoe ahead of this one with Katie perched in the middle, and I wish I had an oar, that I pulled and heaved this perfect projectile of timber downstream with these men, in league with them, in rhythm. I wish this body of enough subcutaneous fat reserves to feed a small village for a week were capable of such work, but more than this, I wish that I could work toward some small goal so elemental as paddling a canoe from one place to another in concert with other men, other travelers, fellow voyagers. It is an odd wish maybe, but one any comfortable man or woman in the civilized world has felt as an inchoate urge, some desire that tingles along the back of the arms and in the wrists, an atavistic spasm in the hands that never quite reaches

171

the level of consciousness let alone the level of language. It is the desire for an elemental labor and to belong to some endeavor both practical and endemically poetic, both communal and aesthetic, like making love but with some less obvious and less immediate objective, like dancing maybe. A labor that is equal parts purpose and joy.

The sun is warm on my head in spite of my cap, and the sound of the water and the oars swishing and rising and dripping then swishing again is mellifluous as Gregorian chant, so I lower my chin to my chest and sleep a short while sitting up. I awaken with my heart pounding when I nearly fall forward and catch myself as if I were plummeting from a cliff or a plane. I look over my shoulder at the man behind me, half expecting him to be laughing his ass off at the antics of the stupid white guy in the wilderness, but he only smiles warily, almost benevolently, without missing a stroke with his paddle.

I had forgotten how dense the high jungle can be. A wall of green runs right up to the river in places, with the tree line even reaching out into the shallows here and there. We stop for lunch for all of ten minutes, some cold coffee passed around and tortillas coated with beans, then back into the river. Just after we launch the canoes, we round a long bend with lianas stretched out into the current and then hit an open spot in the trees, a mere cove in the vertical green where grass is knee-deep; and there, in the center of the small clearing, is a great cat, a jaguar. It is up to its forelegs in the carcass of a white-tailed deer, blood up its front and spread over its lower face.

The men immediately stop rowing, but they do not point. They all see the animal and make no move to go forward or to remark the creature's presence to each other. Katie has noticed now too and stares with her

172

mouth open at the jaguar covered with the essence of its prey. The big cat is looking back at us, breathing heavily in the heat, the blood caked in its fur. Its eyes are stern but otherwise seemingly impassive, certain of its strength perhaps, of its place in the universe. Then the jaguar screams and backs reluctantly out of its meal, turns and disappears into the shadow of the trees in a single movement so quick it is almost as if the creature disappeared into the air.

The rowers move to a kneeling position facing shore all at the same time as the canoes begin to list in the current. They face the boats upstream and bow simultaneously in the direction of the cat's retreat, their oars in front of them in the water to keep the boats from turning. Then, all of them look at me for a long moment as the boats swirl and threaten to turn back wholly toward our destination even in this lighter current near the shore. The Mayans look almost expectant, as if I could explain why this nocturnal and paramountly secretive beast should show itself to us today. They look at me as if I had something to do with its presence, and when I do not speak, for a split second, I think I see fear in their eyes. Then they turn us back downstream and resume their rhythmic paddling.

"*Que pasa, amigo?*" I turn to ask the man with the missing teeth behind me, but he waves off my question between strokes and refuses to look anywhere but ahead of us. Katie looks at me with a puzzled expression but turns her eyes to the front quickly to watch as a patch of rough water approaches, more afraid of her circumstances than curious about this minor spectacle. I doubt she knows a jaguar is so rare and wary that many Indians who live in this land all their lives have not seen one, but I suppose our companion's behavior toward me must have seemed strange even to an urban lawyer in khaki more stylish than practical. I can only assume their reaction has something to do with the old man's, Chan Lin's, vision of me, and I decide I may not want to know.

The slender canoes negotiate the fast water easily, the rowers keeping the boats close to one bank as much as possible, then portage around another set of rapids with boulders the size of import cars and water too fast to negotiate safely, the water compacted to a fist and shoved through a tight canyon. From this point, the water is more shallow and generally quicker for several miles. The men lean harder into the paddles and have to keep watch for barely submerged rocks, and then the river opens up and slows again and the rowers fall into a brisk and powerful rhythm once more, dancing together and with the river, pushing us further north as the sun falls slowly to our left in a dying arc.

As the river falls into crepuscular shadow, we enter a small channel that runs into the Usumacinta, almost a canal, and pull the boats up onto a sandy shore covered with sparse grass perhaps half a mile from the river proper. We eat more tortillas and beans, and the Mayans spread out over the ground wrapped in bright blankets, which were covered in tightly woven reed mats on the boat trip to keep them dry, and sleep the good sleep of physical exhaustion. The only words from these men is the news from the leader, a big-shouldered man of thirty or so who was the front rower in Katie's boat, that we'll walk from here, three days into the mountains to Chan Lin's village.

I gather some fallen limbs and driftwood and make a fire for light and to drive off the mosquitoes at least a little. Then Katie and I sit up a while, to unwind from the day's constant motion she says, because she feels like she is still bobbing along, and me because I am in no hurry to enter the land of dreams where the dead will not leave me alone. Katie is obviously still pissed over

174

our conversation last night, but small talk bores me anyway, as would any Monday morning political rant from the likes of her. Night-bird song and bat wings as they turn and shift on the dark are fine by me.

The bats are quick shadows against the stars that explode above us, a second's respite only in a world of murder and torture, flaming corpses and men and women and children gone forcibly blue in the face, of ancient trees stolen and other debauchery only a demon could invent – God laughing at his own joke. I imagine the exploding sky is God's dream, my exploded life and the violence we call human existence just a minor punch line in a far bigger comedic project. We spin wildly through the void, hell-bent on nowhere, amid planets and boiling gases traveling at velocities we can't imagine, our life like a bullet made and shot and its target gone under so fast it is all of a piece: from unmolded lead to a rotted corpse fast as God can envision it. The only truth we can know for certain: the end, nada, zilch, blackness stacked on blackness and a silence so profound the heart quails at the mere thought. The bleakness of these metaphors almost makes me laugh.

"Do you know the stars?" Katie asks, her neck also craned upward, her arms around her knees to steady herself. "Their names, I mean." She looks almost girlish against the darkness, and for a moment, I am tempted to imagine us both as children in some suburban backyard. But I can't afford such mundane middle-of-America crap, some vision of the inanity of life lifted to the level of religion that none of us lived anyway. And I shake off the notion.

"I know some of the constellations and a few stars, mostly the ones to navigate by in either hemisphere, primarily Polaris in the northern and the Southern Cross in the Incan lands of course, and a few others for more

175

accuracy, like Orion and Sirius the Dog Star. But the locations of many stars depend on the season too, and it has been a long time since I had to know these things. Hell, it has been a long time since I looked up at the night sky, a long time since I looked up at all."

"Strange how a city dweller could go a lifetime without seeing the night sky," she says, "how we lose context that way. Maybe it allows us the illusion that we, human beings, are the focus of all existence because everything we can see is manmade and right in front of us. Our own creations, skyscrapers and public art, are the biggest things in our midst, and the fact that we made them is primary in our minds, in our association with the world constrained by what we've made instead of anything so big as galaxies and stars, which must remain abstractions, a myth the astronomers both propagate but also diminish by reducing it all to numbers, that most esoteric of languages. City dwellers have even made the ground we walk on, all the concrete and blacktop, and produced the smells around us so nothing of nature intrudes but our own bodily stink, which we also mask. Maybe this is our way of coping with our finitude, a way to stand our tiny presence in time."

I don't answer because I know she is not really talking to me. This is a soliloquy, which is the way modern humans address the great unknown that is perhaps the great absence we name *God*. Such a speech is the vestigial remnants of prayer to the vestigial remnant of Deity. We can only manage to talk to ourselves of these big things, never expecting an answer. We stare into the exploding dream of the sky a bit longer, then roll out our sleeping bags from their waterproof gear bags and climb into them without another word. The Mayans declared the tent too big to haul in the boats, so Katie made a gift of it to the fragrant burro man. The stars wheel and burn over our heads the night long, and I stare into them, falling asleep after the last birds have ceased to call and the bats have gone home to roost.

Justine is there behind my eyes, holding out her severed ear and imploring me to attach it to its vacant and bleeding moorage on the side of her head. Then Chanelle is there too, her arms crossed and her toe tapping, the picture of an irate woman, a scolding mother. She does not speak, but I know she is unhappy because Mankin has not yet paid for maiming and killing her sister. I apologize, but this only makes her weep. She holds her face in her hands and cries bitterly as her sister strokes her hair with blood-covered fingers. They sit that way in my dream, rocking together beyond my reach, until the sun comes up.

Chapter Twenty-One

I have been promoted to bogeyman.

We walked at a quick pace, as fast uphill as two soft and stumbling urbanites can manage, for the next four days. The Mayan leader of our little group apparently thought his previous estimate of three days to trek from the river to the village was adequate, confident he'd taken our lack of physical conditioning into account, because the four men marvel endlessly that this trip that is normally a day and a half should take anyone so long. And they are apparently marveling for our benefit because they do so in Spanish rather than the Quiché they speak to one another most of the time. Apparently, even their old and very young can make this journey in two days. The leader sends a man ahead on our third day of climbing to let the village know we are running a little behind.

The Mayans never grow impatient with us, however, merely smiling and shaking their heads as we stop every few hours to catch our breath and rest our legs. Katie developed blisters almost immediately, her high-end boots not really the proper footwear they appear to be, but one of the Mayans stepped from the trail and into the trees, disappearing instantly, and returned a half hour later with leaves he chewed into a mush and applied to her wounds. Within an hour of stopping, she declared herself healed and we pressed on. The Mayan worked on her feet with chewed plant pulp every few hours the rest of the trip, and she has had no more trouble walking.

The fourth day we step into a clearing, which is the first open space of any size we've seen the entire trek. I have to stop a moment to let my eyes adjust to a little distance, and to let my mind adjust to the end of the claustrophobic feeling I developed two days into our march because of the seemingly endless lush density of the forest pressing in on the trail. Perhaps a hundred feet from the forest's edge are the long, slightly elevated houses of Chan Lin's village that are made of the tall trees that grow at this elevation, logs stacked with mud to fill the chinks. Smoke rises here and there from among the dwellings. A line of faces also awaits us, children mostly and a few old women, all dressed in white peasant clothes with their hair cut bluntly at shoulder length, but as we approach, they withdraw to keep the same hundred feet between us. And as we enter the village proper, the spectators walk parallel to our path, using the houses to separate us.

When I ask my toothless companion why the locals are so wary, he hesitates and then replies, "*Señor Azul* walks the night and steals the souls of the living. You are Lord Death's minion, his foot soldier and his assassin, and the people are afraid. Anyone who can touch Lord Death and not die himself is indeed powerful."

"But do they fear Valasquez?" I ask.

"Yes and no. He is one of us, so less alien, but he goes to the white world much and does unspeakable things there, or so we hear. His path is an arduous one, a bloody one, and he is on that trail for us. He kills and suffers for his people because Chan Lin, the greatest of us, and maybe the greatest holy man our people have ever known, has asked him to – because Chan Lin says our people are doomed without the assistance of the Jaguar. But we also know the Jaguar is deadly, that he carries the weight of thousands of souls maybe, so

179

we step aside when he walks by. Some take to the trees until he leaves the village again. None of us takes the death of another, whether winged or furred or human, lightly. So we take the magic he represents, the accumulated souls he represents, very seriously."

Just then a boy of about ten runs up to me, touches my forearm, and then disappears around some wooden rain barrels stacked between a couple of the houses. I look at the Mayan, who smiles sheepishly, then proudly as he speaks. "*Mi hijo,* and he is very brave. The old one has told me he will take the Jaguar's place when the time comes." He is a little sad as he says this, perhaps because he knows how lonely his son will be, the fear he will inspire in his own people.

"And what is the Jaguar's place exactly, his role?" I ask. "You both fear and revere him, and one day your son will become him. I'm not sure I understand."

"He is one of the twin warriors made manifest in our time. He is the twin we call Little Jaguar Sun, and you …" The man looks down as he speaks, uncertain.

"Please continue," I say, half knowing the role he will assign to me.

"You are the twin we call Little Hidden Sun, or the Blue Man Who Speaks to Lord Death. Chan Lin has called you the Blue Man Who Will End Time, which makes some among us all the more afraid because we don't know what that means. There are lots of other names too, but these are the ones we hold to be most important, because Chan Lin says these names are part of our destiny."

I can see the Mayan's son peeking around one of the houses ahead of us. He steps into our path as we pass and greets his father, who looks sidelong at me and touches the boy's head tenderly as we walk by him, but we do not stop. Katie, who is walking behind us several feet, touches the boy's head too. He has

180

now turned to watch us just as I have turned to look over my shoulder at him. The kid's gaze is intense, focused like the jaguar we saw eating the white tail, as if he too knows his place in the universe and is confident in his role like few human beings ever achieve; but there is something primal in his gaze too, like he could pounce with the same single-minded ferocity as the big cat. He lifts his chin in my direction, then turns and speeds off toward the forest edge at a dead run like a feral creature seeking the safety of the wild after a brief visit to the human realm, perhaps a visit to remind him of what he is and what he is not, of what things human he is disallowed.

We stop before a house at the far edge of the village. The house is bigger than the others and raised a few feet higher off the ground. As we ascend the wooden steps, the leader of our expedition emerges and says something in Quiché to the toothless man, then descends the stairs without looking at Katie or me. The toothless man asks us to wait. He says that Chan Lin has been ill for months and is just waking from one of many naps he takes every day, and the old one will see us in a few minutes. Then he excuses himself, bounds down the steps, and walks quickly toward the forest where his son entered the shadows. I can just barely see them embrace, the man squatted down to the boy's height, the boy talking quickly and waving his hands in accompaniment.

After a few minutes, an older woman and a girl of perhaps fifteen greet us. The older explains that the two of them are Chan Lin's first and last wife, that the others are away working the fields. The young one is shirtless, the buds of her breasts pointing as straight ahead as the old one's point equally straight downward through her thin shirt. The old one leads us through a large front room with no furniture, then down a short

181

hall to a sunny room with an iron bed and a tick mattress and pillow. The old man is rustling the corn shucks as he struggles to lift himself into a more upright position. The old woman scolds him in Quiché, and both women rush to help him sit up a little. Then they leave us alone with him.

Chan Lin addresses Katie first, thanks her in Spanish for her service to his people, then directs her to a house two doors away where her colleague, Jack France, is staying. He says the man is down with a fever but receiving the best treatment the tribe has to offer and should be up and about in a few days. She looks concerned as she turns for the door.

For several minutes after Katie leaves, Chan Lin stares at me intently, and then he closes his eyes and I think he must be sleeping again. But before I can leave quietly, he speaks. "*Hola, Señor Azul.* We've been waiting a long time for your arrival."

I start to apologize for our tardiness, for my lack of physical prowess in this rough country, but he says, "Your arrival was prophesized many generations ago, more than 500 hundred years by your reckoning, when the Spaniards were our greatest threat. You took your sweet time," he says, and he smiles.

The old man's face is creased, fold upon fold of ancient flesh, but his shoulder-length hair is thick and jet black. I think of Ron Reagan, his old countenance under bootblack hair, but before me is that old man's dream of himself that he projected outward as best he could, as any actor does, achieving verisimilitude at best, but still frighteningly unreal, a death's mask disguised poorly with the trappings of youth. I can see nothing calculated for effect in the old man before me, no self-delusion. Chan Lin is staring at me again, and his eyes are clear, his gaze strong and intelligent. I am wondering how to use his mythology to my advantage. I don't want to hand this people's mahogany trees over to the timber company consortium, but I don't want to be killed before I carry out my real mission either. If this old man thinks me the incarnation of a mythic warrior, then he won't have me run off and Mankin won't be the wiser.

The old man is still smiling. "Yes, I know you are here to steal the trees, that there are heavily armed men waiting in the forest not far away to see if you succeed or fail. If the latter, they will kill you, and I assume they will step up their terror tactics again, steal women and children again, maim our men again." The old woman peeks in the room and then leaves without speaking.

"If you know so much ..." I begin, but Chan Lin cuts me off.

"I know that this is the difference between your people and mine. Yours believe their civilization the center of everything and would wreck the universe to keep it going if that were possible. My people know that the universe has a destiny, that our paltry way of being, as glorious as its history, as much as we love it, as in tune with the universal order as we strive to live, is destined to be sacrificed in order that the stars may travel the very trajectories they travel now. We know that without such sacrifice all would go awry, all would end." The old man clears his throat, which brings the old woman to the door again, but he waves her away with a smile and continues.

"We know that our end time is not that far off, not by our way of measuring time anyway, perhaps another few hundred years – at least *I* know this. The rest believe we will triumph over the dark culture, the monolith of power and wealth and sameness that is Western Civilization. But this is only partly true. In fact, Western Civilization is even now winding down of its

183

own accord, and we are merely helping it along in some small way in order to bring about what must be, to insure that hell does not reign up here in the light of day; because if your civilization does somehow survive its own stupidity, that hell will come about because everything will be the same, a bleak and final banality that knows no destiny but its own boring existence.

"Most of your fellow members of that civilization believe the opposite, of course, that they are in the ascendancy because capitalism is going global, or so Jaguar tells me, this being the language he puts to my dreams, because they control most of the planet to one degree or another, use most of the resources, employ far too many of the rest of us as cheap labor or hold us even as slaves – and of course they kick the shit out of whoever objects. But as those odd Christians are fond of saying, the Lord works in mysterious ways. If they knew but half the truth of that statement they'd all jump off one of those tall buildings the Jaguar has told me about and I've seen crumbling to the ground in my dreams, jump in utter despair. It must be such a shock to know that all of existence does not revolve around you when you have believed the contrary for hundreds of years. Frankly, I'm not sure I can imagine it because the size of the delusion is beyond me."

The old woman comes in again, straightens Chan Lin's pillows and shoots me a harrowing glance as she leaves the room.

"She doesn't seem to be all that afraid of the Blue Man, harbinger of the end times," I say.

"No, that old woman is afraid of nothing at all. My first wife, whose name translates as Whisperer in Dreams, is a sorceress, a *bruja* of enormous strength and creative energy who thinks all this talk of the destiny of the universe is so much pig shit." The old man smiles broadly.

"She is a holy person too, but not engaged in a battle to ensure the destiny of the universe?" I ask, not without a little sarcasm in my voice, though I did not intend it.

"She works at a more local level. Her enemy is evil alright, but as it manifests itself in the trees that steal children or in a man's enemies, those who invoke Lord Death to poison his crops or kill his livestock. Lately, she is working hard against the men in the forest who were taking the people one at a time until recently. She is a healer and caster-of-spells of the first rank, but she is not concerned with these larger issues."

"But the word is that I work for Lord Death too, as I assume the men in the forest are working for him. In fact, I'm told your people are frightened of me for this reason."

"They know you are a killer, *Señor Azul*. The rumors of your mythological implications are widespread, it is true, that you are the incarnation of the warrior that is also the moon, but more than anything they sense about you the many souls you've taken from the world, hear them sighing in the air around you, as I can hear them now. Any Mayan, even one hypnotized by the Christians, is still close enough to his ancestors and the old ways of knowing to understand this without having words to explain it. Now you are a soldier in the service of Lord Death, but in this instance, you are also in the service of Quiché, the Goddess who is also the people and our dying language, as well. Your Christian roots tell you light and dark, evil and good, are polar opposites, and in some limited sense they are; indeed, my people generally believe the same thing, but we know these things must exist in balance.

"But your people also tend to associate death with evil, which it can be. More to the point, it can be a tool of evil, as you know all too well. But the trip to the

185

Underworld is part of the human path too. A *brujo* also knows that both the people and the Lord of the Underworld serve the same ultimate goal, the destiny of the entire universe, and to that end we work together sometimes, although Lord Death's immediate aim is to fill the ranks of the dead with more dead, of course. Even Lord Death, who is happy to have all the brains for *piñole* he can get, is disquieted by the tendencies of Western Civilization to usurp destiny, to spread over the planet like a disease of nondifferentiation, a malaise of uniformity, hell on earth but ruled by men and not Lord Death. In short, he is a jealous deity."

"In my culture," I tell him, "we call this a rationalization, when the ends justify the means, no matter how brutal. The powerful of Western Civilization you vilify as your enemies use this same tactic with impunity." My tone is all sarcasm now.

The old man smiles at this and calls out in Quiché. The old woman enters carrying water in a clay pitcher as blue as the sky. She pours him some in a cup of blue enameled steel but does not offer me any. He drinks, then goes on as she fusses at him some more in Quiché, an enormity of consonants, on her way out the door.

"The Jaguar is relatively young, so he is uncertain, even after all the years of our association, when I tell him to follow the white assassin to a particular town in America, to find a blue man there and to speak to him, that you, *Señor Azul,* will both steal our trees and end time because Lord Death told me so – the Jaguar is uncertain as to my sanity. But then he finds you and goes about the business of my people by helping to destroy yours in ways both subtle and invidious. But he rationalizes nothing. He knows that his business is bloody and his tactics extraordinarily dark, and he knows that his work will help to bring about ruin and

186

terror and a terrible despair. But he also knows, because I have taught him so, that his own ruin is part of this plan, that he will die ignominiously, as will I, as will my people who will only outlast yours to replace them as the preeminent purveyors of evil in the struggle between the various forces in the universe. I know this. I have seen this.

"In the end, which is not really an end, the stars will turn over a cold earth, and the mythological beings like you and the Jaguar's successors will live here alone with no one to tell your tales, no one to propagate the truth in stories. But only for a time, because it will all begin again with a new race that will again propitiate the ancient gods, who will again sing and dance and rejoice in their being without dividing the world into good and evil, believing they serve the former when they really serve the latter. They will live here without trying to swallow it all, control it and turn it to their own ends. They will know their place in the universe as only a few old *brujos* know theirs at present."

My head is light and I struggle not to stumble when I stand. I don't know what I expected based on what little Valasquez told me, certainly no noble savage, maybe an eccentric and toothless old man merely trying to defend his own against inevitable genocide a little longer, but now I can't help but believe Chan Lin as mad as any ideologue who sanctions the suffering of others in the name of a higher order – and maybe he is more mad than most given the scale on which his vision dances. Before me, maybe, is a nihilist whose cold logic outpaces even the men who birthed death camps or mutually assured destruction or any pogrom. "So this is your apocalypse," I say, "which varies remarkably little from the Christian version. You kill off all the non-believers so the chosen can again have dominion."

"Oh, but it does vary, Blue Man, in important ways. There will not be an Edenic ending for any chosen few, no return to some pristine garden, nor will there be an autocratic rule of a single godhead, but a true rebirth. It all starts again. The Christians want the entire universe to coalesce into a barbaric sameness, the world inhabited by a single race following only the Christian god. We want as many gods as can fit into a world this size, as many races, which include the four-legged and the winged races too. This is what I mean when I say we want the universe to achieve its destiny. We want an endless variety here, a great multitude with each aspiring to achieve their own destiny that is also the destiny of the universe. And that can only happen when the lingering taint is gone: us, all of us. Because the evil will persist out of balance unless it all starts anew. Existence is a messy and chaotic dance, Blue Man."

The old man sighs. "I don't like what I see in my dreams, *Señor Azul*, but I have no more choice in the path I am taking than you do. Our paths are merely part of a larger path, and the Lord Death and Quiché themselves are now directing us. There is little comfort that, in the reckoning of my people, we live in the fifth world now, that the world has been destroyed utterly four times since the creation and always it is reborn again, but it is all that I have to keep me going forward." Chan Lin sighs deeply again, as if trying to catch his breath.

"But first things first," he says as he closes his eyes, looking even older than when I entered the room. "I will rest a while and you will stay with the others of your kind. The Jaguar arrives in two days, and the people will make a great ceremony in honor of the Twins, of you two, and there will be a funeral. The Jaguar must deal with the immediate threat to the people, the men in the forest, to gain the people an exit, and then the people will move again, yet further into the trees for sanctuary – a temporary sanctuary. Then you must begin your journey to end time. I want you to visit Olvidero first, a diviner who may or may not be able to give you guidance."

Chan Lin slumps forward a little, and the old wife and the young wife are immediately at his side, entering the room in a flurry as if they were watching from the doorway the whole time. They ease him down onto the tick mattress and cover him tenderly with a brightly-colored blanket, blood-red and the same deep blue I was when I woke up in the alley. Then, in Spanish so that I may hear the exasperation in her words, the old woman directs the younger to take me to the door.

I sit on the steps to the old man's house for a long time. I watch the children and the black and white speckled pigs and red chickens wandering about between the houses. I watch the people look sidelong in my direction to make sure I'm not moving toward them. I watch the smoke rise up against the surrounding green, all the more gray for the contrast. I look into the palm of my hand and imagine it blue again. Then I flex my fingers methodically as in the old days, the fingers of a killer in search of a weapon, the only tool of value in the decaying world according to the old man, the only human tool I have ever been allowed in any event, and I am more sad than I have ever been in my life.

Chapter Twenty-Two

I have all but lost the old instincts that kept me alive in the field back when I rode the geopolitical range. I heard nothing before being awakened in the jet blackness with a hand over my mouth and a hushed "shhh" in my ear. I can barely make out a man's head above me, some apparatus on his head, night-vision goggles I suppose.

I can smell something like metal on Mankin's breath as he whispers, "The old man is out of the way now and it is up to you to accomplish this mission, and soon. The timber people are tired of waiting and Custer has sent word there are Mexican troops headed this way to put down some radical indigenous types to the west. Do what we hired you to do, Blue, or next time you will wake up to discover you are dead. Remember, if you screw this up, the remaining sister will be dealt with too. I'll add a piece of her to my collection, hang it right next to the first sister's ear." Then he is gone.

I sit up and get my bearings, listening to the soughing of Katie's sleep-breathing across the room and to the sick guy's more guttural sounds where he sleeps not far from her. Then I slip my boots on without tying the laces and head toward the window, a square cut in the logs and covered with a piece of striped cloth. The plastic ends of the canvas laces click across the planks of the floor as they whip loosely about. I climb through the opening as quickly as I can and circle to the front of the house. I look around the corner just as Mankin slips out the front door and heads down the steps. He is moving quickly but quietly toward the trees.

I have to wait until he disappears behind another house before I can follow him because of the night-vision goggles he wears. There is only the wisp of a moon showing through some high clouds, which means he can leave the goggles on, a major advantage, but the moon is big enough to give sufficient light in spite of the wispy clouds for me to move without tripping over the sleeping pigs. A dog barks at the far end of the compound, but otherwise it is quiet, not even night birds calling.

I step to the edge of the forest, to where Mankin entered, but inside the trees it is pitch black. I step forward a few paces and squat so I won't be seen against the lighter background of the clearing, and I listen. I am hoping that my eyes will adjust sufficiently so I can follow the assassin in a few minutes, find where he is hiding and take the bastard out before he can make good on his threats. But the wall of darkness remains impenetrable and I feel a rising sense of panic. I can't help but fail to get the trees because I am too old and inept and Mankin will make good on his promise to kill Chanelle. Even if I hear him and manage somehow to follow, this killer is among the best on earth. My heart pounding is the only noise. Even the buzz of insects has ceased.

Then I hear a small sound like deadfall brushing against a pant leg, and I focus my attention in that direction even harder, but the sound does not repeat. There is nothing but forbidding blackness. The night is once again so still that it recalls my dreams of the Underworld, wherein the very quiet itself echoes, wherein the vastness I cannot see but sense stretching away from me on every side makes my heart ache with preternatural fear, a sensation like falling into an abyss with my feet firmly on the ground.

I hear my own heart thumping again, and then I hear something out there in the dark once more, light footsteps, but they come from behind me. I turn to see the toothless man's son walking nonchalantly toward me in the moonlight. He stands before me a long minute, then turns his back and I can hear him pissing on the ground. When the sound of water hitting the forest detritus stops, he takes my hand and we walk back to the village, to the old man's house. The old woman is sitting in the dark on an ancient ladder-back chair as if waiting for us.

"*Chan Lin. Muerte,*" she says, emotionless, then tells me that the old man's head was cut from his body and placed on the porch for everyone to find in the morning, that she has retrieved it and returned it to the rest of him so he will not be in pieces in the Underworld.

I start to tell her I am sorry, but she says the old man knew this was coming, that he had even told her it would be tonight. He told her his death was necessary to unite his people in a single intent, so they would follow Jaguar to a new home further north in spite of his youth. She says the old man told her that he was dying anyway. She tells me these things impassively, as if we discussed the trail conditions to the Usamacinta River.

I ask her what she intends to do about his death, and she snorts in reply. "I cast spells, Blue Man," she says, "and I will do so for the next ten days to send the assassin responsible for this to Lord Death himself to be dealt with for all eternity, but you are the bringer of the killer's actual death, his sacrificer. Quit acting so stupid." Her tone is flat, all exasperation without a hint of anything else, as if the old man's death and my ignorance are the same foregone conclusion and both merely make her tired and testy.

As the old woman rises to go in, the boy, who has

192

not let go of my hand, reaches into a pouch at his waist and hands me a worked stone object a foot long. The artifact is blunt on one edge and sharp on the other, so sharp I feel blood trickle down my thumb after I touch the blade lightly. Then he turns toward the village and disappears in the dark.

"You will need this ancient knife, Blue Man," says the old woman from the doorway. "The Jaguar has one like it and will tell you of its meaning and its value. You will take the assassin's heart with this blade and bring the blackened piece of shit to me so that I may conjure him in hell." She slips quietly into the house as the dog at the far end of the village barks again then quiets almost immediately. I feel the air pushing in on me, now the heavy fetid air of the Underworld. My fantasies of vengeance for Justine's death aside, I have spent many years trying to forget the very things the old woman says constitute my future: blood on my hands, the smell of a man split open, the last inevitable spasms of a corpse. I walk down the steps, take two paces toward the house where my bed awaits, and vomit loudly over the ground. A night-black pig awakens and is eating the remains of my last meal before the final bitter bile hits the earth.

Chapter Twenty-Three

Valasquez the Jaguar sits on the edge of Chan Lin's bed and stares into his bloodless face as if he expects the old man to speak, or maybe as if he hears the old man whispering the last strange instructions he will ever receive from him.

I am here to see what Valasquez plans to do and to relay Chan Lin's last message if necessary. The Jaguar walked straight here the minute he arrived at the encampment and has been sitting by the old man's body since, a half day. I am here because I am haunted by visions of gutting Mankin and stealing his heart for the old woman, which are both satisfying and sickening, not so much a tug of war for my visceral response as a disconcerting simultaneity. Perhaps at last, with the Jaguar's help because he will want to take revenge for this old man's death, I can ensure Chanelle's safety and avenge Justine. But the thought of getting bloody again, of adding to the faces I see standing in rows in the night, no matter that this new set of accusing eyes would belong to a sick bastard who doesn't deserve to breathe the same air as the rest of us, has my bowels churning.

Chan Lin's head sits on his chest like an oracle. I would have thought that his wives would put it back atop his shoulders and pull a blanket up to his chin to give the illusion of wholeness. The old woman has been in the room twice in the few minutes I've been here to stroke the old man's hair and run her thumbs over his sunken eyes, to hum some words I can't quite make out as words, perhaps a pre-lingual spell for a safe passage to the other side. The sobbing of many women, Chan Lin's other wives I assume, comes from somewhere in the house, a drawn out sibilance that is half weeping and half singing. Not so much words as the incipient shape of words, the eggs from which words hatch.

Valasquez does not answer when I speak. He merely stares into the shriveled face. So I stare into the old man's crumbling visage too, for an hour or more. All I can see in my mind's eye are the endless dead, the rows, the ranks, the continuous dead unto the horizon. Then Valasquez stands and walks to where I sit in a ladder-back chair the old woman brought for me, and he takes my arm and helps me to stand as if I were infirm. We walk together, his hand still on my arm, through the low sobbing that fills the house like a continuous exhale and out onto the porch. I realize that I can hardly stand let alone walk without Valasquez to steady me, that I feel drunk.

He helps me sit on the steps, letting me down easily, almost gently, and then sits beside me. We watch the pigs and chickens walking about, suddenly in patterns that make sense, perfect pig and chicken patterns, and then the Jaguar speaks as if from a dream in which I am the only one real, the dreamer sick to his soul.

"The old man said you would take his death hard, Blue, harder than a stranger or one from your world normally would, because of what he called the death-sickness. He means that you are weighed down by the many souls you have harvested, by the knowledge of your role in my people's destiny."

I raise my hand to protest, to stop him so I can speak, and it takes all my strength to lift this hand, to say a word. "Stop," is all I manage, like a semi-aphasic crossing guard.

There is not a human being moving in the compound, not a human sound, no singing or talking, save the grief of the women in the house behind us, and their grieving may or may not be human, but a caterwauled warning from the other world no one hears but me. A brightly-colored bird, tanager-red with white on its wings, flits from rooftop to rooftop, stopping long enough to send a single call note rising through the sunlight as if he has lost someone he must find before it is too late.

The Jaguar says the words I have longed to hear and dreaded simultaneously since I left San Cristos de Silva: "We will kill Mankin, and the others with him, soon – to gain some time. The old man told me that you must take part for reasons that have to do with the role you play in this ... what did you call it in a previous conversation? Passion play? Which is perhaps accurate in as much as the many who have been, and those who will be, sacrificed are indeed giving their blood for the sins of the fathers as well as for their own sins, if you prefer to look at our destiny through that lens. But you must take part for psychological reasons too, because of this malaise you suffer." This killer pats my arm paternally, like he has a right to comfort another killer because we share the lineage.

"Only murder will cure what ails me, huh?" I manage to say in a harsh whisper. "More murder because I am sick of murder?" I mean to be sarcastic, to offer up rhetorical questions of indictment, words dripping with malevolent irony, but the words come out a flat declaration, as if I spoke the truth and as clear as a summer day in the dry heat of Nebraska. The Jaguar continues as if I had not spoken, as if thinking aloud.

"I must move the people to a sacred place three or

196

more days' walk to the north, an ancient city the Olmecs built that I stumbled upon as a child, and we must do so without Custer and Bagby's spies watching where we go. I am also certain they will move soon because of the Mexican troops headed this way, because the troops will move us to get to the trees and then there will be no payday for the assassin and the rest."

"You are abandoning the mahogany trees?" I ask.

"There will be no mahogany trees when the road is finished and the trucks roll up to the vacant encampment."

"Scorched earth," I say. "How trite of you."

"Don't be a smartass, Blue. Until you are faced with destroying something dear to you so the enemy can't use it, can't make high priced dining tables and other upper class commodities from trees so old some were here at the time of the conquest ..." The Jaguar's voice trails off. "It won't matter soon anyway. My sources say that the government is preparing to seize more tribal lands than they have already taken, which is well over half of the ground my people could lay claim to only fifty years ago. That is why the soldiers are coming, actually the 13th Brigade, which is part of a larger force that is a combination of soldiers from the Mexican Army and state policemen, the culmination of the New World Order – a martial unit built with the express purpose of controlling the people within a country as opposed to defending them from outside aggressors. The 13th Brigade is essentially a well-equipped army that is all but owned by the timber and mining interests."

The Jaguar stands and walks down the wooden steps, then turns to look at me. "I don't really know why you are here, Blue, beyond the old man's riddling anyway. But you are in this up to your chin now. I doubt I need to repeat that I expect you to do whatever it is the old one has lined out for you, or whatever he has seen of your role, or whatever the hell is the proper way to say this, and if not …"

"I know. Death waits for me everywhere I go, Valasquez. If Mankin dies before he can get to me, then you will certainly do the job for him after I have fulfilled my purpose, whatever that might be. Strange how you assholes are in the same line of work whether you like it or not, how the facts of my life and death seem to prove it over and over."

"I don't have Chan Lin's gift of sight into dreams and into the future, into the myths of my people, but I'm far from stupid, Blue. I have a very big job to do that may or may not include your help, that is all, and that is all you mean to me. I kill the enemies of my people, cut their throats or poison them a bit at a time with their own insatiable desires that all add up to the desire to die anyway …" Valasquez's voice trails away again and he looks toward the forest edge as if he expects someone to step into the clearing. He stares into the shadows for several seconds, then walks a few steps toward the trees and stops to stare a while longer into the forest. He turns to me again.

"The old woman told me she gave you one of Chan Lin's ancient obsidian blades. The tool's lineage goes back to the Olmecs, perhaps three-thousand years. The knives were used in temples that, for the most part, fell to dust years ago. The blades were used at Palenque by the old man's ancestors, and before that they were used by his ancestors too, priests all. Now he has given the last of these blades to you and to me. I have spilled more blood with mine than I can remember; but, no … that is not completely true. You and I both know that we never forget a single drop of blood we've shed. If nothing else, the dead come to us

198

in dreams to remind us of what we've taken from them, no matter that one may have sacrificed them in the old way and to an order that is beyond them."

"More rationalization, Indian. You, we, are merely killers, not sacrificers to anything except political and economic expediency or self-protection, and even these may be rationalizations, illusions. A death is a death is a death: the absence of life, the end of all possibility."

Valasquez is amused. "All death is a sacrifice, Blue, to Quiché."

"You told me years ago that the choice of whether one's death is a sacrifice or simply an empty fact is up to the victim, to the one dying."

"But the warrior who has chosen to die this way, as a blood sacrifice to the universe, must also kill this way. Call it a rationalization if you wish, and I certainly could not live with the acts these hands are responsible for without this belief, and so you may be right in some way. Every day I ponder the possibility that this is all a lie, but I pray for the safe passage of every soul I have ever taken, to send them on their way as honorably as even the stupid and the sleepwalking and servants of evil surely deserve. I even pray for those I kill from a great distance via my transactions you know nothing about …"

"Ha! You pompous, moralizing fuck." I have my voice back completely now. "You are a killer, plain and simple, like I am." The venom in my voice surprises us both. The Jaguar is no longer smiling.

"These volcanic glass blades," he says, and from somewhere behind him he produces a black stone knife that is semi-translucent just like the one the boy handed to me, "were made by shamans three-millennia ago from shards carried many miles, and the few blades like them that have fallen into the hands of Western archaeologists to measure and catalog and put on display somewhere have been purported to have a cutting edge that is a single molecule thick. This is a stone tool made with other stone tools and yet it has been sharpened to tolerances unmatched by moderns using lasers. You now wield a weapon imbued with magic, Blue. That is the only explanation possible. If the old one is right, the nonchalant carnage we are both guilty of has not prepared us for the path we now walk, and any question of illusion pales by comparison to the size of his vision, the amount of time involved, the number of souls."

Valasquez stares at me for several seconds with his blade at arm's length as if sizing me up for the grisly work ahead, as if aiming it at me. "Come," he says, "the old one told his wife we need to see Olvidero."

The heat is oppressive outside the shade of the trees as we walk through plots cleared for gardens but now going back to forest by degrees, sweating and swatting away the swarms of flies and mosquitoes that rise from the grass as we pass. Then we walk through active gardens of corn and tomatoes and sweet potatoes until we enter the forest at a place where I can see no path until we are in it, a barely present trail with lianas hanging in our way and trees drooping great branches we must push aside to pass. This is hilly country, like what we walked through for four days to get to the encampment, and we go up and down endlessly, although the up is the part I remember most about the trek from the Usumacinta River because the climbing hurt so, made my legs and lungs ache as if a single organ. I stand at the bottom of a ravine and bend to catch my breath, my hands on my knees, before climbing back out again. We walk for two hours and then come to a long, raised log house in a clearing only slightly larger than the structure. I can see a small planted plot through the trees behind the house. A woman and a man are working there, bent over and tugging at weeds that they deposit behind them. They both stand and look at us for a long time, then wave back as the Jaguar lifts his hand in their direction. The man walks toward us as the woman goes back to tugging at weeds.

Olvidero is a short man of about my age, stout and grinning continuously as if his face muscles know no other contortion but this one trick. He slaps me on the back when we are introduced, like a Rotarian with too many martinis in him, shakes my hand vigorously. "Good to know you," he says, and he winks. "Good to have the warriors of the sun and moon at my house at the same time."

He directs us to his covered porch where we sit at a rough-hewn plank table and drink cold water from unglazed bowls. He removes four crystals, each about the size of a fist, from a pouch on his belt and places them side by side on the table in front of him without being told that Chan Lin sent us, without Jaguar saying a word, which he hasn't except to introduce me formally.

"These are how I see the world," he tells me. "I stare into the multiplicity of the stones and, sometimes, I see images there in the translucent walls, signs I must interpret much as one sees things in dreams. Whether I see anything or not, the next time I sleep I will dream in images that demand I interpret them too. If I have seen nothing in the crystals, the dream images are stark, confusing. If I have seen signs in the crystals, then the images are as bright as *Señora* Olvidero's weaving," and he nods toward the loom at the other end of the porch.

The partially finished cotton cloth is brilliant red interspersed with an equally strident yellow in thin lines, and these are interspersed with thinner lines of green, in what anthropologists call the classic style. The weaving is Guatemalan in origin. When I mention this fact, Olvidero is pleased and claps like a child at a birthday party.

"Many Mayans now in Chiapas are from Guatemala," he says. "The fighting in our homeland killed perhaps 200,000 of us. The government calls most of those deaths *collateral damage*, which are the words they use when soldiers throw explosives into a crowded market or other places they think guerillas might be. We used to call this practice fishing with dynamite. All the fish float to the top and you take home only the edible ones, the ones you were really after in the first place, but all the fish are dead just the same." Olvidero never quits smiling as he says this as if it is just part of his shtick, macabre comic patter, and still the Jaguar does not speak.

Olvidero continues with his explanation as if we had not discussed anything else but his divination, all the dead bodies merely markers in a cosmic joke followed by a barely audible rim shot – bada-boom and the gods laughing unto tears. "If I see something in the stones, my dreams tonight will be an elaboration on what I see in the crystals, some further signs to corroborate those other signs in a complex dance. You can stay here tonight so that I can tell you what I dream."

"Are you ever wrong?" I ask.

"Oh, hell yes," he says, and he laughs. "You try looking into the bowels of a rock and see how much you get of the universe. I watched a Yaqui healer read the intestines of a goat once. Shit, I told him, that's easy. Try looking into the mineral viscera of a piece of quartz and tell me what you see." Olvidero is obviously enjoying his own stand up routine. He slaps his leg and laughs an exaggerated laugh, the fool's laugh who knows the rest of the world should be wearing his harlequin's clothes and not he.

"Be careful Olvidero," says Valasquez, speaking for the first time since introducing me. "*Señor* Blue is pretty white and therefore pretty serious in a stupid kind of way. He'll be telling everyone you sacrifice rocks to read their spleens."

Olvidero guffaws again, a prankster gamboling for no one's benefit but his own. He adjusts his rocks on the table, a clear quartz and three others shot through with rivulets of pink, like veins in transparent hearts. He stares into the first for several minutes, then into the next, and so on until he reaches the last quartz an hour after the first as Valasquez and I watch. He stares intently, his brow furrowed but the same grin like a mask on his face. Finally, he closes his eyes and rubs them through the lids.

"As the old one, Chan Lin, warned me," he says, and he opens his eyes and looks at Valasquez and then at me, "the two of you are indeed hell on earth. These messages are clearer than any I have ever received: a pall of black follows you, storm clouds black as bile, as the guts of Hell, the end of everything. You do not need me to tell you what I dream tonight. My dreams will threaten my life with what they say." He collects his rocks and stores them gently in the pouch on his belt, then walks down the porch and back through the trees to help his wife with the weeding, still smiling, the apocalypse a joke on the race, bloody slapstick. A Three Stooges movie with automatic weapons fire.

"Well, Chan Lin said Olvidero may or may not be very helpful," I say, uncomfortable with this man's bright

203

demeanor and dark message, the incongruity.

"Oh, but he was, Blue. One more time I have been told that this path is the only one I am allowed." There is a strange mix of resolve and something heavier in Valasquez's voice, not exactly despair but close kin. "It begins in earnest now, Blue."

Chapter Twenty-Four

"*Que soñaste*?" are the words that wake me. Jack France, Katie's associate in indigenous rights, stands over me. He is haggard, thin, his eyes swollen and his complexion pallid, but he is up and walking around for the first time since I arrived. Katie sat near his bed on the floor most of the time, worried as only a lover could be.

Believe me, I think to say, you don't want to know – an offhand fact most mornings. But I say instead, "I was much too tired to remember any dreams at all." Which is true for the first time in many months. Even stone-drunk I dream of the dead standing at attention in a loose eternal kind of way, like so many empty folders in a filing cabinet, their eyes blank and staring, mirrors of the nothingness outside and in.

France says he was sent to wake me for the midday meal. The Jaguar and I walked back to the encampment in the dark because he wanted to talk to Olvidero for a while, and so he had joined the couple in their garden until sundown, helping them pull weeds while I dozed on the porch. We then ate an excellent meal of chicken and potatoes fried together with green vegetables I didn't recognize and the best mushrooms I've ever tasted in my life, nut-flavored and slightly sweet. I thought we'd sleep there, but Valasquez insisted we enter the encampment in the dark to keep Mankin guessing, wondering what errand required that we return under cover of night. In the pitch black we had stumbled uphill and down on the same close path that we'd walked to get to the Olvideros' in daylight, and I felt as if I'd had my ass severely kicked by the time we crossed the open space to the houses of the village. The branches and vines were brutal opponents in the nearly total dark of most of the trip, except for a few small clearings when the moon was high enough overhead. How Valasquez could make out the trail at all I am not sure.

The boy who will replace the Jaguar someday as his people's premiere hit man met us an hour from the village, stepping silently into a small clearing to greet us, a dwarf apparition by tenuous moonlight in his white peasant smock. He led the way from there, stopping frequently to listen, then stepping lightly on. The trip back took three times as long as the journey to see Olvidero, and I fell into bed and slept like a dead man, my usual dreams unable to get through the white noise of utter exhaustion.

Jack France talks a lot, perhaps in an attempt to say everything he would have over the last several days if he hadn't been nearly comatose. In the short walk to a communal open-air kitchen he tells me his primary interests are indigenous rights and ancient lifeways, that he has degrees in anthropology and philosophy and journalism, that he thinks he has hit upon an idea for a US media campaign to help the Mayans in all of Mesoamerica – serious headshots overdubbed with a deep tenor describing the desecration relative to the richness of the culture – a campaign he admits Katie is adamantly opposed to but for reasons he says she cannot articulate, which I doubt. At least in my experience, she is as loquacious as France and as prone to polemic as any lawyer, but I do not doubt aloud. He tells me that there are nearly eighty insurgent and terrorist and indigenous movement groups in the region according to the CIA, all lumped together, as the

Agency is prone to doing, oversimplifying an incredibly complex region and its politics by assuming all of these groups are the enemy when in fact the governments that screw the locals continually are made up of fascists and thugs. He tells me that, of the 200,000 Mayans killed in the Guatemalan civil war, for example, nearly 95% were taken out by the government while the remainder were the handiwork of the guerillas, but that in fact a handful of these insurgent/terrorist/indigenous groups have taken to the drug trade as a way to make money, becoming as rich as mid-sized corporations in the process, the communists too. He tells me that these groups feel it their right to fight back against imperialism, and perhaps extinction, by any means available.

He says that Chan Lin's death is a travesty in many ways, not the least of which because he had allowed France and Katie unfettered access to the *Lacandones* for interviews and study so they could build an adequate defense against the Mexican government without understanding what that means exactly; but he said it was also a shame because it is rumored that Chan Lin may have been killed by a Bolivian drug lord who saw the Mayans as competition when anyone who knew him could tell you the old man would never engage in such a tactic, no matter how he loathed the very auspices of Western Civilization, which would make his murder a mistake of the first order. France tries to talk on, but I stop him before we climb the steps to the kitchen that has a roof but no walls, like the covered picnic tables at the local park when I was a kid but big enough to hold about half of the encampment.

"Drugs? Who has connected the drug trade to the Mayans?" I ask. Some things the Jaguar said are beginning to make sense to me now, the quip about destroying people with their own desires that really all

207

add up to the desire to die anyway, his assertion that Custer and his cohort think they know the source of one Mayan revenue stream, to use the term of the corporate age, but not the depth and breadth of that stream.

"Katie heard the rumor in Peru, and then coincidentally met *Señor* Valasquez there in a hotel dining room. That was the chance meeting in which he asked that representatives be sent here to help his people. When she asked what brought him to Lima, he said business, but that could mean many things, of course, and Mr. Valasquez is a very busy man by all accounts."

France and I watch children playing a game much like soccer but seemingly without a goal or rules of engagement. One child trips another. Then when the boy who fell to the ground gains his feet again, he kicks the girl who knocked him down in the ass as hard as he can and shoves her out of his way as he heads for the scrum around the ball, which is woven reeds around an unknown core, perhaps more reeds. The girl rubs her ass indignantly, smiles in our direction when she notices that we are watching, then heads for the scrum as well, grabbing the boy who kicked her by the back of his shirt and throwing him aside.

"Then I heard the rumor in Mexico City," France continues. "Actually, I overheard a conversation in Quiché, I guess because the participants, two well-dressed indigenous men in sunglasses, assumed no *Norteño* would know their language. They talked openly about a shipment of contraband that sounded suspiciously like it must be coca, of a man named the Jaguar who had killed their rivals to help them achieve a sale they would not have made otherwise, of unbelievable sums of money. Then they mentioned Chan Lin's encampment and the ceremony to

208

consecrate the incense burners that was to take place in a few days. Idle conversation maybe, moving as conversation can between disparate topics. There was no overt connection between these *Lacandones* and the drug transaction, but the mention of both in the same conversation raises suspicions at least. But, as I said, Chan Lin would not take part in such a terrible trade, and I doubt anything could happen in this encampment without his knowledge or even his blessing."

"Who says he may have been murdered by Bolivians?" I ask.

"A couple of the women who tended me when I was down with yellow fever. Katie had stepped out, and I assume they thought I was too delirious to hear them. They said they knew that the Jaguar's war on the Americans, North and South, involved the sale of drugs. Whoever this Jaguar is, a local self-proclaimed warlord who has embraced the trade to fund his insurgent troops perhaps. The women's assertions about Chan Lin's murderers were phrased as suppositions, as quandary, but it is not inconceivable that all this talk may have led a drug lord in Bolivia or elsewhere to assume a coup is in the offing in their bleak world, and it is not beyond thinking that they would send killers to end the threat, real or imagined. Don't you think so, Mr. Blue?"

The kids playing ball have separated now, and one small boy is running and kicking the ball, outpacing children twice his size. He kicks the ball soccer-style all the way around a house just in time to run into the group lagging furthest behind and another scrum ensues.

"This is the first I've heard of the association of drugs with these people, but anything is possible I suppose," I tell France. But I know this must be part of the Jaguar's plan of attack, and I even understand his reasoning. Why not kill the *Norteños* by giving them exactly what they want and use the proceeds for further mayhem, real and virtual, the overtly bloody variety and the more subtle kinds: fraud, embezzlement, the funding of environmental and indigenous rights groups, lawsuits? Who can say how the vast quantities of cash from the international drug trade could be leveraged against financial institutions or against the more obvious enemies of the people, how much damage could be wreaked upon them? Maybe instead of just funding indigenous rights and environmental groups he plans to buy into the timber and mining industries and work away at them from the inside. Maybe the Jaguar intends to buy into the timber consortium to dismantle it.

The thought nearly makes me laugh: the Jaguar in his thousand dollar suits entering boardrooms and salons, cocktail parties where the rich plot to fuck each other's wives and to steal 400 year-old mahogany trees. Jaguar the Mayan hit man extraordinaire with his Glock firmly holstered in the midst of his enemies, and instead of killing them, writing checks and contravening in ethereal financial transactions, the majority investor in companies to dismantle them. Destroying profits and the machines that generate them would be a ploy utterly beyond the ken of reason for his foes.

The word "madness" doesn't begin to cover their dismay before Indians generally, their perception that any anti-profit motive is unnatural, hell that it is unholy. They could never understand that the man in their midst with the sloping nose and high cheekbones who dresses as they do is not so much their enemy as their antithesis, themselves in a funhouse mirror, and so they can't possibly understand his motives let alone predict his strategy from one moment to the next.

The Agency used to play just this kind of financial havoc with the enemies of US foreign policy, real and fantasized, control money markets to devalue currency, set up dummy corporations to launder ill-gotten gains and to circulate the money to groups Congress doesn't know exist. But the most *takin*-drenched maven of monetary shenanigans would be appalled by the whole idea of using money to destroy profit altogether, to bring on the apocalypse and destroy the destroyers of rainforests and cultures, *them*.

The boy who will replace Valasquez walks down the steps of the kitchen and takes France and me by the hand to lead us to the midday meal. I ask his name for the first time as I take a seat across from Katie at a long plank table, but he does not answer. He smiles and says in Spanish that Katie sent him to retrieve us, then dashes back down the steps. I expect him to stop at the latest melee over the reed ball, but he bolts by the other children and disappears into a house. He reappears seconds later with a bow and arrow and runs back to the kitchen and to our table. He tells me that he will wait for me in the small clearing on the other side of Chan Lin's, and when I have eaten I should join him to do some hunting.

"My name is Heart of Sky. In your language, Hurricane," the boy says in concise English. Katie and Jack France and I all turn to look at the boy more closely, to see if there is anything else we may have missed about him, this being the first English words we have heard in this village except our own. "I am named for a great king who will tear at the earth until there are no more evil ones, no more usurpers of Mayan life."

"Will?" asks France, but the boy only smiles darkly and bolts from the kitchen and toward Chan Lin's house. "Will?" he says again and looks at Katie, who says perhaps the boy's English is still not perfect as

211

regards tense.

"Nor past perfect. Nor conditional except imperfectly," she says and laughs at her own joke.

The day is less warm than yesterday, a few high thin clouds floating over the sun and the slightest hint of breeze as I walk around Chan Lin's former residence and into the clearing behind the house. The boy says we will hunt squirrels, and he will let me use his small bow after he has taken the first animal to show me how it is done, that his mother will cook what we bring back. We stalk through the trees on a game trail for several minutes, first to the north then swinging around to the west to make a circle back toward the encampment. When we are near enough to hear children laughing, we head back to the north again to make the same circle so that we cover overlapping pieces of ground in a cloverleaf shape.

The boy points out nesting birds I would have missed otherwise. He also points out several snakes. Some he says are quite poisonous, harlequins of red and yellow and more obscure varieties that I have to be nearly stepping on to see, some as green as everything around us on all sides but up. It occurs to me that I must have walked near hundreds, perhaps thousands, of snakes on the trail from the Usumacinta and between the encampment and the Olvideros' house and I'm lucky I haven't been bitten on the ass when I squat in the woods first thing every morning.

The boy, Hurricane, spots a squirrel in the lower branches of a tree, one of the few with limbs that don't begin thirty or more feet from the ground in this part of the forest. He tells me to sit quietly and watch as he stalks closer so that he can get a shot. The squirrel jumps from branch to branch, oblivious of the boy's approach. The Hurricane disappears into a thicket, a section of understory growing up where a garden had been not that long ago I assume, given how quickly the forest encroaches on every vacant space. I stare into the wall of green but cannot see any movement at all.

"Well, Agent Blue, if it isn't."

I turn quickly to find Mankin sitting on a rotting log not fifteen feet away. He has an automatic rifle across his lap, a camouflage bandanna around his head, and he is wearing the same expensive aviator-style sunglasses he wore when stalking me in the rust belt of the United States. The only weapon I carry is the obsidian knife, which is in a sheath the boy gave to me before we left. He insisted I carry it so we will have something to use to gut the squirrels. Hurricane positioned the sheath on my right side and to the back, so I could reach it easily he said.

"What do you want," I say, but I'm sure he is here to kill me for failing to get the trees, that the ruse is over. I am more sad for not having fulfilled my promise to the twins than afraid. He looks at me and then leans to one side to see around me into the trees, looking for the boy I suppose, and suddenly I feel panic. I can see the boy's toothless father in my mind, grieving for this loss beyond imagination.

"Rumor has it that the *Lacandones* are moving, Blue. Whether to stay ahead of the soldiers marching this way or because of something you've done remains to be seen." Mankin looks at his fingernails, then picks away at something there I cannot see. "But we get our payday, and that is what counts, after all."

Now I know he is here to kill me because the job is done. There is really no other reason but this one that he has decided will suffice, because he doesn't know what else to do with me. I have failed Justine and Chanelle is my only thought. No fear. No sadness now, except for what may happen to Chanelle and what will

213

certainly happen to Hurricane, but then Mankin probably won't bother to find Chanelle again and the boy is simply collateral damage, the inevitable detritus of war who awaken to find themselves among the ranks of the dead. In fact, there is a single moment that I am almost relieved that it is all about to end. Terminal impasse will finally bring down the curtain on this darkness that is my life – traded for the absolute darkness that comes after. No more thinking and no more dreaming, the conceptualization of life or its projection into symbols to haunt me. Just the absolute monotone of the void, forever and ever, amen.

Mankin looks at me over his nails as if freshly manicured and inspecting the work. "Custer, however, is willing to give you the benefit of the doubt. He says you have been quite useful, as he thought you would be. He says you are to meet him in three days' time at the Usumacinta River where you took leave of the burro man on the way here, so that he can pay you for your services."

"He will just let me walk away? Unlikely," I say, with nary a tremble in my voice. I will not show any emotion, no stupid acceptance of such bizarre rules of engagement to this asshole. I resolve not to give Mankin any satisfaction before he shoots me dead.

"Now Blue, why such a gloomy outlook? He really does think you've pulled this off, and in any event, you are a resource that may come in handy again one day. You know how Custer likes his collections. Well, consider yourself collected, cataloged, and on call."

I hear a disturbance in the air that moves from behind me and just past my ear, then toward Mankin, the aerodynamic *swoosh* of something moving so fast I can't focus on it. I hear Mankin grunt and a slow release of air from his punctured lung as he looks down at the bright red feathers of an arrow sticking from his

214

chest just above his right pectoral. He looks at it as if examining a piece of lint on a suit lapel or a strange butterfly that has landed there. The small look of perplexity on his face turns immediately to the controlled rage that makes him so good at his craft. He pulls his weapon up to the level of my chest just as the boy steps up beside me. He has another arrow nocked and is beginning to pull the bow up to fire when Mankin speaks, obviously surprised by the size of his attacker.

"A kid," he says, half with disgust and half with mocking incredulity. He flips the safety and lowers the gun toward Hurricane in a single motion, a practiced killer even on the doorstep of his own death. I realize that my hand is flexing compulsively at the same instant I reach behind me, grab the stone knife, and throw it underhand all in the same movement. The blade enters Mankin's chest a few inches above his heart and disappears to the hilt. Mankin looks at the hole left by the knife like he looked at the arrow, slightly perplexed, as if his own blood were new to him, the substance streaming down his chest nothing like the stuff spilled down another man's chest. Then he smiles as if he just now understands a joke told to him years ago and falls forward to the ground.

I hear a gurgling and a mighty suspiration that fades to the tiniest wheeze in a second, the last wet exhale of a tenantless body as the frayed illusion dissipates that this tiny spot of time we lay claim to meant something. Then there is only the anticlimactic absence, the animate having become in- as the essential disperses on the wind to leave behind the inextravagant fact of the material: the lights gone out and the band gone home, the last kiss goodnight ice-cold air in an endless black corridor. Then I imagine that there must be no cold and no dark, just the iron grip of nothing wrapped around nothing and ten generations of worms belching and farting and fat on this side of the divide.

Then I am retching but nothing comes up. I am retching as much with memory as for this bloody thing in front of me or for Mankin's spirit walking into the final obliterating dark to join all the others, where I seem destined to send many more. By this hand, by this hand, by this hand … The words won't stop echoing in my head.

Chapter Twenty-Five

These are the days of butchery, and not in any metaphorical sense whatsoever, but the days of the actual cutting up of bodies. Rudy is a blithe man with a knife, a blithe man in an apron and yellow Playtex gloves cracking wise and cutting pieces of flesh from a man as if filleting fish to be fried in a vat of hot oil for a Sunday get-together.

Two of our Guatemalan charges walked into a remote church with automatic weapons and cut down a priest and a nun and an old man taking confession because they heard a rumor that the priest was an insurgent sympathizer, a disciple of Paulo Freire wielding liberation theology more dangerous than any gun. We had warned them: the hearts and minds of the masses must be in turmoil, must be gripped with fear. Above all else, the masses must *not* be allowed to focus on any ideology that would give them a space within which to calculate terror as a tool of state, to incorporate the chaos we inflict upon them into a vision of normalcy that could stand in opposition.

And the normalcy the priest threatened is the peasants' ability to think beyond the rudiments of good and evil in the face of murder and missing limbs because they might understand these acts as a function of power instead of merely the work of the devil, whom they can *only* fear. They can only cower before *his* work and pray for deliverance, but power wielded by men is another matter, and armed insurrection, violence in answer to violence, their probable reaction.

"Christ!" says Rudy when we hear what the civil guards have taken upon themselves to do. "I could almost be proud of these morons if the PR weren't so damned awful."

His answer is to have the soldiers scrub the church of all sign of slaughter, as much to punish them like errant schoolboys for their misdeeds as to hide the evidence, and then we will dispose of the bodies and add these names to the roll call of the disappeared. But there isn't a helicopter handy to haul the corpses to a lake, and no large bodies of water are near enough anyway. Rudy says he is afraid the bodies might be dug up by dogs if we bury them in the traditional shallow graves, and to dig deeper graves takes time without machinery, time to be discovered digging, time for the dead to be missed and a search to be mounted. Such are the machinations of the mind of a true killer for the State, a civil servant merely doing his job.

And as every good Baptist knows, Rudy tells me, "These damned Catholics are a bunch of idolaters anyway, especially down here in spickland where the statues take on human qualities, where Christ writhes in perverse agony, and not only in every little piece of shit building they decide is a church but in every house and on every damned dashboard and hanging around every spic neck."

So Rudy's plan calls for the parish's pigs to eat the corpses. He says he'd seen it done in Vietnam, a captured VC Colonel forced to watch as his favorite houseboy, a kid of perhaps twelve, was devoured by three pigs in only a few minutes; but three adult bodies between eight pigs, per Rudy's calculations, will take too long unless the corpses are in pieces. So we cut them into chunks the pigs can manage more efficiently.

We cut them into quarters on the altar as the two soldiers responsible joke about blood sacrifice and their Indian ancestors and mop up the puddles of blood.

The pigs devour all but the heads, bones and all, in the hour or so it takes to butcher the dead. The heads Rudy lets the pigs have for a few minutes to obliterate the facial features, and then he bundles the mangled remains into a canvas bag and sends the soldiers on a hundred mile drive with instructions not to deposit them by the roadside until well out of this region, in fact, on second thought, to leave them at a particular crossing outside a village rumored to provide recruits for the guerilla movement.

"Why waste a perfectly good corpse?" he asks me as the soldiers drive away. "Body parts as signs of foreboding to the populace are an ancient means of communication. These dumbasses sure shouldn't have killed these folks without running it past us first, but hell Agent Blue, when handed lemons, make lemonade."

Valasquez pulls the stone knife from Mankin's chest as if he were pulling it from water. He wipes it on a handful of leaves and gives it to me. Chan Lin's oldest wife has come with him and stands above the body chanting with her eyes closed. "She says you are to take his heart as his sacrificer so that she can conjure this assassin in the Underworld. If you hand her the knife and tell her you would like to give her the honor, you may not have to do this. I know you are squeamish in your old age," Valasquez says in English and with no hint of sarcasm or irony.

I thank the Jaguar for this first kindness I have known him to show anyone but his blood kin and do as he suggests, but the woman is adamant. I must take the killer's heart. It is the destiny of the Blue Man to take this heart, she says, and she refuses to even look at the knife I hold in front of me. I look at the Jaguar for help, but he only glances back at me impassively, then turns his gaze on the corpse as if his line of sight were my road map, my guide to what I must do.

For a moment, I think of merely turning and walking away. This task can fall to the Jaguar whose taste for blood runs deeper than mine, but I think of Justine, picture her turning blue and bleeding, and step to Mankin's body, put the blade back in the wound it made, but halfway, and pull it through bone and tissue. The stone knife slices both effortlessly. I will my gag response away and hold my breath for the seconds it takes to remove a square of the assassin's chest and to cut out his heart from the blood-filled cavity, the knife having cut his ascending aorta when it entered him the first time. When I am done, the old woman takes the heart from my trembling hands, wraps the bloody mass in a strip of her skirt she has torn away, and walks toward the encampment without saying a word. Silently I wish her luck in conjuring, so that Mankin may suffer the combined pain of all his victims.

Hurricane arrives from the opposite direction the old woman took. He stares into the open cavity of Mankin's chest for a moment, then smiles a thin smile I cannot read. Or perhaps I do not want to read what it contains, what this mere boy has already become in his apprenticeship as his people's assassin. Maybe I can't even imagine the creature he is already, let alone name him, this hybrid of ruthless reason and animal cunning, this child who will become the perfect man for our age perhaps – the surreptitious mover of history in an era when those in power have declared history at least passé, if not dead, a decided fact. While they are not looking, when they can only see themselves and their tiny portion of time, like rich people on some temporal

220

cruise ship talking of stock options and fondling drinks with tiny umbrellas, maybe he will manage to turn the entire ponderous ship by wiping out the majority of the crew and then working on the passenger list.

The boy takes the knife from my hand and turns the blade over, feeling its heft, its balance. He touches the single molecule of separation between the living and the dead, then gently pushes the knife into the sheath on my hip. He beckons for me to bend to his level, and then he wipes the tiny line of blood on his thumb on my forehead and smiles.

Hurricane tells Valasquez in Spanish that the men who were with Mankin have already left for the Usumacinta River and it looks like they have been gone for several hours. Valasquez tells me we will not hunt these killers now, as he would prefer, take them out as a warning to Bagby and Custer, because the Mexican soldiers will be here in only a few days, which means that my trek to the river could be more hazardous than it would be otherwise. I might overtake the mercenaries because they are waiting somewhere on the trail for Mankin to catch up, or because they will see much smoke tonight and perhaps backtrack to investigate.

He hands me Mankin's weapons, an M-16 and a Glock, both with extra clips, and tells me I can leave for San Cristos de Silva in the morning with the boy and his father as my guides. He says that he and the people will leave the following day for their new home, but that I have work to do in the US. He says Chan Lin had told this news to his oldest wife the night he died. But the Jaguar either chooses not to elaborate or knows no more himself. He tells me that France and Katie will go with the *Lacandones*, because the Jaguar wants to make sure they make it safely back to the US himself, after he has shown the people where they will live. He wants to make sure they make it safely in order to file the appropriate reports to the newspapers and briefs with the Justice Department in a protest that is perhaps in vain but which must nevertheless be done. Katie will then go to Mexico City to try to stop the government from taking more Mayan lands via legal action, another hopeless but necessary task I assume.

"But first," he says, "I must move my people to their new home because I am the only one who has seen it, because Chan Lin is dead, because the people are afraid." He turns to walk back to the encampment with the boy at his heels, and I follow them because I do not know the way, because I have no other choice, leaving Mankin, sans his heart, to rot into the ground where he fell.

Chapter Twenty-Six

The world is on fire, a conflagration of hot-blue and orange flames and black smoke to indicate the end times and the Underworld too, which have become the same thing. Two men in brilliant capes made of feathers have just emerged from a trapdoor in the ground, in the midst of the burning forest, and walked proudly but casually through a small breach in the flames. They now stand with the fire and acrid smoke as backdrop and are fighting off a hoard of attackers, men and women covered with mud and leaves and wielding swords and flaming brands. The men fight valiantly, sending each muddy attacker to his or her death in turn with a flourish.

The line of their enemies seems endless, but the two heroes do not falter. They swing with the same strength at the end of the line as at the beginning, and when the last attacker falls, they embrace and bow to the crowd of onlookers who stare in rapt attention. The men are very close to the flames, but they seem unaffected by the heat. They lock arms and walk back through an opening in the flaming trees to the trap door and raise a kind of bower, a gate, a doorway that is made of woven sticks and vines and is aflame. They carry it to the opening, then set the gateway down and ceremoniously step through it, away from the flames and toward the people watching.

As they do, a creature of enormous size, a man in a headdress formed of wood in the image of a snarling monster, a man carrying a halberd with a screaming head made of stone for a blade, steps up to the two warriors and smites them. They fall, and the monster raises his halberd in victory. Then he steps into the flaming gateway, walks through the flames to the trapdoor, and climbs into the earth.

Only then does the crowd react. They clap wildly and chant together in Quiché and carry the miraculously revived heroes on their shoulders toward the communal kitchen where many pigs are roasting with potatoes and ears of corn covered with red pepper, the celebration of the Twins' victory over the agents of the Underworld, of the emergence of the people into the light of day.

Jack France and Katie are ecstatic, holding each other and laughing with tears running down their cheeks. Valasquez is explaining what they have just witnessed: "The twin heroes of my people, Little Jaguar Sun and Little Hidden Sun, both gods and also incarnations of the gods on earth, go into the Underworld to save the people. They must fight many battles, play in rigged ballgames in which they must outsmart the Lord of the Underworld in order to stay alive, dodge the many traps set for them. Sometimes the traps are just jokes, but they are always deadly jokes, like when Lord Death tells them that they must choose between four doors, only one leading out of the Underworld and the rest leading further in, when in fact all four doors lead deeper into the bowels of Hell.

"In the end, the Twins are triumphant, but not in the way you might think. They must die in some versions of the story, even willingly embrace their deaths, which are horrible – Lord Death flaying them to make gruesome clothing. And the Twins only *seem* to die in other versions, fooling the Lords of the Underworld even in this, becoming fish and then vagabonds and

224

then the sun and moon. But in either event, it is their deaths or perceived deaths that permit an unfolding of the world as it was deemed to unfold at the creation, a blossoming that was the time of the Mayan high civilization, that will be the blossoming of that civilization again."

"It was hard to tell from the play what is above earth and what below, what is of the world of men and what is of the Underworld," says Katie as she dries her eyes on Jack's shirttail, his exposed abdomen fish-belly white. "The convolution could only be my lack of appreciation for Mayan stage values, but it seemed almost a willful mixture of symbols – the Twins fighting in this world but also in the land of the dead."

The Jaguar looks at me for a long moment as if waiting for her words to make sense to me. "Your observations are very astute," he says to Katie. "The people tend to believe the Underworld an actual place, the place of the dead, the lines between the light and the dark clearly drawn; and indeed, perhaps this was so in the golden age of my people, but I doubt it. Chan Lin would tell you that the doorway is symbolic only, that the Lord of Death walks this planet in the light of day and the majority of people are dead without knowing it, that the heroes must battle Lord Death endlessly, through the generations.

"Yes, there is a succession of ages, the golden age falling into the dark to be reborn again, but the twin heroes who serve the people fight the forces of the dark in order to keep the light and the dark balanced, and they fight every day of every year through all time so that the world may blossom as it should."

"And do the heroes ever serve Lord Death?" I ask.

"What an odd question, Mr. Blue," says Jack as he

takes his arm from around Katie's shoulders to wag a

long white finger good-naturedly at me. "How could the heroes ever serve the greatest enemy of the people, the enemy they had to defeat to free the people in the first place?" He takes Katie's hand now, the picture of love and the sincere desire to do right in a world wherein it is too late, wherein their activism, as laudable as it is, is also naïve. But then they could not act if they knew the darkness of the worldview Velazquez was only skirting the edges of in his synopsis – if the old man is to be believed anyway – the darkness that Velazquez himself represents. That I represent.

And I have no doubt that Chan Lin is right. The world exists in a hard-won balance that is presently threatened, and men like the Jaguar work in league with Hell precisely to keep the darker hell of banality from becoming human reality entire, the world we sleepwalk through, of television and advertising and consumption and attenuated desire that means that disappointment is also attenuated and therefore it all remains the same because no one ever gets pissed off enough to act in the more extraordinary sense of the word. There is no revolution because all is failed satiation. Desire met and unfulfilled at once. This is the hell an enlightened capitalist strives for: when the third world joins the first in having all wants met and not met in a single swipe, when all wants are reduced to the same list, then all is truly lost, all is the same, and a hell even beyond Lord Death's dominion in terms of its bleakness will become human life.

"The old man told me that things are not so simply bifurcated," I say. "He said that even Lord Death desires that the universe unfold as it is supposed to, desires that the universe achieve its destiny."

The Jaguar smiles a half smile of impatience, a rare thing in a man who must think in terms of millennia – the thousands of years his people had an empire and the thousand they have been bereft. "You must forgive *Señor* Blue," he says, "but he is the twin Truth, the Blue Man Who Will End Time, the Little Hidden Sun, and his path is as bloody a path as any man who walks."

Jack and Katie look confused, half discomfited by the final dark revelation of the role of the Twins and half uncertain as to whether this is a bleak joke or not, their host convoluting the drama they have just witnessed yet further by including a living being in the cast, someone they thought in the audience only. And a *Norteño* at that.

"And you must forgive *Señor* Valasquez," I say, "but he is the Little Jaguar Sun, the twin Death, and I beg to differ, but his path is bloodier than any man who walks, and indeed his path will be so awash in blood that we are all drowning in it, until human blood sweeps us all away and nothing remains but the earth as it was before we invaded it, infected it with our strange need for dominion."

The Jaguar and I stare malevolently at each other for several long seconds as Katie and Jack struggle to speak, stutter then laugh uncomfortably and look at each other and then at me and ultimately at the Jaguar, waiting for his answer to my terrifying prognosis, which must sound like an indictment somehow too. They need this to be a joke that is just beyond them in order to survive their lives. Then Valasquez laughs long and hard. I do not know whether he recognizes this fact or laughs at his guests' discomfort or the hubris in my wanton instigation of a pissing contest with the chosen assassin of the Mayan empire as it struggles to put off extinction another few hundred years even as the people themselves are on the brink of annihilation.

"Let's eat," he says, and he slaps Jack on the back as if they were aging frat brothers and offers Katie his arm, like one of the rich Mexican gallants he so despises, all effete manners and a willed ignorance of the blood that is spilled in their name. The stand of 400 year-old mahogany trees burns on into the falling dark. He looks over his shoulder once as I stare after them, walking like friends out for drinks, but he is looking past me and into the flames, sadness passing over his face for an instant and then gone.

Chapter Twenty-Seven

The walking and the good food and lack of booze seem to have lightened my step and given me back some of the wind that age and more than two decades of indolence have taken from me. We left at first light, an odd line of the ten-year-old heir to the Mayan assassinship in his white tunic and huaraches, his father, identical except for his size, and me in the rear in my fatigues and heavy boots.

We are the unlikely visual aid for a history of weaponry. The boy carries his short bow and a quiver of fifty or more arrows fletched with yellow and red and turquoise feathers, the same weapon he used on Mankin or I would think this a pathetic instance of the boy imitating manhood, the wrong time for games as it were. His father carries a single-shot rifle of unknown vintage, .30 caliber I suppose, that was old when he was born. And I carry the weapons of modernity that can fire more rounds per second than my companions could manage in half an hour, range and carnage that defy comparison. Death measured in geometrical integers. If the bow is a one, the single-shot is a three, four tops, and the M-16 is not on the same scale, ten to the power of something beyond comprehension. Or so it *should* be. I remind myself of where we are headed, to what uncertain fate but also of the magnitude of death outside this forest. In here, there are predators like the jaguar we saw on the Usumacinta, snakes to kill you in your sleep should you roll over on one, and even the mosquitoes are virulent to someone unaccustomed to the microscopic invaders they carry. But outside these green walls are men like Custer and Bagby, men with whole villages of blood on their hands, whole civilizations either directly or indirectly because of their management of operatives like Mankin and their manipulation of men like me.

And then I remember the Olmec obsidian blade on my belt, the modern killer carrying the sacrificial weapon that precedes even the boy's bow in terms of when it was invented, its actual age measured in thousands of years, and the blood it has spilled a congealed ocean stretching beyond the horizon. The circle of history is symbolically closed in the weapons on my person, and I become the most perverse of signs: the mass murderer as sacrificer in the name of holy chaos. My destiny, like Oedipus's, proof of the savagery of god.

We walk for several hours in silence, the sun indicating that it is still before noon. The boy never slackens his pace in spite of the extra steps he must take to keep up with his grown companions. The heat has risen with the sun, and the birds that made so much noise at sunrise are now quiet, except for a few that flit about us, scooping the mosquitoes from the air as we raise them by our walking, that we attract with our blood, which the insects apparently smell through our flesh. We walk through great clouds of gnats that stick to the lips and in the eyes, and the swallows call to each other with brief notes between bites to indicate where the swarm hovers and flit back and forth through the cloud lessening its numbers in small gulps of bug flesh.

We stop for lunch in a glade that is quiet and relatively free of insects. The boy says he will scout the trail and return, but his father insists the boy sit to eat and that he will scout ahead. The man's name is Ortiz, and he calls his son *mi hijo* or *joven*. He does not call him Heart of Sky or Hurricane except when he says he will go forward while the boy and I rest and eat. He smiles at his son almost every time they speak, but not when he says these names. He is solemn and not without the hint of a profound sadness in his manner as he reaches to stroke the boy's hair, as if remembering someone lost to him, as if fingering a photo of a dead son rather than touching this one in front of him who is chest-deep in the tall grass of the clearing. He nods to me and walks quietly down the trail ahead of us, stopping after a dozen paces to listen, then walking out of sight. The boy and I sit in the shade twenty feet or so from the trail and drink water and eat the tortillas and beans his mother and a few of the other women of the encampment packed for us.

The Hurricane says in English between bites, "The Jaguar says you are a reluctant participant in your destiny. What does this mean?"

"Where did you learn to speak English?" I ask.

"The Jaguar teaches me when he's in the village, but that is not often. He travels long distances north and south for the people. Chan Lin told me. I have also been to school in Mexico City, but I was lonely for my people and the noise was terrible, so the Jaguar brought me home with a tutor, a teacher from the school. But he grew lonely for his people, and maybe he missed all the noise, and after a time Chan Lin had my father take him back to San Cristos de Silva to ride the airplane back to Mexico City."

The boy takes two ears of corn sprinkled with red pepper out of the satchel he carries and tosses me one of them. "You are a very bright boy," I say, and I mean it, but I also mean that he is more incongruous than any child I've ever met. He is not merely precocious or good with words, but there is a hauntedness to him I have

231

only seen in some middle-aged men and a few very old women, people for whom life is a burden they cannot put down, a series of responsibilities that will only end with death. A fact they know beyond doubt.

The boy has taken a few bites of his corn and now gnaws all the way around the ear over and over without further chewing or swallowing until he has reached the end. He opens his mouth to show me the mass of kernels, trying not to smile, but then has to close his mouth quickly to keep his harvest from spilling out of the corners of his upturning lips. He chews and swallows the mass, then chases it with water from the inside-out stomach of a pig that serves as our canteen.

"So what does the Jaguar mean that you are a reluctant participant?" he asks again, wiping his mouth on the back of his hand. "Is this what a person means when they say someone is avoiding the question?"

The boy's insight into my motive almost makes me smile. "I have been told that I will play a part in a people's future who are not my people," I begin, not sure how much of my story, if any, the boy will understand – smart and with the soul of a much-tested middle-aged man or no.

"But isn't the fate of your people tied to the fate of mine?" he asks. "Aren't the fates of all peoples tied to the fates of all others, connected so that what happens to one spreads outward to all, touching the nearest most forcefully and those furthest the least but nevertheless touching them in some way, changing them?"

"Yes, I suppose," I say. "But Chan Lin suggested that I am to have a hand in destroying my own people. I have killed many men, as I'm sure you are aware, and I'm responsible for the deaths of many more, men and women and children, and I am very tired. So maybe I just don't want to kill anyone." I can feel the weight of

232

the sun bearing down on what little I've eaten and stretch my legs out into the tall grass to relieve the pressure on my stomach. If I pretend to sleep the boy will not be able to ask these hard questions, but then, maybe he deserves to know what he is up against.

"You wish to retire," the boy says flatly.

"I didn't think the *Lacandones* had such a concept."

"We don't," says the boy, and he grabs a fly out of the air and shakes it to hear it buzz then releases it again. "But the priest who ran the school in Mexico City was going to retire. He too said he was tired, of praying and performing rituals I guess, although Chan Lin did these things and he was much older than the priest at the school. The priest explained to me that retiring meant doing as he pleased, doing nothing if he chose.

"I always do as I please, except when my mother makes me sit still to eat sometimes or my father will not let me go hunting with him, but I can't imagine the desire to do nothing. Even the very old ones walk out to the gardens to teach the young how to plant and which plants are weeds, and even the smallest children carry vegetables to the kitchen or refuse back out to the gardens between their games."

"In my culture, *nothing* is what many people do best, even if they still have a job," I say. I am unsure if he will understand the concept of pay, that to retire can conceivably mean to labor as one wishes without worrying about a paycheck, or if he can understand the daily inanities of most modern work that men and women are subjected to unto death if they can't retire, the ridiculous ways they must spend their precious time in return for money. I am sure he can't imagine Chan Lin as a greeter at Wal-Mart wearing stupid smiley faces on his lapel, perhaps capitalism's most invidious invention, defying you to be unhappy amid all the gewgaws, or his mother as the bored matron at the post office or the maid or the teller or the counter person at Burger King. I'm sure the boy can't imagine a person wilting into the ground by degrees while still in harness, still pulling away at the big sled that someone else is driving: the faceless rich, the politicians, or maybe nobody now, the sled on auto-pilot. And how could I explain retirement to a child whose culture labels the abstraction that is money *shit-of-the-sun*, how explain social security to a person in a culture that cares for its old?

"They must practice doing nothing diligently," the boy says without irony and drawing out the syllables to the last word, feeling his way along its consonantal length.

He throws the vacant cob he has been fondling out into the small clearing and reaches for more pepper-drenched corn. "Chan Lin told me that all human actions have an effect throughout the world," he says, "that what we do day-to-day, minute-to-minute, matters, and so we must walk with all our attention on the world about us, eat as if we feed the rest of the world, savoring every bite so that the world will know the joy in our eating."

I think of the boy's trick with the corn but don't mention it. "Chan Lin had a higher opinion of human action than I do," I say. "All gestures seem pretty empty in the face of eternity, even in the face of the size of the population in the world – so many people spread over the globe that it is hard to care for even a fraction of them. So the death of a single person looks pretty small, in spite of my desire not to take any more of them out of this world, and the life of a single person, as most live it anyway, seems miniscule too. Maybe if there were fewer of us it would make more sense to me that we are all tied together, but that rippling outward you mentioned has so far to go now, so many lives to

234

touch, that it seems ridiculous to think that anything we do matters very much at all." I feel like an idiot waxing cynical with a ten-year-old, but the world he is inheriting, his role, and his odd old-man demeanor seem to invite it. How else will he know what he is running headlong into?

"But humans are the way the world knows itself, *Señor* Blue. Without us," he says and sweeps his arm across our field of vision, the tall grass, the wall of trees perhaps thirty feet away, the birds that flit through the shadows, the sunlight that beats upon the foreground, "all this would be here but sad, lonely, because it could not know it is here, amid all the other parts of this world. Without our eyes and ears and hands, without our words, the rocks would sleep, the trees would only know of the world what they can touch when the wind blows, and the birds would only sing to each other."

"Did Chan Lin tell you this?"

The boy looks at me and smiles so wistfully I can't imagine that he is not really a far older man disconcertingly disguised in this short, lithe body. "No, *Señor* Blue. This I just know."

I look at the boy as he gnaws off the last kernels of corn and tosses the empty ear out into the grass, a manchild who has had a hand in at least one death, who will kill many more if he truly fills the Jaguar's gore-stained shoes. I think to ask him about all those deaths, how he can believe in the importance of the minutiae of human actions but take out an actor. In this model of ultimate integration and interaction, what enormous changes must take place in the world because of a single absence? If he believes eating and drinking and walking create ripples in the cosmic fabric, murder must be a tidal wave. But the boy answers even as I think to ask.

"A human death is therefore an extraordinary

235

responsibility. If the person's actions end, and all those who would have been affected by that person are not affected as they would have been, and so they live their lives in a completely different way than they would have had this person lived to old age, or whatever was to be his end if you or I had not killed him, then the person who kills another has altered the universe in a very big way."

The Hurricane looks at the red and black ants crawling up one leg of his pants, picks up each in turn and places it in the grass to his right. "I think about this all the time, *Señor* Blue, because I am a mover of the world toward its destiny, as you are, as Jaguar is."

"Chan Lin and the Jaguar may be wrong about your role," I say, thinking how easily a kid of ten might be brainwashed, thinking how thoroughly convinced he is a bloody player on the field of history when he need not be. If anyone has a future filled with options, surely a child of any culture, regardless of all else that is placed upon him, can find a way out, a way to his own idea of himself.

"Neither has told me what my role is, *Señor* Blue. I told them when I was six that I am the one they have been waiting for and will take the Jaguar's place but also exceed him. I told them that I will restore all the old holy places, which will stand again until the utter end 200 years hence. I told them they must teach me so that I may be the Hurricane, and so I have had training in the many arts of destruction, training few children ever receive."

The Hurricane's head is down, but I can see his face through the curtain of his dark hair. He looks more than burdened now. He looks sad, as if he could weep like the child that only his body indicates he still is.

"I understand now," he says, "what the Jaguar meant. We are all reluctant participants in our destiny

236

maybe, everyone who has ever breathed, but especially those of us who must move history, those with the most responsibility."

The boy's father walks from the trail and through the tall grass. The Hurricane runs to meet him, embraces him about the waist, and rests his head against his father's abdomen. Ortiz strokes his son's hair and speaks softly to him in Quiché as if to comfort him. As if to comfort a child awakened by a nightmare.

Chapter Twenty-Eight

The swirl of night through the small opening in the forest canopy. The stars turning over us like buzzards, some making the great round in a single night, but most on longer journeys, all changing positions over the long flight outward if we could only look long enough as the universe blows to pieces from its ancient singular kernel. Chunks of rock hurtling. Chunks of light returned to the eye over distances measured in billions of years. And on our smaller scale, slightly different celestial arrangements depending on the worldview of those doing the naming, the arranging. The Olmec and Incan and Mayan princes cut out the still-beating hearts of slaves and held them against the darkness to ensure the stars keep to their seemingly chosen trajectories, to ensure that the text of the universe unfolds as it is destined to unfold.

Ortiz's breathing crackles and sputters wetly from his buckled lung, the distance between each raspy in-breath and each stuttered out-breath lengthening a full second at a time, a unit of measure not even perceivable in the timetable of that larger round, the turning of the buzzard stars. But an eternity too. In a few more arduous minutes, he will be dead.

We were surprised by Mankin's men when we walked into this small clearing in the dark. The firefight lasted only seconds, and then they fled into the dark, leaving two men behind I wounded with Mankin's M-16. I doubt Ortiz got off more than one .30 caliber shot before he was hit. When the shooting stopped, the boy took the obsidian knife from its sheath on my hip and stepped up beside each bleeding man as quick as any night creature. Even by starlight, the men looked perplexed at the tiny person standing over them, at the rapid movement of his hands as the boy cut each man's throat without any outward sign of malice, as if putting wounded game out of its misery. The mercenaries did not fight his tiny hand on them, as if this were a gesture of love from a strange child they had never seen, their deaths somehow the culmination of this cherub's innocence – this deadly wielder of the knife.

The boy then knelt next to his father and stroked his hair, saying something in Quiché, then stood and disappeared into the forest in the same direction that Mankin's men had taken. Before he left, he stepped so close to me where I knelt that I could smell the *piñole* on his breath that he had eaten a few hours before. I could just barely see his face by the dim light of the moon, and there was no grief there, no child's fear, but a man's rage, a focused intent that leaves no room for protest or reason – and for a second I was afraid. Not of the boy but of this world, the drear alchemy that can transmute unsullied youth to bloody purpose. "Wait here," was all he said in his overly concise English, and he followed our attackers without making a sound as he went.

It takes nearly a full minute for Ortiz to inhale and exhale once, then he does not breathe again. I listen intently, but I hear only a few birds rustling in their roosts like sleepers turning to get comfortable again before going immobile for the rest of the night. The hours creep past, the stars turning even more slowly than is their usual habit, the quiet of the night nearly total. Then, after an eternity, as waiting with the dead is always an eternity, the birds begin to waken before first light, a few isolated calls and then a cacophony. The stars that had circled the dead like carrion eaters are now themselves devoured by the new day rising.

I close Ortiz's eyes to save him the clichéd blank stare into oblivion. Then I cover him with his own serape to keep the bugs off a little, or maybe so I won't have to see him, the man-gone. Then I sit with my back against a tree in the shade, the M-16 across my lap, and sleep fitfully. I awaken once to see the boy sitting next to his father's corpse and playing idly with the fringe of the serape that covers him, but when I awaken briefly again later he is gone, and I am unsure whether I dreamed him here or not. I doze and wake this way until the sun is high overhead and hot on my knees that extend out of the relative comfort of the shade.

I stand and stretch and walk to the edge of the trees to look for the boy. I can't see more than ten feet into the trees, and I return to our packs for water and some drying tortillas. I walk to the other side of the clearing to eat away from the flies buzzing the corpse as they seek out a niche in which to reproduce, and the boy steps silently from the trees, haggard and covered with blood. He steps up to me ceremoniously to hand me the knife and walks to his father's body. He kneels on the ground for several minutes, then steps into the shade, puts his small bow and half-empty quiver aside, and goes to sleep curled on a decaying log.

Except for the blood, in sleep he is a boy, merely exhausted from climbing and running and shouting to hear his voice echo back to him, a human boy before the world turns innocence to delusion, the boy to something frightening. He is not the night-stalker, not the executioner in the name of Mayan ascendancy, in the name of destiny, whose arms grow heavy with the weight of killing and the responsibility out of which he cannot imagine himself. Like all the rest of us maybe,

240

like the grocer and the truck driver and the postmistress and the auto worker and the electrician and the prison guard and the waitress, just a little bloodier and therefore more tired, more in need of sleep.

Chapter Twenty-Nine

Buffalo Bill Custer looks peeved even from a few hundred yards away, and like a living, strutting cliché, some perversion of the famous Charlie-don't-surf captain in *Apocalypse Now* and George C. Scott's Patton. He is wearing camouflage fatigues, but the pants are puffed-out English riding trousers stuffed into tall black paratrooper boots that reflect the jungle light like a mirror, and his getup is cut so sharp that I imagine a valet with a hot iron hiding in the surrounding forest. His oversized cavalry hat, like his namesake could have worn, is cocked to one side, just barely touching his aviator's sunglasses, and the moron is even sporting matching silver automatics with snow-white handles in night-black holsters. For contrast, I suppose, a deadly fashion assertion of some symbolic kind.

This jester, pacing up and down the bank at the exact spot where I spent the night with Katie the indigenous rights lawyer and Mendoza the Mexican flower prior to our canoe ride to the Mayan encampment, would make me laugh if he weren't so deadly. Bagby – also in fatigues but the more staid Special Forces variety – peers upstream and then downstream with binoculars, sweeping the tree line on our side of the river in long methodical arcs, scanning for movement, for signs of life, for danger maybe, maybe for someone to kill – me.

The Hurricane and I walked most of the way from the encampment because the boy couldn't possibly help portage a canoe. I wasn't boatman enough to get us upstream very far from where we'd left the canoes on our trip to the encampment anyway, dumping us twice in a half mile, and so we opted to walk. But about five miles from here, the boy led me a short distance up a tributary where we found a very small canoe he said his people use to cross the water at this point on the Usumacinta, and we paddled to within a half mile of this location just in case Custer and Bagby have men stationed along the trail. Then the boy insisted that we pull the canoe out of the water a half mile upriver to take advantage of the forest cover, and we buried the boat in the brush.

We are now upstream from Bagby and Custer's location a few hundred yards, and I am lying on an embankment thirty feet above the water and hidden in the thick forest that starts immediately at the top of the steep bank of bare dirt. I told the boy to stay back several feet while I crawled on my belly to this spot to watch these two with a pair of high tech binoculars I took from one of the dead men in the clearing. The lenses zoom in and out electronically, whispering as they go, their focus so tight I can see the day's growth of beard on Bagby. Custer looks clean-shaven. Maybe he had Bagby carry a charged electric so he could maintain appearances for the wildlife, or maybe being beardless is part of his perpetual-boy motif, a biological complicity in his arrested development.

The Hurricane has defied my request that he wait back in the trees. When I look over my shoulder, he is behind me about five feet with a red-fletched arrow nocked and a look of intense concentration on his face. He is peering upriver through the trees toward Bagby and Custer's location, but I doubt he can see anything from where he is sitting. Maybe he is picturing these guys' heads on a pike. Maybe he is just making sure no

243

one comes at us from another direction.

I have been staring down at Bagby and Custer for fifteen minutes and scanning the tree line around them, but so far there is no sign that they aren't alone. There could be an entire brigade just inside the tree line and I wouldn't be able to see them, which makes walking or floating up to them – hell shooting them dead from here risky. I can't imagine why Mankin would lie about meeting Custer here to be paid – he had me at the end of his M-16 just before the boy sent an arrow into him – but the Hurricane may have missed one or more of the mercenaries without knowing it. Certainly, these assholes are all highly trained soldiers with enough knowledge of how to navigate through rough terrain in the dark to elude a boy, no matter his innate prowess or his training at the hands of the Jaguar.

I tell myself that I have to get up off my ass and do something. I also remind myself I have to stop walking around nonchalantly as if I'm not chin-deep in lies and mayhem again. I have to stop taking anything for granted and live like in the old days. Stay sharp, I tell myself. If the old instincts don't return at least in some diminished form, if I continue to deny that I'm once again a player in this stupid game, regardless the new rules or utter lack thereof, then not only will I die but so does the kid. The boy will do whatever he must to kill Bagby and Custer, and their army as well if they brought one. He is serious about his role as Mayan avenger, and maybe he wants revenge for his father. But as deadly as the boy might be, he's still a hurricane in a child's body and carrying stone-age weapons. He might manage to sneak up on these two come dark, but he won't stand a chance against any others lurking in the surrounding forest. Too many throats to slit. Too much firepower and high tech gadgetry like night-vision goggles or some other whiz-bang adjunct to the death trade invented since I was in it last. I tell myself to shut the fuck up, but my mind races with a thousand possible endings.

If I *don't* take these guys out, just walk around them and then to San Cristos de Silva to catch a plane, I assume they will follow me to the end of my days. Not that I care whether the end is sooner or later. But the boy, the boy, the boy ... And what of my promise to avenge Justine?

This confusion is pathetic: some part of me sick to my infested soul of killing and some part dreaming them dead for Justine and some part wanting to save the boy and some part wanting to surrender and let them put me out of my misery now that Mankin can't hunt down Chanelle just for spite. There is also a part of me that hopes they really are going to hand me a pile of cash so I can find a place to hole up until the money is gone, one last drunken hurrah before an inevitably bloody end. I don't know what to do next, so I just lie here looking at them. Christ, terminal impasse. Rudy would be amused and tell me another joke: a dumb Mick walks into a bar filled with straight-up killers, and what does he do? *Nada.*

So this is destiny: the unavoidable in karmic overdrive bearing down on me until I surrender to whatever comes, maybe whatever I *have* coming. Valasquez was right. I can't get out of what comes next, regardless of what it is, no matter what I do. I have free will, choices, but the outcomes are all equally horrific. Terminal impasse ... but with no one to take out to remedy the situation ... nobody but me.

And maybe that is the null set here, death by my own hand. The rest of the players in this bleak drama would just have to fend for themselves, and my role, whatever the hell it is, goes unfulfilled. At least the boy will be spared his destiny of dreaming the long ranks of the dead by joining them. The Jaguar will go on killing and running drugs in the name of Mayan sovereignty, or rather, the dream of recapturing it. Custer and Bagby will go on destroying people and cultures – and if not them someone else will fill the void because capitalism hates a niche market or a resource squandered. I could just step up to the riverbank and put a round in my own brain and this would all be over, for me anyway. How many times have I dreamed it already, the black hole under my chin, the top of my head gone, a lightning flash of pain and then nothing at all, forever and ever amen. I envision my body tumbling down the bank and into the river, a macabre baptism into the Underworld. But I don't take my eyes off the opposite bank.

Bagby is looking at me now, or at least he is looking in this direction. Maybe he saw me move, or maybe my binoculars glinted in the light when turned just so. I sink down a few inches and keep my glasses trained on him. He stares at my position for a few long minutes, then scans a little way past where I am lying and stares again, looking for some movement within his field of vision. I look back over my shoulder to check on the boy, who nods his head for me to follow him and crawls further into the trees on all fours. When I look back at Bagby, his gaze is now further up the bank and I back out of the undergrowth and slink back into the forest as quietly as I can move with one leg asleep and my back aching.

I expect the Hurricane to stop after we've retreated into the trees far enough that our whispers can't be heard echoing in the green light, but he walks through the deep brush to a game trail, and we travel for ten minutes, then for twenty. And still we walk. I try to catch him to ask where he is leading us, but he is always several paces ahead no matter how fast I move. He

246

has to duck under fallen limbs or lianas hanging in our way on occasion, which means I have to crawl on my hands and knees, the M-16 slung across my back and gouging me. He always stands twenty or thirty steps away as I struggle through, then all but bolts as I get upright again. I think to shout for him to wait, but I don't dare, and then I think perhaps the kid has a plan of his own, some escape route that must first lead away from the river. I finally grow weary of the voice in my head and just stumble in whatever direction the kid leads me. Then, after thirty minutes of walking away from the river, he is standing in front of me in the trail, grinning benevolently. "Here is the entrance to the Underworld," he says, as if he were just a boy and showing me a secret place where the other kids never find him at hide-and-seek. As I step up beside him, I can see the remains of an ancient temple, one of the Mayan pyramids wrapped in lianas and the piled up deadfall of hundreds of years of forest detritus. Part of the pyramid is covered completely to form what one would take for a hill if standing only a few feet from the path, but the shoulder directly in front of us has two windows about fifteen feet from the ground and a door at ground level that look very much like eyes over a gaping mouth.

"Why are we here?" I ask. I feel a sense of dread in the presence of this stone face that I can't explain.

"We can rest here out of the sun and plan for tonight," the boy says, and he plunges through the mouth and into the dark. I stand a long time in the sunlight, waiting for him to return or to shout that I am to follow. Nothing stirs inside but the bats whose shit I can smell even outside. I plunge into the dark too, which is lessened by the windows for many feet, but then there is a corridor and utter darkness leading inside and down. I cling to a bat shit-covered wall for several paces, then I say the boy's name aloud. He says he is still ahead of me, a small voice with stone echo, and I travel further, running into a wall. I can hear the boy singing softly to my left and feel a slight breeze coming from that way too, and I hug the wall and shuffle in the dark, imagining an abyss before me just before each footfall, until I see light flickering ahead of me.

I step from the corridor into a long, low room lit by a single torch the boy holds with both hands, dried lianas twisted tight and dipped in pitch to judge from the acrid smoke. I can see the golden eyes of bats watching us from their upside-down perches, and anywhere there are not bats, figures are incised, covering the walls and the ceiling. Mostly scenes of bloodletting: monarchs and their spouses with thorns and lancets through their tongues or sacrifices rolling headless on the altar or warriors hacked and bleeding on the battlefield. Every inch of the walls and ceiling not obscured by bats or bat shit appears to be covered with the sacrificially bleeding and the dying. I couldn't take it all in were it broad daylight in here rather than midnight-black with uncanny shadows cast by the boy's torch.

The Hurricane points toward the dim light coming from a corridor at the far end of the hall and we walk together through the echoing chamber. The light comes from a skylight, a square hole cut in the shoulder of the pyramid perhaps twenty feet above us and on the opposite side from where we entered. We can see well enough that the boy smothers the torch in the dirt. Dried leaves and vines that fell through the hole in the ceiling cover the floor, and the boy uses this material to make a fire. I am not sure why because we have nothing left to eat let alone anything to cook, and there are few bugs in the air, I assume because of the bats, but I don't ask. He travels around this space, which

248

must have been an anteroom of some sort – where the sacrifices waited their turn perhaps – collecting leaves and twigs to keep the small fire going.

I suggest that it would be good to have something to eat, thinking perhaps the boy can find us some roots or kill us a bird or some other forest creature. He reaches into the pouch he carries at his waist and produces two small leaves the size and spade-shape of the mint that grew next to the hollyhocks in all the yards of my childhood. These, he says, will keep me from thinking about food. I assume the leaves are a relative of the coca plant, which some Mayans suck on for energy on long marches or hunting trips. I take the leaves and chew them, placing the remnants under my tongue as directed. Within a few minutes I know that I have not taken some tribal version of speed. The room tilts and the darkness in the big chamber we walked through previously begins to roar as if the room were a beast.

The anthropologist Rudy and I collected on the train all those years ago told us that the Mayan pharmacopoeia contains some forty psychotropic plants that the holy men and women use in various rites, and I can only assume the boy has given me one of these. I want to ask him why. Some part of me is hurt that this semi-feral child would betray me. But I can't formulate words. A series of grunts and sputtered consonants in no meaningful order come out of my mouth instead, an animal meander of meaningless vocables.

The boy says in Spanish, "Jaguar says you must come here, to this entrance to the Underworld, and chew the holy leaves so that you might better understand your destiny." I want to laugh at that word from this child's mouth, this forest boy whose destiny is perhaps darker than anyone's. I want to laugh for this poisoning he has carried out as deftly as any agent too, but I can only spit and drool as my lips make noises like an airplane, or rather like a child imitating an airplane in the waning Nebraska light.

The air is now an electric tangle, a hesitant blue shot through with dust motes, angling, sidling, turning like planets on microscopic axes, rising and falling. The boy watches me watch the air – I can feel his eyes. Then, when I turn my attention away from him for a moment, or an hour or a day, he disappears and I am alone. Panic rises in my chest.

I vomit. Then I vomit again. Black bile and then blood. I notice for the first time that the antechamber is lined, floor to ceiling and over the ceiling too, with bas-relief skulls, skulls incised in the stone in profile as if a million, ten million, skulls beyond counting, are stacked here at the gateway to Hell. I am enthralled by the infinite blankness of so many eye sockets empty as outer space. I am enthralled until the skulls begin to move, to float like the dust motes, spinning and rising on random arcs of light and shadow, until the stone skulls begin to speak.

I hear Justine's voice and she is crying incoherently. I hear Rudy admonishing me to beware terminal impasse, to act, calling me a dumb Mick fuck, a moron, stupid as any Indian, telling me to kill somebody so the impasse passes. I hear my mother searching for me, her voice a long echo down a summer block. My father opens his bare-bone jaw to speak, but only the air of decay escapes – taciturn even here. And I hear my own voice speaking Quiché. Then the voice is the old man's, Chan Lin's voice saying in Mayan that I am the destroyer, the Blue Man to End Time, and I understand every word, though not what this same riddle I've heard a hundred times means. Then his voice is overwhelmed by the chaos of the voices of all the dead by my hand

250

or by my intent or my failure to act or my silence or my absence – all the deaths I caused or did not prevent or merely wished for as casually as a prayer for rain.

The room spins into darkness, and I have disappeared into it, become it, the disembodied body of the dark, and I am resting in my own black arms. Certainty itself. An inchoate clarity aware of its own scattered existence and nothing else. Because there is nothing else. But the calm lasts only a split second before the world floods back, or rather, I flood back into the world, once again embodied and puking blood and bile, afraid and filled with self-loathing.

Now the room is the world and the world is ticking. I see skyscrapers tumbling, people falling from them with arms and legs akimbo, falling like rain as when the World Trade Center towers fell, but this is all the towers in every city on earth crumbling, all of them, and there are battles in urban wastelands, and prisons to replace the crumbled apartments and office buildings, and people are starving and dying of addiction and broken hearts. I wonder if I am merely watching the 6 o'clock news, a docudrama, a movie, a television event – all the horror of our time just another form of entertainment. All of the carnage a cliché now, an empty gesture of crumbling because the crumbling has become our reality in toto, the crumbling its own closed system, death itself made manifest, as any alternatives, any dreams beyond this single bleak dream, are strangled at birth.

And I am the center of this crumbling vision, not just as a point of reference but its axis: the Blue Man Who Will End Time. I see myself in the chaos, unmoved, blood on my shirt and a tangle of bodies at my feet. I am calculating the distance from the earth to the clouds as measured by corpses stacked one on another. I am trying to figure the time it takes for this perverse ladder to melt back into the earth, how long before the flesh and blood markers are replaced by actual human beings again, how long the mute earth can bear not having voices speak its beauty and its horrors. And I am telling myself stories about the Twins, Little Jaguar Sun and Little Hidden Sun. The world is quiet except for my voice and the sounds of carrion fowl as they gorge. No one to hear but me. No one to speak but me. But then the Jaguar's voice rises from the piled dead to tell me I can't die, that I will reach old age carrying the ever increasing weight of souls on my increasingly bowed back, that I will serve the destiny of the world in this fashion and no other will suffice.

I want to weep: for the world, for my pathetic self in my youth dressed in delusions of freedom, of heroism, for any delusions of peace in my old age I might have entertained or the sweet rest of death if I can have nothing else. Then the boy is rolling me over, out of my own vomit, and he is speaking in tongues as he beats me on the back to clear my airway and pours water over my broken lips from the inside-out pig stomach. And then I am weeping uncontrollably for the first time in my life, and I understand the movement of time. The human body a single *tick*, the mind a single *tock*.

Huge red numbers in an endless digital row descend at the speed of light in the air above us, and when each column is at zero, the last row having run down in the blink of an eye to leave a row of zeros glowing red for as far as I can see, there is a pause, a split second of utter quiet, long enough to think, "What a clichéd image imagination projects. How trite unto meaninglessness." And then there is a roar and a conflagration all around me to make the devil weep with fear, and I hear myself shrieking, the millions of voices of the gone-under rising in a single call note issuing from my raw throat, the long tremolo of human grief and anguish and sheer astonishment at our hubris and our mortality that we thought but a rumor. At our sacrifice to the destiny of the universe, which is a breathing being.

Then the boy is leading me by the hand through the room-of-sacrifices, his torch making the bas-relief figures of the sacrificed and the sacrificers jump and collide just before they disappear into the dark to be replaced by more sacrificed, other sacrificers. Then we are in the green light of the forest and walking back the way we came, toward the river, toward Bagby and Custer.

Part III

Inside the mirror an Other waits in ambush…
I have dreamed the sword and scale…
Praised be the nightmare, which reveals to us that we have the power
to create Hell…
Whoever looks at an hourglass sees the dissolution
of an empire.
Whoever plays with a dagger foretells the death of Caesar.
Whoever dreams is every human being…
Everything happens for the first time, but in a way that is eternal.

Jorge Luis Borges

Chapter Thirty

The woman sitting across from me on the train to Baltimore is a sound machine. I stare helplessly at her lips moving, the small droplets of spit flying, and her teeth flashing like inane semaphores. The constant rumble of words is unconnected to any further thought beyond the most rudimentary association, just a turgid mix of noise only nominally forced into some syntactical, some semantic order to make minimal sense. Like randomly switching between TV channels at twenty-second intervals, her rant is nevertheless all connected somehow. Like that tumbling mix of electronic images and language, the limited sign set forms and reforms, the message merely the same one repeated in various ways on all channels at all times. Maybe her rant is what passes for conversation these days.

I sat here because she is pretty. No, because she reminds me of Justine, the same round eyes and the same distance across the bridge of her nose and the same inviting lips. I wanted to ask her when I first sat down if her nipples are offset, the right slightly higher than the left. But the resemblance ends with her face. At first the melody of her subtle Brooklyn accent was enough, all e's and i's the same diphthong to my ear. Not the comedic-TV-overacted cross between a debauched Yiddish accent and street slang, but the real thing, an accident of melted languages that makes a delightful song. The joyous sibilance, the overstated nasal, the sideways glide of one word into the next. It was extraordinary at first just to hear my native tongue spoken by someone who doesn't sound like Dan Rather, his Texas drawl willed to the banality of Ohio diction and just barely audible as background noise he has failed to tune out. Then her lack of referential depth turned cloying, like a single note held in perpetuity until it is obnoxious, like a civil defense siren someone is testing and can't find the off switch.

She opens her mouth and out comes nonstop commercials and soap opera: "And I says, what you doing with that bitch, Tyrese. We both know she got designs on your dick. Then he shows me his new Nikes this girl bought him, you know those red and silver high-tops you can buy only at Steward's Athletic Emporium, that new store in the mall that replaced the old one, what was it called? Then I told him I need to stop at the Save-Mart and get some tomato sauce to go with that garlic in the fridge, which is beyond aged now, though aged garlic is good in spaghetti sauce according to Martha Stewart, so he says to me you know how that shit you mix all together makes me nauseated, that's the word he used, nauseated, and he claims he ain't never even had dinner with this bimbo even though I seen 'em at McDonalds and Burger King and Jenessa seen 'em at the Village Inn. I told him I was gonna fill those new Nikes with spaghetti sauce, that shit I mix all together instead of taking it from a can. You know, you can only get those shoes at Steward's, which used to be, what is the name of that store, on the corner of the mall there across from where the ladies undies boutique was at, which is now Pets- on-the-Mall or something like that? And that other shoe store used to carry those little pumps I like with the matching handbags – red and blue and green and any other color you can think of like that star on *Friends* always wears, and I've seen the reruns so many times I know the dialogue by heart. She is my favorite, even though this show is all white people, because she got so much style she could be a black woman, except for that ditzy act of hers that no black woman would ever sink to ..."

Local geography and local history reduced to a tour of the mall, past and present; personal history but a disconnected facet of the market, the merchandise scenery; TV the road map to it all, to nowhere and everywhere at once.

Heart of Sky, the Hurricane, is sitting near the front of the car talking with an elderly couple who are obviously engrossed in what he is telling them. They obviously want to hug him, take him home, keep him there like a pet. He is dapper in his suit – a three-piece affair with creases sharp as razors that he insisted I buy so that he could look like the Jaguar – his new haircut and the shiny black shoes he polishes every night before he goes to bed. He looks slightly ludicrous from here, pretentious rich, although he is neither rich nor pretentious. The disguise is just part of the gig, the ruse he plays on the rest of the world, part of the deadly game.

He tells everyone he meets that I have adopted him to save him from a life of poverty and violence in the streets of Mexico City, that his name is Bill. I asked why he chose the name, but he only shrugged and deemed it as good an Anglo name as any he'd heard, which he says are all pretty meaningless anyway. He says he originally took the name to be a foreshortening of something like "the bill is overdue," but he has figured out since that this is not true, the truncated meaning of his name anyway, although he tells me with a rueful smile that he likes the idea that he might serve as such a marker for his people among mine: Bill the bill collector.

So the boy and I travel the country, usually by train

so Bill-the-Hurricane, the summoner, the midget third-world collector of past due judgments on the first world, can talk to the other passengers at his leisure, so he can enthrall them with his odd mix of childish innocence and adult urbanity. The kid obviously enjoys this part of his work. Some days I think him merely curious, as any child might be in such a wholly different world than the one he comes from, and that his gumption and intelligence lead him to explore other ways of being his elders could not tell him about. Other days I think him as perverse as any agent in the service of power, however defined, and he merely enjoys the subterfuge, making fools of the people he meets. Although they will never know how foolish they look to him, which makes his ongoing prank a cynic's joke because he knows everyone else is too stupid to understand.

I struggle daily to understand what the hell I'm doing here at all, why this child-assassin is now my companion and where our adventures in mayhem lead. To Hell, I suppose. All signs seem to point there, to some ignominious end and eternal suffering, which is maybe eternal banality as I stare outward into the darkness with all the other dead standing idly in ranks as far as the eye can see, staring blandly as any corpse in my dreams.

These are the days of Buffalo Bill Custer in his jester suit, in his George C. Scott-doing-Patton garb, on his knees and begging for his life. Henry Bagby, Hank Butterbuns the meek, the compliant, the ostensible sycophant, stands over him with an automatic aimed at his frontal lobe. Custer is weeping and can barely speak. If he lifts his head, Bagby cuffs him hard enough to open a lesion with the butt of the pistol but not hard enough to crush his skull. One of those tricks of the trade, the legerdemain of suffering: to judge a blow for the damage it will do and the amount of pain it will yield before delivering it. The killer as craftsman, perhaps a class title now in the course listings at the School of Assassins.

Custer looks pathetic, his blood-soaked beret in his hands like any other penitent, his face tear-streaked and sweat-streaked and blood-streaked, and the crotch of his pants steaming wet in the humidity – the effluvial streams of the human body becoming the same stream. I almost feel sorry for him in spite of all the spilled blood I know he is responsible for, including Justine's tangentially. But then that is the working definition of collateral damage: tangential death and tangential responsibility, the victims somehow responsible for their own carnage even, or perhaps victims of destiny more than any other culprit – in the wrong place at the wrong time and somehow also meant to die here on the spot where they now stand, which is also where they will fall.

But now Custer knows what it is like to enter the big room where they spill your blood and brains over the ground. He knows what it is like to stand at the altar, in front of the altar rather than behind it, and say, "No thank you. I really don't want to play anymore. Don't you think there could be an exemption granted this one time? Can't I please just abdicate and go home to play with my gewgaws stolen from every culture on earth? Can't I just say I'm sorry for all the crushed windpipes and battered skulls and lopped limbs and electricity to the pudenda?"

Now he has some inkling of what it is like to wake up blue in an alley and discover the layout of the big room had been an illusion all along, which means your whole life had been an illusion. At least the enormity of the altar and the truth of who is really standing behind it to administer the blood and brains of the sacrificed to the masses was a big awful joke, and that means your chosen identity had been a big joke too – and a cosmic guffaw echoes through your brain for the few moments you have left.

Right this second he is learning the absolute punch line like I have lived it. Not the actual blueness, but the simple-minded desire to sleepwalk through the battlefield of good and evil. Right now he is wishing that the greatest burden he ever has to carry is the burning sensation of self-administered anesthesia deep in the belly, opening the old ulcers one more and one more time, at most a few night visions of the dead staring implacably. At this moment, as he bleeds and pisses himself and weeps, he has some small idea of what it is to wake up blue and hung over and feeling as stupid as any man who ever lived: like Christ on his cross, like a soldier in the split second it takes a landmine to sweep away his lower half, like the poet dead for truth, like the suicide for love as he tumbles asshole over appetite to the concrete. Right now, he is living those few moments into which a lifetime of realization are compressed to one big shit sandwich that he has time to be force-fed by gravity before he hits the ground.

The Hurricane and I watch this little play from less than thirty yards. We backtracked and used the short canoe to cross the Usumacinta at twilight, and then crawled to the forest edge where we could get the drop on these two. But this is what we found in the circle of light cast by their small fire, which has a blue aura, as does most everything but the two killers playing out some scene born of decades of their strange dynamic. I assume the blue aura is caused by the drug the boy gave to me that has yet to wear off completely.

"You have made one too many mistakes, Bill," says Bagby, projecting as if he were saying this to the gallery seated somewhere in the dark, his ever so slightly falsetto voice deeper than usual, his delivery mock oracular like overwrought summer stock. "You insisted that Mankin *not* take out Agent Blue, that we pay him instead and keep tabs on him after he goes back to the States, and now our best men are dead – except Simone here and he has a wound that will take some time to heal. Who the hell can we send after Valasquez now? You? Who the hell will carry out the next assignment in Bolivia? Again, you? You have put the whole operation at risk, so what other choice do I have?" Bagby feigns sadness, a mockery of emotion that must offend even a dolt like Custer.

As he says this, a man in fatigues with blood over his chest steps into the firelight. Simone, I assume. He looks pale from loss of blood even in the dim firelight. I peer in the direction of the boy, who is next to me and not two feet away, but I can't see his features through his curtain of hair in the dark. I can't tell whether he is horrified that he missed this one or if he knew one got away and did not tell me for fear I wouldn't allow him to go further, or maybe this is his contribution to the game. Maybe he sent back just one alone and bleeding to tell the tale, a way of saying "your move." I touch his arm and begin to pull back into the trees a slow inch at a time. The boy retreats more quickly, more quietly too, and is leaning against a tree in the shadows when I am far enough from the fire in the clearing to stand up.

As I reach the boy, there is a single shot that makes me jump and my heart to beat one big thump, sending adrenaline to my brain, even though I knew the shot was coming, inevitable as sunrise. The shot echoes only slightly because of the closeness of the target to the gun. Immediately there is subtle movement to our left, to the north of our position, and the boy and I both slide slowly down to a crouch. For a moment there is nothing, and I wonder if the noise roused some slinking beast, a jaguar perhaps who is hungry for human flesh. Then I see the silhouette of a man against the stars through an opening in the trees; then he is gone again. We do not move for several long moments, hearing only voices in the direction of the river, unable to make out a word. The boy moves forward before I can stop him, but he returns only a few seconds later while I am still deciding whether to wait or to follow him.

"There are at least six," the boy whispers in my ear. "Maybe more in the trees still. We must have moved around them in the dark."

I imagine Custer's houseboys walking up to the scene in the firelight, the gallery for whom Bagby was projecting I assume, their nominal boss sprawled face down on the ground, which means they are now Bagby's houseboys. Insurrection is not an issue for a hired gun as long as he gets paid, and I suppose that is the reason-entire behind this little bloody tragedy in the clearing: to keep the help happy and engaged by sacrificing Custer as the maker of the mistake that cleaned out half the crew and perhaps put the next payday out a bit.

But then we hear Custer bawling loudly, like a calf I once saw eviscerated accidentally by a passing piece of farm equipment when I was a kid, a howl only an animal suffering more than we can stand to witness produces. The boy is crawling forward again before I can stop him, so I slink to the ground and follow.

Custer is still on his knees, still howling, and the howling is pulling at my stomach until I vomit as quietly as I can. Six more men stand around him now, all dressed in fatigues and their faces painted green and black, all heavily armed. Bagby is gesticulating wildly above the racket, and then I notice why Custer is bawling like a split calf – both his ears are gone and he is bleeding heavily down the sides of his face. There is

264

also a gunshot wound in his side, another old trick of torture: to shoot the body in a place where there are no vital organs, the slow-bleed so the victim can see his death coming from a mile away, or in Custer's case, from just up the block, for his blood is pooling quickly in the dirt, perhaps because Bagby nicked a vein.

Without thinking, I stand and step forward, telling the boy as I rise, and in a whisper just loud enough to get through the wall of sound coming out of Custer, not to move. I step into the clearing, and before any of the mercenary houseboys notice me, I level off and put a single round through Custer's heart, the irony nearly overwhelming even as my finger twitches and the recoil enters my shoulder: I have assassinated this asshole as I swore I would, even after I lost my taste for the blood oath, nearly choked on it, and I did it to put him out of his pathetic misery, pain he deserved as much as any man on earth.

Or maybe we all deserve what Custer was experiencing by virtue of being alive at all, and I robbed him of all the pain in any life compressed to a few moments. Everything we have ever suffered congealed to a single in-breath, a single exhale, that pain a deserved last rite to be savored because it is the end of our being human, the last experience of the flesh. Maybe I robbed him of the last few delicious seconds of the wind on his skin, made more delicious by virtue of its ephemerality, its intensity as an adjunct to the chaos of pain and his blood pumping out of him and running down his face and down his pierced side, as he feels the enormous dragon of panic rise to look him in the eye and then subside. The only elements of the world left to Custer the pumping that will slow and then cease, the hot liquid going cold as it drips from his fingertips to the ground, the sweet breeze over the blood and tears on his cheeks. A final slow exhalation.

Then a silence deep as the heart of God. Not the abrupt closure of slivers of splintering lead through the aorta, utter blackness in the split second it takes for the synaptic switch to be thrown.

Custer's eyes focus on me for an instant, a last brief flicker of recognition, then go blank as he lurches forward into the dirt. The report echoes very briefly, followed by utter silence, all the more quiet for the demonic wailing that came before it. As I approach them, the eight men aim automatic weapons at me in unison. I walk forward with the M-16 lowered in that pack-like display of symbolic obeisance all of these men have been taught to recognize, but which they may not honor either – the word *honor* a travesty even as I think it, the set up for a joke that is its own punch line.

I step to within three feet of Bagby, who lowers his weapon and stares at me for a long moment, a look of confusion on his face, which is replaced instantly by a smile. At his good fortune, I suppose. Now the only problem I represent is how best to kill me, how best to satisfy the employees so they keep killing for Bagby in spite of the mock organizational shuffle they just witnessed. I start to worry about what the boy will do, if he will put an arrow through Bagby, which will mean the Hurricane's end as well as mine, but the thought barely rises and then there are gunshots, incoming automatic weapons fire from across the river.

The dirt flies around me and I can hear rounds skipping into the trees and bouncing through the air. Two of the houseboys fall immediately and do not move. Two more are hit and head for the forest edge dragging broken legs behind them, bone and gore protruding into the night air. One falls with a red-fletched arrow through his Adam's apple. Bagby and the rest are diving for cover, and I hear curses from

266

across the river in Spanish. I retreat to the trees slowly, almost stroll back the way I came. I feel nonchalantly immortal, as if this second of time were all of time and would take eternity to unfold. The blue world explodes around me, a conflagration of sparks, and I walk by the boy without looking at him and head up the trail. Toward what destination I cannot say.

The Hurricane and I are traveling around the country to stay one step ahead of the assassins. One is on this train now: Simone, the only one of Mankin's men to escape the boy's vengeance back in Chiapas and perhaps the only witness to Bagby's overt ascension to the head of the organization to survive the attack by guerillas of one faction or another at the river – and who knows how close Bagby really stood to the center of the circle. As he told me before the natives cut him to pieces, there are others more veiled and yet more sinister than he, evil an endless well of anonymity, or Simone would not be here now.

The assassin, disguised ever so slightly in a ludicrous false mustache and glasses, sits in this very car. He is wearing a three-piece suit and carrying a valise as if he were just another commuter headed home from a rough day of corporate shenanigans; but the disguise seems purposely flawed, purposely transparent. I suppose, once again, so his victims can see death coming from a mile away, his gesture not so much part of a game – we know who he is and thus make more interesting prey – as torture. The victim haunted by the final surmise, which he can only intuit will come without knowing what it might actually be, except in the last instant of consciousness flickering out: *so this is my destiny.* I imagine a mild surprise preceding utter night, something akin to grief but sardonic and touched around the edges with fear.

Simone is seated near the old couple, just three seats back, and trying hard to appear to be reading the *Wall Street Journal* and to look like he is not watching the boy, who is certainly aware that this is Simone. I have witnessed many an odd espionage *pas de deux,* but this may be the oddest – the corporate assassin doing a bad imitation of himself and the tribal child-assassin doing a self-conscious impression of a rich Anglo kid.

In reality, the boy is perhaps the most deadly person alive, rivaling even his mentor, the Jaguar, and perhaps the only one in the same league. Even at so tender an age, the Hurricane is a preternatural killer, better than any pro I have ever known. He has proved it over and over in the several months we've been together. And Simone must certainly know who killed his comrades in Chiapas, perhaps who killed the previous three assassins sent to find us. And he has no doubt heard rumors of dead Mexican diplomats and dead Guatemalan politicians and dead Peruvian corporate presidents in every town we visit: Mexico City, Washington, New York, wherever we find them. In fact, this may be the way they keep track of us, merely by reading the obits in major newspapers.

But then maybe a man like Simone is incapable of recognizing the incongruity of the killer in a boy's body, and maybe he is right not to see the kid as anything other than what he is, a mirror image of Simone but shorter and better at this trade than any before him, dangerous in the extreme and so perhaps a flawless being for our New World Order – animal cunning and a vicious reason wrapped tightly in ideology and disguised as perfectly innocuous.

The elderly couple is laughing now and exchanging awed glances, obviously amazed by the manchild before them as he does his erudite kid act, his cute but knowing imitation of an all-American boy, his precocious-unto-charismatic shtick. If the Hurricane is not murdered, he will serve his people's interests well.

If he is not murdered: the ultimate conditional, the reckless way of language in our age to say something extraordinary as if it were merely another line of conversation. Insipid patter encompassing only the mall and television characters, as if it mattered no more than what followed or preceded it. Oh, by the way, *if he is not murdered* he will serve his people well. But then the assertion following the conditional is no better, containing, as it does, multitudes – the swelling ranks of the dead in the boy's dreams that will be a blank- eyed army before he reaches pubescence, a small country by adulthood, a world-entire should he make it to old age. The boy peeks around the elderly couple and waves at me as any innocent might. Simone pushes his face further into his paper.

These are the days of a carnival in Chiapas, in the little town of Chamula. About half the residents are dressed in bright robes of many colors and wear masks that are gringo flesh-colored, precisely Caucasian-titty-pink as Chanelle would call it, with bright gold beards and large blue eyes. A man tells me from behind his mask, which includes a golden crown, that this is called the Dance of the Party-Goers and that the masks are of the Spanish conquerors who devastated this land centuries ago. I expect some symbolic tribal revolt, a rush of Mayans brandishing clubs maybe, to ritually set the world aright again; but in the half hour or so that I stand on a dirt street watching the proceedings, there is no such uprising. The party-goers merely twirl in imperfect waltzes, bow and curtsy, flit about the square and act as uppity as any conqueror would toward those not be-masked.

269

I am standing with the boy in front of a church painted the most amazing yellow. Faces of the saints in red decorate the balustrade at the top of the building. We watch as one of the participants in a flowing gown of improbable colors – Latin purple like the Catholics associate with the passion of Christ and the deep red of Guatemalan weaving interspersed with lines of dark green – saunters up to a man wearing a traditional straw cowboy hat and dirty-white peasant uniform, the brim of his hat turned up abruptly on the sides. The one in the mask visibly lifts his plastic pink nose in the air and turns away in an exaggerated flurry of disdain, robes flying, which makes the Indian in the straw hat laugh until tears stream down his face. Others standing nearby laugh too, until there are twenty people laughing and crying and slapping their thighs in utter joy.

"The cosmic joke that is *Norteños* and Europeans," I hear from behind me, and I spin on my heel, my hand on the M-16 and raising it as a reflex. Bagby is smiling affably as if delighted to see us here, as if we were old friends.

After the firefight on the Usumacinta, the boy and I walked for six days until we reached Chamula, where he told me there would be a plane we could hire to take us to Mexico City, San Cristos de Silva now too likely a destination and the plane probably under guard by one or more of Bagby's men.

The Hurricane, Heart of Sky, explained that the Jaguar had insisted before we left the encampment that he go with me back to the States. I started to protest loudly because the boy could certainly get himself back to his people, their new home further in the wilderness or no, and I could not imagine this child in my life on a daily basis or what the Jaguar might have up his sleeve. But before I could speak my disgust at not having been asked about this plan, the boy interrupted to tell me that only he could get me out of the forest alive anyway. A good point, and the death wish that had hovered over me, barely hidden for decades, that descended on me with a hideous crash the day that Mankin murdered Justine, had begun to lift enough after Custer's death that I could tenuously imagine a future somewhere warm with lots to drink until the cash runs out. What might come after that I did not know and did not care.

Bagby is sweat-stained and rumpled, the effects of having tracked us to this village, living off the land, as we have, for the past six days, eating birds and grubs and roots. He has his pistol out but it is lowered at arm's length by his side. I scan quickly to the right and left for more of the mercenaries among the locals, but I see only the party-goers and their audience, who pay no attention at all to the men in fatigues with automatic weapons. I suppose they are used to soldiers of various factions, government and insurgent and probably corporate mercenary, passing through.

"I guess these people don't understand that the weapons you and I carry, the tools that do the real work of the world, could wipe out these fools dancing through the square in their quaint clothes in less than a minute, the entire town in perhaps a half hour – just these two magnificent machines," says Bagby, and he is smiling wanly now. "Before any of them could get away or help could come. Before they could pray to their saints or gods or whatever the hell this particular batch calls their divine intercessors." Bagby does not take his eyes off me. The boy has disappeared. I felt him lift the obsidian knife from the sheath on the back of my belt just after Bagby appeared, and then he was gone.

"What now, Henry?" I ask, and I slip the safety off loudly with my thumb, an autonomic response to danger as in the old days but also a sign for Henry

271

Bagby to interpret, to mull, to wonder at in all its potential significance.

"I'm not sure, Blue. It seemed incumbent upon me to follow you. I can't figure out how you have done certain things, like killing so many highly trained men in your ... Well now, what shall we call it? Your *fallen* condition, perhaps? And Mankin among them. I've known Mankin since we served together in Vietnam, and there are few stone-killers to match his capacity for violence, his skill in a fight, or his acumen in the bush."

"Ah, you are the famous Lieutenant," I say, realizing that Rudy had mistaken rumors of Bagby for rumors of Custer in Vietnam all those years ago. "The rear guard destroyer, the collector of ears." Bagby shrugs his shoulders. I am hoping to keep his mind off the boy. Simone must certainly have reported back to Bagby that it was but a boy who killed his comrades, or maybe he deemed this fact too strange to believe and so kept it to himself.

"Maybe," he says, "but then you know how these small incidents get blown up in the telling, unto myth even, with the perpetrators cast as supermen or demons on earth or some kind of destructive apparitional force. Mankin and I were merely serving our country to the best of our ability."

"And now? Are you serving your country by freelancing for timber consortiums, and I suppose drug cartels and governments who want this land for whatever can be squeezed from it no matter the human cost? Are you serving your country by getting rich at the expense of so many locals turned to corpses?"

Bagby laughs, a sound I realize that I have never heard before. He was always standing off to the side as Rudy and I dealt with Custer, scrutinizing, evaluating, glaring his disapproval sometimes, which I thought merely a function of his close relationship to Custer, but

272

which now appears to be a frequent result of passing judgment on Custer as well. "Oh Blue, you always were such a funny guy, in a perversely romantic kind of way. Of course, we are serving our country. How better than to remove all obstacles to free trade, regardless of the commodity? And after all, that is what drugs are, as are 400 year-old trees, and even these people: their fear, which makes them pliant, and their labor as peons or outright slaves. All commodities of one sort or another. How better than to grow rich and spend the money in the good old USA, like good Americans, in order to spread the money around among our own?"

A party-goer dances by close enough to brush Bagby's automatic with the bright cotton of his costume, and when the dancer turns to look Bagby in his close-set eyes, he laughs high and shrill and spins away into the crowd with his plastic nose in the air.

Bagby scratches his temple with the muzzle of his gun in an exaggerated imitation of a man confused. "The arrogance of the powerless has always amazed me, Blue. That they can manage to hang onto a many-millennium-old vision of their place at the center of the universe in spite of all the evidence to the contrary, that they can stand in their jungles and on their mountains and laugh at us even as we walk toward them to blow their fucking brains over the landscape and take what they have in tribute to those at the top of the seething heap, the *rightful* occupants of the earth, the rightful owners of it all, those on the throne by virtue of a superior guile and intelligence and willingness to spill the blood of lesser creatures."

"And this category includes you?" I ask, astonished that the man I've seen as Hank Butterbuns the clerk, the sneak thief, the functionary could harbor such black and overblown notions of his role on earth.

273

"Of course not, Blue. We, men like you and me, serve those men at the top, the ones for whom these others exist, and we are here to remind these others of their place and to take tribute to their betters. Of course, we ply our trade for a fee, and who can blame us for asking top dollar?"

"You mean we serve other white men generally, I assume, or maybe you mean only *some* white men, those with the juice already."

"Oh hell, Blue! Don't wax liberal provincial on me now. The white camp is my camp at present, of course, and white men have held onto the honorary title, the King of Everything, in a global sense for some time now, but such classifications are arbitrary. Several hundred years ago, these people around us were running things in this corner of the world, and they did so with gusto, blood running over them like water. Power is, and always has been, the only categorical imperative, power the true coinage upon which all else on this planet is premised, power the basis for profit and profit proof of power. It is simple, really. And those with power, and those who aspire to wrest it from those who have it, keep men like us employed."

"Subjugating the masses," I say, as if finishing his sentence. "Just another day on the clock."

Bagby smiles wanly again, then guffaws in an exaggerated imitation of a man amused. "Yes, Blue. We kill them if they don't cooperate, or kill some to convince the rest, or we outright enslave them by standing over them as they bend to their necessary labors, or we addict them to make an instant market, or we invent TV and pipe commodity fetish dreams into their shanties, holding out the prospect of some product falsely associated with their dick or their stomach or some other seat of appetite to make them want their little piece of the action, which is really no piece of the

274

action at all – the present version of glass beads and metal fishhooks."

"So all of us, these people and you and I, exist only to serve some anonymous few." I am trying to sound sarcastic, but the strength of his conviction matches the grimness of his version of the world, which adds up to a disconcerting clarity. And then I realize I've heard this before, lived it in a more subtle rendition. This is America as meritocracy, the world as our oyster, our playground, and before that the divine rule of aristocracy in Europe, and Bagby's is merely the new-age secular version of the same old liturgy minus sanction from any larger authority but the system itself the system its own horrific validation.

"Yes, of course, a beautiful scheme really, complex but so elegant too, simple even, when viewed from the proper perspective, which is the larger scale of evolutionary expedience. This is just our purpose, yours and mine, to facilitate the movement of profit up the scale, and we all fall along the scale somewhere: these poor bastards, these wretched locals on the bottom since meeting their betters some hundreds of years ago, and you and me much further up." As he says this he raises his automatic slowly and sweeps it across the square to encompass the people dancing and the spectators and the mud-and-wattle buildings as if choosing a target.

"But men like us are also *not* subject to the same constraints of the scale as the rest, even those at the top who must strive to have it all because that is their only option, an innate desire they can neither explain nor elude. But men like us ..."

"The killers and torturers," I say, all sarcasm gone from my voice now, as if this were merely antiphonal response.

"Yes, Blue. We are unique among men because we move history in its inevitable direction. We take out whatever stands in our way, whatever confuses us or scares us." And Bagby gets a faraway look in his eye as if reaching for the words to a divine vision, some secular equivalent of beatific realization achieved after years of contemplation, and it is a moment of inattention that I think may be my only opportunity to end this impasse. But then I cannot move to raise the gun to his head, to pull the trigger, and the moment passes.

"We are instrumental on a scale these peons cannot imagine. We enable the powerful to be powerful, but we also enable the one lurking in the shadows who is smarter than the one on the throne at present, who is biding his time. We help him to achieve his destiny and take his rightful place, and then we help his successor and his after that, ad infinitum. Moving history forward by leaps and bloody bounds, and all through history, regardless of who sits on the throne, because they need us, because history needs us to move adequately forward."

"This rationalization of Western Civilization as natural hierarchy is all very nice, but back to the question at hand: what now?"

Bagby smiles wearily yet again, like an impatient man with a secret, a man with intentions he does not care whether you recognize or not. "You seem better at this work than I have given you credit for, Blue, and caused a human resource shortage for me as it were, so a job offer is the only logical option, of course." Bagby lifts his gun slowly and puts it into the black holster on his hip in an overblown show of nonviolent intent that may or may not be true, his terrible smile incongruous and strange. "No hard feelings Blue, but I would like to know what your motives were behind killing so many of my men. Who is paying you?"

As he asks the question, I see his arm tense ever so slightly, which may or may not be a sign that he will pull his weapon when my guard drops. Then I see the boy moving behind Bagby for an instant. The Hurricane is steering one of the party-goers through the crowd in our direction, and I see him peek from behind the dancer's left hip. The dancer seems to think that this is merely childish participation in the ritual and moves rhythmically in a kind of tango with his short partner guiding his steps from behind, as in a conga line in a bad movie.

"And if I refuse your job offer?" I ask.

"Then, given the fact that you killed my men, and you had to hunt them down to kill them at that, I must assume you are working for someone with interests contrary to those I serve. I must assume that perhaps you are in league with the Jaguar, which would be bad news indeed, and I would have to kill you."

"I seem to have the advantage in firepower," I say and wag the barrel of the M-16 at him.

"That remains to be seen, Blue," says Bagby, and he stretches his hand as I used to, like a movie gunfighter, and I hear his knuckles pop. "But I've learned one thing of paramount importance from this rabble: patience. I can hunt you for as long as it takes, if indeed you refuse my offer, which is quite generous I assure you, and you would be working for the winning side. The Jaguar can't hide from us forever, and he is working outside the great scheme of things besides. Valasquez is a fool on a fool's errand to save a foolish people destined for inevitable extinction, a people whose time has passed."

I see Bagby's upper forearm twitch again ever so slightly under the green cloth of his fatigues, and he

277

stretches his fingers outward again, the knuckles popping more loudly than before. I hear Rudy's voice echo in my head: *err on the side of caution – shoot the son of a bitch.* But I do not move.

Time slows to a crawl again as it did during the firefight on the riverbank, and I see blue spots in the air as if I am witnessing the explosion of molecules or tiny universes invisible to anyone else, worlds passing beyond time and space and this sad melodrama of ascension and decline. Then I see the Hurricane's dance partner move up behind Bagby and turn abruptly and saunter off toward a group of onlookers as the boy gently shoves him away. Then the Hurricane steps up to Bagby and swipes downward and across the backs of his legs with the obsidian blade. He cuts fast and deep behind this killer's knees where they are hinged, swinging the blade with both hands as if swinging a little league bat.

Bagby screams as the tendons snap and he falls immediately to the ground. But his gun is out before he reaches the dirt and he is firing even as he tumbles, even as he reaches in vain with his empty hand for the backs of his legs to hold them together. A party-goer falls in slow motion to my left, blood spreading immediately over the bright cotton of his costume, the red a stark contrast to its primal green. Then a woman in gingham and a multicolored shawl falls to my left, closer than the dancer, and I know that Bagby's next shot will hit me.

I put a single bullet in Bagby's sternum, and he rolls over on his back as one exhausted after long labor or strenuous sex, his arms spread like Christ on the cross. He seems to gather himself, and then he beckons me over with the hand that held the gun, which now rests a few feet out of his reach. When I am near enough to hear the air passing out of the hole in his chest, to hear

278

him wheeze above the confusion in the square, he says, "Fool. There are others, and there will always be others, and they will send assassins after you until they find an assassin who is your better. You had this one chance, and now you are the enemy, just as these peasants are the enemy, but you are worse because you are dangerous and because you are one of us. They will kill you slowly, more slowly than I killed Custer," and at this thought Bagby laughs softly, a wheeze within a wheeze.

I step back, and the locals, as if they had been waiting for me to move, descend on Bagby with shovels and sticks, stones and machetes, and they scatter him over the square in only a few minutes. An arm is nailed to the church door. His genitals and one foot are fed to a pig tied to a post. His gawking head is stuck on a stick and paraded around by the party-goers. The rest of him I lost track of in the melee.

One long tremolo of grief after another rises into the air, the variant pitches and rates of warble touching as relay runners of sound or merging with their successors as if parts of a round of sorrow and indignation, of unrelenting pain. A final ocean of grief rolls over us as it is transubstantiated to sound, twenty women wailing in high falsetto, and the boy and I walk to the airfield to find a ride to Mexico City.

These are the days of endless grieving, remorse so deep I know that no amount of booze can numb it, and so I no longer drink, not in three weeks anyway.

In the last few months I have seen Justine's face on many more women than this stranger rattling on non-stop across from me now, and they have all turned out to be far less than her equal, as if to remind me that something beautiful disappeared from the world when she died. And I saw Chanelle from a distance once, as I peered at her apartment from a dark doorway across the alley. She kissed a man at the door, held him for a long moment as if she were afraid to leave him, and then walked more tentatively toward the street than I have ever seen her move. Knowing she could not forgive me, I did not intend to speak, but seeing her afraid broke my heart – my fault, my fault, my fault – and I slipped as far into the doorway as I could and turned my back as she passed. I did not want her to see me, but I did not want to look at her either. I left some of the Jaguar's money – cash he makes sure is at dead drops across the New World, wherever there is someone to be assassinated – with Liebowitz at the dry cleaner along with instructions for delivery. I left no note.

I now dream of my parents every night, and I still see the many dead at these hands, which now includes those in the square in Chamula who fell because I could not act. I know they are not the last. The boy and I will continue our tour of the Americas defending Mayan sovereignty or bringing about the destiny of world, or whatever the hell the old one told us our role is on this planet at the desperate end of time.

All the sacrifices stand in ranks as far as I can see in my dreams. Our destiny to move history through another bloody phase, or into the next bloody phase, something … I would believe that this bloodbath was for some good if I could, but no utopian this Blue Man. Right now I merely seem to have no choice. At the least I was born with this singular talent, to dissimulate and kill, and there are so many who do not deserve to breathe.

These are the days of Simone in his expensive suit folding his *Wall Street Journal*, of the boy rising with great fanfare to visit the next car, shaking the old gentleman's hand ceremoniously, waving fondly to the old woman when he heads up the aisle, winking at me as he passes. These are the days of Simone rising to follow the boy as inconspicuously as he can so as not to arouse suspicion in the couple who still stare happily after the child they know as Bill. These are the days of Simone walking up the aisle, glancing in my direction as he passes to see if I move or not, daring me to follow him to what he believes is my fate as he shoves history imperceptibly forward. I don't so much as flinch.

Only the Hurricane returns a few minutes later. He sits across from me, next to the woman who is still talking, to read a comic book, *Batman* in Spanish. He hands me the 3,000 year-old obsidian knife as if an afterthought.

The End

MICHAEL MCIRVIN was born in the Nebraska Panhandle in 1956. He taught writing and literature for many years at various institutions, including Colorado State University and the University of Wyoming, and for the past several years he has been a freelance editor and writing mentor. His poems, stories, essays, and book reviews have appeared in hundreds of periodicals, and he is the author of nine books: poetry collections, novels, and an essay collection. He lives on the High Plains of Wyoming with his wife Sharon and is currently writing another novel.

Other Books by Michael McIrvin

Optimism Blues: Poems Selected and New (poetry)

The Book of Allegory (poetry)

Dog (poetry)

Lessons of Radical Finitude (poetry)

Love and Myth (poetry)

Hearing Voices (poetry)

Déjà vu and the Phone Sex Queen (novel)

Whither American Poetry (essays)

www.ingramcontent.com/pod-product-compliance
Lightning Source LLC
Chambersburg PA
CBHW030321200626
46816CB00006BA/1879